Acknowledgements

I should like to give my grateful thanks to the staff of the Ringwood and Fordingbridge Libraries, for all their genuine interest and support, during and after the writing of this and all my previous novels.

Graham Adams

Best wishes
Graham Adams
Aug. '17

The Woodman's Quest

<u>Preface</u>

How on earth can a young man, born not only with severe physical problems, but to have been rejected at birth, make his way in the world?

He realised that to remain an island would only hinder his progress, but help comes from an unusual direction.

A heart-warming story of one man's quest to find a way of life that can hopefully result in true happiness for him, here is his story.

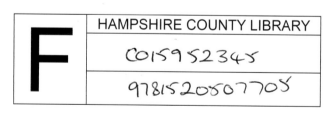

The Woodman's Quest

The Woodman's Quest

By Graham Adams

New Forest Author

Chapter 1

Back to the cottage

'Phaedra darling, how can you not be happy here? We have this lovely house, and in such a beautiful setting of the New Forest too?' The raven-haired mother asked as she walked up alongside her daughter, who was staring outside the mullioned window. Lydiya knew that there was something troubling her young daughter's mind, but she received no answer, not even a sign of acknowledgement.

Phaedra was just looking at the vista of the green clearing that stretched out beyond the window, encircled by a thick stand of mature beech trees in full leaf. Even the bright sunshine was unable to penetrate into the woods and she could not help focusing on those black voids between the white-blemished trunks. Her mind also reflected those thick black shadows, and contemplated the forbidding darkness, even felt the unexplainable pull for her to go and explore it. The blackness of her most recent past had scarred her soul and she knew that she had to find some release from it.

A few years before, Victor and Lydiya had received this wonderful inheritance from a very dear and very rich benefactor; a large house called 'The Gables' situated on the fringe of the New Forest town of Lyndhurst, prior to that they lived in a two up, two down cottage in the village of Burley.

Neither big houses nor any sort of material wealth held any interest to this young woman however. Twenty six years old,

The Woodman's Quest

outwardly she was strikingly beautiful; her black hair was halfway down her back and was full of natural shiny curls framing a chiselled face, flawless with a slightly hawkish nose. The amazing thing about Phaedra was that she had absolutely no idea about the heads that turned when she passed by any man in the town, or even when the chatting would go silent, should she enter the local coffee house. She simply was not aware of the huge impact that the young dark beauty constantly made, wherever she went.

She had a secret, a very big secret that haunted her in every waking moment. Some years before she had been kidnapped in London by a gang of Iranian criminals, who had threatened her very life? She was eventually saved by a close friend of her brother's, but the whole thing had ended in great loss of several other lives. If that was not enough, she knew in her heart that the whole catastrophic episode was caused by her own foolish actions.

Her brother and father had also been caught up in the melee; they had both risked their lives to gain her rescue, which added greatly to her continued anguish and guilt. She was a classical trained singer before the kidnapping, but sadly that promise was swept aside by a stray bullet she received in her throat area whilst making her escape to freedom.

There was only one thing to do now, and that was to get away and rebuild her life. She still wore the snake necklace with a strange mystical stone around her neck that Teddy had given her, and as she held the glowing crystal in her hand, she immediately felt an important decision had been made in her life.

The Woodman's Quest

'Mother, will you ask Dad if he will drive me to my little cottage in Tintagel please?' Phaedra asked.

Lydiya's face dropped. She knew deep down that her daughter would eventually leave the Gables, but this time, there seemed an air of inevitability about her decision, so she didn't argue, and instead disappeared out of the room to find Victor.

'Shall we say first thing in the morning darling?' Victor asked his daughter quietly.

He perceived a slight nod of her head, but she didn't turn around to face him. It would only make it worse, and it probably would have. At the same time Lydiya put her arm around her daughter's waist and led gently her to her room to pack the belongings she needed for the journey, knowing that it might be some time before they were to be together again.

Three months before, their son had left in a much happier fashion. He was about to leave for Philadelphia with his fiancée Marcy. His parents were pleased that their son's life had at last finally got a meaning. His recent letter from America was full of intentions stating that his parents were to be guests of honour at the biggest, fanciest Greek wedding that had ever taken place on the East Coast! All the details would follow in a subsequent mail.

Phaedra took her mother to the local shops in Lyndhurst so that she might obtain enough basic supplies for at least a month at her remote stone cottage, situated on the cliff top on the North Cornwall coast. She had settled in there during the previous winter with a great deal of help from her very

The Woodman's Quest

good friend Ian, who was a specialist in self-preservation. He had fixed up a generator which was fed by a small wind machine attached to the cottage roof. This not only provided power for the cottage, but it also brought up fresh water from a nearby well.

As they brought back the supplies, Phaedra suddenly felt alive again, anticipating the excitement of reconnecting to the way of life that suited her the most. Living alone would give her the time and solitude that her heart yearned for, no more being dependant on anyone. Recently she had to endure those tedious times when her karma was interrupted by constant unwelcome enquiries as to her wellbeing when she strolled around the town.

She did have her own transport, an old Land Rover which was still parked up at the cottage in Cornwall. A few months before she had been visited by her brother Mikhail who had persuaded her to go with him in his vehicle to France, so that they could visit their maternal grandmother in the Alsace Lorraine town of Toul.

The plan was to have both parents take her to her cottage, and at the same time she would be able to show them where and how she would be living. Phaedra suggested that they take the Lexus utility vehicle, as the access to the cottage from the main road warranted a four wheel drive.

Four hours later, Mr. & Mrs. Norman were staggered by the sheer beauty of the setting that their daughter Phaedra's cottage was in. The cottage had no neighbours and was nestled in a small valley between two cliffs, with an uninterrupted view of the dramatic coastline. Her parents

The Woodman's Quest

watched her intently as Phaedra reconnected the generator, and within minutes enjoyed the comfort of electrical power and clear running water again. Lydiya opened the shutters to the small windows in the stone cottage to let in the fresh Cornwall air. Victor unloaded the supplies from the car, and as it was just about lunchtime, asked where he could take his best girls out to lunch?

They agreed on the Castle Hotel, which was an impressive building over the next hill which had an incredible view of its surroundings. Phaedra told her mother that the hotel owner's wife Anna was a descendant of Russian aristocrats which immediately made her mother's hackles rise. Lydiya was herself Russian, but with a fiery temper. This was going to be a perfect storm for the overblown hotel owner, Phaedra thought to herself smiling.

Before they went into the dining room they had to pass through the great hall. On the walls there hung a great deal of paintings, and Phaedra began to explain what they were, when they were interrupted by a tall dark haired woman with a recognisable accent; Phaedra held her breath.

'Please do not interrupt my daughter when she is speaking' Lydiya spoke sharply and in Russian, taking care not to face the woman.

Victor was not at all pleased with his wife and was attempting to speak but Lydiya would have none of it. She continued her tirade of Russian and not until Victor got hold of his wife's arm did she stop. All along Phaedra knew that this was going to be difficult, but not as bad as this. To her great relief, a

The Woodman's Quest

large man in a brightly coloured shirt stood between Lydiya and her adversary and smiled disarmingly at her mother.

'Hello, I'm Brian Horner, and I see that you are looking at one of my paintings, I would be honoured to show you some of my other work.'

Lydiya placed her arm in his, and they strolled around the hall, stopping at each picture, with Brian explaining how he had constructed them. Peace reigned at last; Victor gave an audible sigh of relief and held his hand out in friendship to the Russian owner, who seemed struck dumb.

'Do you perhaps have a table available for lunch today Anna?' Phaedra asked sweetly.

The woman smiled as she led them into the bright dining room where the whole of the sea facing wall was built in glass, enabling a full panoramic view of the wild and majestic coastline in all its glory, and they were shown to a table on that particular side of the room.

'I should like it immensely if Brian could join us for lunch Victor!' Lydiya shouted as she and her new artist friend approached their table.

Husband and daughter had no intention in arguing with her, especially as she was finally smiling again. The lunch went very well, especially for Phaedra, as Brian was a mine of information and thankfully had never asked any pointed questions directly to her.

There were occasions however, when she sensed that her mother was going to divulge Phaedra's information to the

The Woodman's Quest

artist, so she gave her a stern look and gently kicked her mother's shins. To her relief, Lydiya had taken the hint from her daughter and promptly asked Brian another question instead to which he eagerly answered.

After lunch, Victor and Lydiya were soon saying their goodbyes to their daughter outside of her cottage. They both hugged her tight and she knew exactly what that meant, without them even saying a word to their daughter.

'Phaedra, have you seen that huge black bird perched on your roof?' Lydiya was pointing to a huge black raven that was constantly shuffling its feathers as if it was impatient. Occasionally a very loud rasping sound emanated from its fearsome beak. Its black eyes seemed to pierce right through Lydiya's heart, which made her shiver.

'Safe journey home, and please don't worry about me, I'm tougher than you think.' Phaedra said, as she placed a comforting arm around her mother's shoulder.

Phaedra hurried them into their car and within a few minutes her mother's waving arm had disappeared over the horizon. She then quickly went into her little cottage without even glancing at the rooftop.

The Woodman's Quest

Chapter 2

William finds rest

Life on the run was difficult enough for any one, but if one had at the same time, a level of disability, that extra dimension to be unbearable. In the past year he had moved from one place to another searching out any hotel receptionists and prospective employers that didn't question too closely about his background, but these they were getting harder and harder to find.

He had moved initially from London escaping from a gang of loan sharks whose threats for non-payment were just too harsh to bear thinking about. If only that horse in the 3.30 at Kempton had come in first, his troubles would have been over.

William Gilpin was a short stocky man of about 33 years old with a pronounced limp caused by a large hump on his back. Although currently unshaven for the past three days, he still couldn't hide the disfiguring cleft on his top lip. Through his lack of confidence he constantly moved in a stooped position and was therefore unlikely to look anyone in the eye, should they come into conversation.

Brought up in a series of children's homes and orphanages, he never knew his parents, and yet somehow inexplicably there was a great love beating in his heart, if only things had been different........?

The Woodman's Quest

All his life he had been ridiculed for his appearance and because of that, he had never made any real friends in his formative years; this gave him no real opportunity to use his sharp intellect in conversation. His favourite place, wherever he stayed, was the local library. Novels or biographies held no interest for him, as his first love was poetry. Classical poetry often brought him to tears; works from Shelley and Yeats were imprinted on his mind.

There was another asset William had that had served him in good stead, he was immensely strong, and so whatever work he obtained was always done well. As he travelled westwards from London he could always find manual work in the farming industry, but his favourite occupation was in Forestry. Even when he was successful in getting a position, he knew that three months would be the maximum period, before he had to move on.

As he sat in his room in a shabby motel in an industrial estate in the middle of Cornwall he pulled out a book called 'Anthology of verse'. It was a small sized book, one that he could hide in his coat pocket without being seen by the librarian in the Exeter City Library. There were some excellent poems in the book, but not many, as he found that they were mostly modern poets whose work did not move him. His plan was to move on the following day, so having torn out the inside page which identified the library, William left the book in the bedside cabinet for the next guest.

Brightly coloured brochures, from the hotel lobby were laid out on his bed and one of them had caught his eye: 'Legends of King Arthur' and on the next line it urged; 'come and visit the mystical village of Tintagel'. Inside of the brochure there
The Woodman's Quest

was a small map indicating the route, part of which ran along the northern coastline called 'Atlantic Highway'.

William decided there and then, that this place was going to be his next port of call, and this time nothing was going to stop him. Although he had never been in that area before, he felt a sort of excitement in his heart at the prospect. All the places he had visited in the past year did not spark any enthusiasm, and he had often faced rejection from the locals wherever he went. Would this destination be any different this time? Only time would tell, he mused to himself.

'Get the 510 to Wadebridge, and then the 595 to Tintagel'. The young receptionist told William curtly.

He tried to smile in thanks but she just turned away, obviously not used to looking at his deformed stature perhaps. He just nodded his head and made his way to the St. Columb Major bus stop. His army style rucksack that he had slung over his shoulder, only accentuated his disability, as he trundled across the hotel car park.

From the top deck of the 510 double-decker bus, he was able to get many glimpses of the sparkling blue North Cornwall coastline which raised his spirits as he neared his first destination of Wadebridge. He read the brochure from cover to cover about the Legends of King Arthur, and hoped that the mystical element of the stories would be reflected in the type of people he would get into contact with. He particularly hoped that people would accept him for what he was, not how he looked.

The Woodman's Quest

The little skipper bus number 595 was a sharp contrast to the previous one, and there was certainly a good reason for it being so small. The roads were very narrow and had many sharp blind turns in them. The driver seemed oblivious of the state of the roads, and he drove the little bus full speed incurring innumerable near misses to oncoming traffic.

Finally the little bus came to the top of a steep hill that overlooked a little village nestling between the two cliffs, surrounded by an azure sea shining in the midday sun. William turned to look at the other three other passengers, and lo and behold they smiled at him knowingly. He almost burst out laughing, he was so happy at that moment.

Whenever he arrived in any town, his first task was to find somewhere to stay for the night. The bus driver had directed him to a community notice board in the centre of Tintagel, which was likely to provide the best chance of a bed. It was situated at the entrance to a large car park and it was one of the largest notice boards that he had seen.

One small card which was attached by four rusty pins caught his eye;

'Small caravan for hire, furnished with all amenities, only £100 per month.'

Beneath the message was written a phone number and a name; `Creswell'`, but there was no address on it.

He knew there was over two hundred pounds stashed in his rucksack; enough to pay the first month's rent and to give him time to hopefully find work of some sort. He did not

The Woodman's Quest

possess a mobile phone of course, so he detached the card from the notice board, and went to find help.

There was a row of little shops next to the entrance to the car park and the second one had its door open. Above the door was written; '*Mystique*' which intrigued him so he walked right in, clutching the advert.

William had never been in such a shop before; it was dark inside, so dark that he needed time for his eyes to adjust from the bright sunlight. The first senses that met him were the soft smell of incense sticks and when his eyes finally focussed, he saw that it was a tourist styled shop that sold crystals and coloured stones.

'Hello, can I help you sir' came a small voice in a dark recess.

He turned around and smiled, waiting for the person to turn away, but surprisingly she didn't.

'Er, I have this from the community notice board and I wondered....' William hesitatingly passed the card to the pretty young woman.

'Ah yes, old George still has that old wreck of a caravan to rent does he? A hundred pounds a month, that's daylight robbery even for you!' The young woman put her hand to her mouth knowing she had been very rude. 'I didn't mean it like that sir!' She blurted out apologetically.

'I've had worse said to me miss, no offence taken I'm sure.' He answered.

The Woodman's Quest

She took the opportunity to introduce herself as the shop owner called Zeta Rosdew and offered her hand. He carefully shook it, and remembered not to grip too hard.

'I'm William Gilpin from... er, St Columb. I'm looking for somewhere to stay, and I hoped that Mr. Creswell's caravan might be ok for me. Do you think I could use your phone to ring the number and perhaps.....?'

Zeta thought for a moment and looked at the strange man in front of her. Without a word she rang the number on her mobile phone and as luck would have it, there was a gruff voice speaking on the other end of the line.

'Is that you George?' She asked. 'Well, I have a possible tenant for your van here, but he's a friend of mine so you aren't going to charge him a hundred are you?'

After she had closed the line, she looked at William in triumph. She had negotiated the rent at only £50 per month, but she warned him that she knew of the old caravan and it was no 'Taj Mahal'. He laughed at that remark saying that he was sure that he had slept in worse.

Old George had agreed to pick William up from the shop in half an hour and take him to his new abode. The visitor to the town expressed his deep thanks for her help, and promised to return and purchase something from her shop as soon as he was settled.

Without a doubt his new address needed some attention but it did have some clean linen for sleeping on, and as it was heading into summer, here was little need for any heating.

The Woodman's Quest

That was fortunate, as there was nothing on offer in the caravan at the time. George soon found out that William had spent time working on a farm in the past, so quickly offered him some part-time work as a herdsman on his small dairy farm.

The caravan itself was parked in a small depression of land just south of the ruined church that stood on the cliff top overlooking the old Tintagel Castle, fabled to be the centre of the legend of King Arthur. William just couldn't believe his luck, on his first day he had found a job, a room with a view and a new friend called Zeta.

The Woodman's Quest

Chapter 3

A helping hand

Spring rolled into summer, and the little town of Tintagel became very crowded with tourists, all drawn to the beauty of the little town, and some just wanted to be touched by the aura of magic in the air. The majority of the visitors would congregate in the high street, and frequented the little trinket shops who took advantage of those who searched for the smallest clue of the mythical king.

Of course some more adventurous tourists would scale the cliff and visit the Old Castle ruins, whilst others would search out the magnificent Castle Hotel for afternoon tea. All these things William Gilpin observed from the top of his cliff, unseen by them.

The nights were shorter at that time of year and after milking, he often had time to watch the sun slowly disappear over the horizon leaving a crimson glow in the sky which eventually gave in to yellow ochre. Finally the dark blues enveloped the sky and silence descended. Often William would lie on the grass on top of the cliff after his work and let the sounds of the night envelop him. For once in his life, time had lost its meaning.

He didn't have a day off as such, the cows needed milking twice a day, so he often found himself wandering the cliff tops in the afternoon, dreaming of being a poet and conjuring lines of verse to himself. One afternoon he wandered to the opposite cliff where in the distance he could just make out a single grey stone cottage roof, which seemed about a

The Woodman's Quest

kilometre away. He sat on the grass deep in thought, when he was nudged from behind quite softly. On turning he smiled to see a goat's white kid which seemed to be only a few days old, which was trying to butt him with its tiny bumps on its head.

It then began to bleat and looked agitated, so he stood up and as he did, the little goat ran off to the nearest cliff edge. William followed and then heard another bleat, but much deeper. He looked over the edge and could just make out the head of a goat, obviously a nanny, and the kid's mother. He lay on his stomach and reached down with one hand a far as her could, without falling over the edge. He felt the rough curve of the goat's horn on his index finger, then stretching as far as his arm would let him, he finally grasped the horn.

William's powerful arm was soon pulling the brown goat onto the grassy verge and as he did, immediately noticed that she had severely broken its back leg in the fall. Meanwhile the tiny kid stood patiently at his side making a soft whimpering sound. He gently lifted the large goat over his shoulder and walked towards the stone cottage that he noticed earlier.

When he was about halfway to his destination, a strange thing happened. A very large raven swooped down, almost knocking him over, and he waved his free arm at it angrily. The bird circled twice and then flew in the direction of the cottage and landed on the roof.

William then stopped for a moment as he witnessed an even stranger occurrence. He was standing with the goat on his shoulders and watched as the door of the cottage open and someone with blue dungarees came out. Immediately the

The Woodman's Quest

huge bird swooped down from the roof and landed on the person's shoulder. As he approached he could see that the raven was cawing menacingly at him, which initially made him shudder in fear.

'I need some wood to make a splint for this goat's leg; it had slipped over the cliff!' He shouted as he approached.

She lifted her arm and the raven flew back onto the roof, and for the first time gave William a reassuring smile.

'Bring them inside let's see what we can do.' She said stepping aside.

William was sure that the goat understood that these humans only wanted to help her, so she obediently let him lay her on her side so that her broken leg could be looked at closely. The nanny goat seemed even calmer when her little kid began to suckle at the exposed teat. At this sight, the two helping humans smiled at her kid's cheekiness.

The woman then went outside for a moment, returning with two pieces of wood and William quickly shaped them with his pen knife, to perfectly fit the goat's leg. The woman then had to turn away as William quickly reset the leg, and then tied the splint with some white strong string that she had produced for the task.

In a few moments, he had stood the goat up on its remaining three legs and it immediately hobbled quickly out of the open door followed by her doting kid. The whole operation probably took about half an hour.

The Woodman's Quest

'You've made a friend for life there er....?' The young woman said, referring to the injured goat.

'My name is William Gilpin miss; I work in the farm over the next hill. Really sorry but I've got to go, it's milking time already.'

'My name is Phaedra; you're welcome to return for a well-deserved cup of tea if you wish.' She said as he quickly scuttled out of the cottage door.

'Ok thanks, see you tomorrow then.' William said and dashed up the hill to his waiting cows.

William thought a great deal about the young woman that he had met in those strange circumstances that afternoon. The cows were especially difficult that day, and William had to man-handle them into their milking stalls, it seemed as if they knew he didn't have his mind on the job in hand. Finally he took the last of the milking machines off of the last udder, and as he cleaned up the milking parlour, he continued to ponder how Phaedra could live out in the wilds in that little cottage with the only companion being what looked like a bad tempered raven.

The following day after the morning chores, he left his contented grazing cows and found himself heading once again to the little cottage nestling in the next cliff top. The sun was beating down on his thinning scalp and his back felt very hot. After knocking on the door he waited, but there was no response, then he heard something at the back of the cottage and scurried round to investigate. An old dark green Land Rover Discovery was parked under a wooden shelter

The Woodman's Quest

and inside was the young woman sat in the driving seat with a puzzled look on her face.

'It won't start William, won't even turn the engine over!' She shouted through the windscreen.

He opened the passenger door just as she turned the ignition key again. All he could hear was a faint 'click'. She told him that the car had been unused for quite a while and looked at him as he nodded knowingly.

'Sounds like a dead battery to me, lift the bonnet up Phaedra.' William answered confidently.

William disconnected the battery and proposed that he take it into the town and gets it checked for her at a local garage. She warned him about the difficult terrain between the cottage and the town and suggested that he look up her friend Zeta in the crystal shop called 'Mystique'. He took the opportunity to tell her the story of Zeta's kindness that she had done for him already, and then promptly put the battery under his arm and made his way into Tintagel.

Although it was hot, William had reached the shop in no time and had no trouble in enlisting Zeta to take him and the battery to the local garage. The owner confirmed right away that it was beyond recharging, and the only solution would be a replacement one. William paid for the new battery and loaded it into Zeta's car and soon they were making their way back to Phaedra's cottage. Amazingly, William had left and returned to the cottage with the new battery in less than an hour, to the amazement of Phaedra.

The Woodman's Quest

Whilst the two young women were catching up with their news in the cottage, William fitted the battery, and the engine was soon fired up and ticking over as smooth as silk. He left it running whilst hobbling into the cottage to report his success. As he walked into the main room, he sensed that there something different. The two women stopped talking as he stared at the massive black raven perched on an old dresser, bobbing its head at him menacingly.

'Don't be afraid, William, Bopoh will not harm you.' Phaedra said softly, and spoke to it in a strange language. The bird strutted on the cabinet for a moment and then launched itself out of the open door without a sound, but William looked puzzled at the young woman.

'What did you say to it Phaedra?' He asked.

'I told him to find us some fish for tea, you will stay won't you? She asked.

William's eyes were open wide, part in fear and part in disbelief. He was just finding his voice to answer her, when the raven flew in with a very big fish in its beak; it was still alive, flapping its tail furiously. Bopoh dropped the fish on the table then jumped back onto its perch cawing deafeningly. Phaedra promptly killed the fish and began to prepare it for cooking. Meanwhile, Zeta looked at William as all this was happening, and without a word just smiled at him, as if to say that the whole thing was a commonplace event.

'Er... my cows, I must get back to them, er... time for milking.' He excused himself, quite unable to take it all in.

The Woodman's Quest

'Goodbye!' He shouted, as he high tailed it up the hill, to sanity.

He heard the sound of the two women laughing in the cottage as he made his escape and it has instilled even more fear in his heart.

The Woodman's Quest

Chapter 4

William to the rescue

Apart from the two women he had met, there seemed little opportunity for him to get to know any other locals in the small town; everyone seemed wrapped up in making money from the tourists. Even the entrance fee to the ruined castle seemed far too high for him; in fact the whole idea of myths and legends was beginning to turn him off somewhat.

George was no better, if William ever saw him it would be to pay his rent for the dilapidated caravan, and all he got in response was a 'grunt'. He was paid well enough though, there was a little brown envelope was pushed through his door containing several twenty pound notes, most of which William saved in his rucksack. After taking out his meagre living expenses he had soon amassed a tidy sum, but with no friends as yet, he had little reason to spend it.

He often thought about visiting Zeta at her shop or Phaedra at her cottage, but neither gave him the impression that they would have welcomed him and particularly it seemed that all Phaedra wanted to do was be on her own. Secretly he admired her for that, but was also a little concerned that an attractive woman living alone would be courting danger, but then he remembered Bopoh the raven. Not many would be able to tackle him.

One particular Friday afternoon William decided to walk into the town and be a tourist by visiting as many as the local

The Woodman's Quest

shops as time would allow, between the milking schedule. The shop owners were courteous, but not particularly friendly, so each time he was soon back on the high street again.

'It's William isn't it?' A voice came from behind him.

He turned around in surprise to see a rustically dressed old woman with a walking stick standing there, smiling at him.

'I'm very sorry, but do I know you?' He answered.

'Not me personally my dear, but Nellie was very glad that you rescued her that day. It was a very good job that you did on her broken leg. By the way my name is Aggie Smith.' She held out a bony hand for him to shake.

'Would you like to have a cuppa with me, Aggie?' William asked, pointing to a nearby teashop.

The old woman recounted that she had previously been to the 'Mystique' shop and Zeta had told her what had happened, but it had been some time since the rescue of her goat, it was only Zeta's description of William that enabled Aggie to recognise him. He asked about Nellie's white kid and the old woman told him that it was growing strong but would never leave her mother's side.

'I expect you are finding it difficult to find friends around here my boy, am I right?' Aggie asked.

William just looked and smiled at her, wondering where the question was leading. She invited him to a special meeting of a few friends who met in the back-room of Zeta's shop every Saturday evening at around six pm. He said that he would

The Woodman's Quest

think about it and just turn up if that was agreeable. She nodded and smiled in agreement and scuttled away refusing his offer for tea.

Across the High Street there was a large clock which indicated three thirty, so he decided to limp up the busy street for a few more metres before making his way back to the farm. The next moment there was a great deal of shouting, and people were running up the hill towards a crowd that had gathered in the middle of the road, opposite the old Post Office.

William picked up speed and was soon in the crowd. He could hear the sound of a horse in great distress so he separated the crowd with strong arms and soon the scene opened up to him. A large bay horse was lying on its side with its legs thrashing in the air. Beneath the rump area, a young girl was trapped and lying unconscious, her helmeted head lay on the pavement.

Someone in the crowd said that the horse had been surprised by the exhaust noise of a motorbike; it had reared up and fell on top its rider, this young girl. People were looking at the scene but not doing anything, so William pushed them aside and levered both his arms beneath the horse and with one mighty shout lifted the prone horse upwards whilst two onlookers quickly pulled the girl free.

The deafening sound of a fire engine approached, followed by an ambulance. This was a sign for William to make his exit, and he deftly disappeared into the crowd and limped down the High Street out of sight. Without thinking he had performed this act of bravery, but as he made his way back

The Woodman's Quest

to the farm he contemplated how lucky he had been to move away without being noticed. He knew that the worst thing for him would be to be recognised and perhaps those thugs in London may have got wind of his deed.

The following Saturday was the time of the 'meeting' that Aggie had invited him to. He pondered whether or not to go to Zeta's shop, especially considering that it was so soon after the 'horse' incident. The afternoon's milking completed, he guessed that it was close to six pm, and on the spur of the moment made his decision to go to Zeta's shop.

As he entered the shop door he noticed that a young schoolboy greeted him at the small counter and pointed to the back room which was poorly lit. Zeta came out of the room and met him with a smile.

'Hello William, Aggie said you might join us but I didn't believe her; welcome.' Her smile was genuine which put the visitor at his ease.

Four people were sitting around a table which was lit by just one candle, there was an empty chair at one end, and William with some difficulty sat on it.

'How are your arms today William?' Aggie asked smiling.

He didn't answer her; he had no intention in admitting to anyone that it had been him that had lifted the horse. In fact he was already beginning to regret even coming to the shop at that moment. Aggie was very astute though, she had read in William's face that it was a bad idea to mention what had happened the day before.

The Woodman's Quest

It was of course very hot news in the village, that someone had done such a deed, so Aggie diffused the atmosphere by explaining the whole incident to William, as if she had no idea that it was him. He caught on quickly by showing a false interest, even asking as to the welfare of the young girl.

Apparently the young girl had been flown to a specialist hospital in London where an operation to her spine had saved her life, but without the hero who had lifted the bay horse at that moment, she would not have survived. There was a countrywide search on the television to find the hero.

'Have you seen the appeal William?' One of the other members of the meeting asked.

William just shook his head; Zeta told the assembly that he didn't have a television. She then changed the subject and introduced the other two strangers to William.

'This is Myrtle, and this is Bertha.' Zeta said, and they both offered their hands.

William had enjoyed the evening, although it was the first time he had ever been to a séance and he open mindedly found it quite interesting. He was grateful that Zeta and Aggie had been most helpful and they were quick to put him at ease. No-one had enquired into his own past, which was of some relief to William. Most of the events of the meeting did go 'over his head', but he was just happy watching and listening to the ladies talking. The most enjoyable thing of all was that they had accepted him and wanted him to visit their group again, to which he gratefully promised that he would.

The Woodman's Quest

As he made his way back to the caravan, many things went over in his mind. Why did Aggie say about his arms? Perhaps she was testing him, in her wisdom she knew that it had been William, but knew that he wasn't to be drawn into talking about it. He really respected her for that gesture.

He walked down the pathway to the bottom of the valley; it was still dusk and his heart missed a beat as he noticed three men standing on the footbridge that he had to cross to get to the caravan. They stopped talking as he approached them, so he said goodnight and squeezed through. When he started to hobble up the steep stony track that headed for the cliff top, he heard them talking again. It was louder this time and they were laughing.

When he looked back to the bridge from his higher vantage point, they had just lit up cigarettes and then he gulped as he watched them begin to follow his route up the steep path. Although he had reached the top of the path, they were catching up to him, nearly halfway. He noticed that their accents were not local; they sounded more East End of London. He swallowed into his dry throat and thought rapidly.

The light was fading quickly and he could just make out where the little pathway split into two at the top of his climb. To the left was his route to the caravan, the one to the right headed for the ruined church. He remembered that the right fork had a large dry stone wall close to the cliff edge, and it was not more than fifty metres from where he stood.

He managed to crouch behind the wall and listened, as the three men approached the top of the pathway. One of the three wanted to abandon their plans but the other two were

The Woodman's Quest

intent on proceeding. He caught the comment about needing the money and a chill ran up his spine. Were they considering robbing him, or perhaps they had the old farmer George in their sights?

His fear then subsided as they realised the obvious danger of the steep path, coupled with the pitch black night. Sense had countered their valour as they decided to abandon their quest and head down, back to the town. As their voices receded, he peered over the wall, and then stood up to see the lights of their cigarettes in single file heading back over the bridge.

In a matter of thirty minutes he was safely back at the caravan, breathing heavily from his effort. Sleep evaded him as he recalled the incident which had soured all the pleasant feelings he had prior to that. His first thoughts were that the men were connected to his past, but he quickly discounted that. He was happy to accept that those three men were just opportunists, looking for easy prey.

He pulled the rucksack from underneath his bed and felt for the bulging wallet. Four months of toiling at his milking job had produced nearly fifteen hundred pounds, a fair catch for the robbers he pondered. He then considered again that if they weren't focussing on him, could they be planning to rob the old farmer, his employer?

George lived a little further down the hill, alone in a run-down cottage, he was fair game. He decided to tell him the next day, and then perhaps George would let the authorities know.

The Woodman's Quest

He finally dozed of in his bed, but awoke with the bellowing of the cows, impatient for milking. So he sprang into action, hoping that George hadn't noticed his oversleeping.

'Hey Bill, what's going on here then?' George shouted angrily. 'You haven't been on the booze have you?' He shouted again.

William didn't like to be called 'Bill' but he didn't answer as he made himself busy shepherding his charges into their stalls. Each cow knew which stall to go in, and as they all knew their handler, some even offered their noses for him to rub as they ambled by. They had forgiven him, but old George was suddenly, not quite so friendly.

In retrospect, he felt that he was being taken for granted, particularly by the old farmer. From the first day as a herdsman, he had never asked for a day off, and wondered how the old man had gotten along, without his dedication to the animals. He suddenly felt strongly about that thought, so decided to go and seek out Phaedra again and perhaps get some advice from her, about his concern.

The Woodman's Quest

Chapter 5

A friend in need

The clouds scudded across the sky as William made his way towards the little stone cottage again. He felt troubled in his mind, and yet for the first time, grateful that he had made a few friends that he felt able to confide in, and hopefully receive some wise answers to his mounting questions. As he stopped for a moment to survey the area, Bopoh the raven suddenly swooped down over his head, but this time William felt no fear.

As he approached the cottage door, he heard the sound of singing from inside, that made him stop in his tracks. He stood by the closed door and quietly listened as the song continued. After a while he recognised the song, it was the aria 'One fine day' from 'Madama Butterfly' by Puccini. At first he wondered if the radio was playing, but realised that there was no sound of the orchestra. He waited until the singing had finished, and gently tapped on the door, Phaedra quickly opened it, and greeted him with a smile.

'Was that you singing that song Phaedra?' William asked.

William sat on her easy chair and she explained about what happened to her in the past, and mentioned how disappointed she was to have a promising career dashed by the injury in her throat. William looked perplexed with her comment about her dashed career; because he considered that the rendition he had just heard was wonderful.

The Woodman's Quest

'Would you like to hear another aria William?' Phaedra asked. 'I haven't sung this one for many years, but I hope you like it. It's called 'Habanera' from the opera 'Carmen' by Georges Bizet.' William sat in the chair, utterly spellbound.

'Your career is not over Phaedra, I'm no critic but your voice is definitely back!' he shouted and applauded when she had finished.

William then asked her why she was living in the little cottage as a hermit, with little or no contact with the outside world, but then realised that perhaps he had gone too far with his questions.

Just like himself, there were probably good enough reasons to get away from society, and perhaps she would not want to share them with him, a perfect stranger.

As he expected, she had declined to answer his searching questions, but was pleased that he had enjoyed that little private concert she had performed for him.

What with the singing and general conversation, there had been little time for William to tell her the real reason he had visited her. Instead, he had to excuse himself and get back to his work at the farm. Prior to leaving though, he did explain that he would like to get some advice from her, so they agreed to meet up again the following day.

On his return to the farm, he was surprised to see old George with the cows, shepherding them into the milking stalls. This was the first time that it had happened although William was not concerned; he just stood close by and watched.

The Woodman's Quest

'I thought that you might be late again Bill, twice in one day.' George grumbled.

'But I'm not late am I?' William asked softly.

The old farmer quickly turned on his heels and scuttled down the hill, leaving the real job of milking to William. As he cleaned the milking parlour floor after the last cow had departed, he pondered over this latest action from George, and as he thought, he was beginning to feel ill at ease there. Perhaps if the old man was looking for confrontation; it would be a long time before he got that, William thought to himself.

As it was still summertime and the evenings were still light, he decided to wander into the little town and look into the shop windows. Halfway along the high street Jones & Co., the local electrical shop portrayed a television in the window which, being early in the evening showed the local news. Mr Jones had set the screen with text at the bottom so that the news could be understood by any passer-by. William watched several topics until one sparked his interest;

'Fifteen year old Hannah Deville has returned home after life-saving care. She was involved in a horrific accident where her horse fell on top of her on the high Street in Tintagel. There is still no sign of her rescuer, who single-handedly lifted the horse in order that the poor girl could be dragged from underneath it.'

The screen showed the girl still in a wheelchair being pushed into the entrance of her home. He also read at the bottom of the screen that during an interview with her doting father, he underlined his intent to search for his daughter's rescuer, but

The Woodman's Quest

also understood that if this person preferred to remain anonymous, he would respect that.

William warmed to the man's wisdom and noted that he was someone to be respected. As he limped away from the shop, he decided to put the whole incident to the back of his mind and get on with his life. At that time anyway, he had other things on his mind, such as the way old George was treating him.

He began to retrace his steps when a small red car pulled up alongside and he was relieved to see that it was Zeta who invited him in her car.

'William, I'm just going for dinner at The Kings Arms, would you like to join me?' She asked.

'Do you mean me, to join you?' He was astonished that someone would ask him.

They didn't sit in a dark corner of the public house as he expected, but right in the centre of it. William was so proud of the young lady sitting opposite him. The reactions of the rest of the clientele were predictable, but Zeta took absolutely no notice of their stares, instead she showed great interest in him.

In their conversation, he told her about Hannah, the girl in the horse accident, mentioning that she had returned home. Zeta mentioned that she had often been in her shop, and told William that she was hoping to offer Hannah a Saturday job there, even though she was wheelchair bound. As casual as he could, he asked whether Zeta knew where they lived, and

The Woodman's Quest

was told they had a large old house in its own grounds on the northern edge of the town.

He really enjoyed the very first meal with anyone, since he had arrived at Tintagel. Zeta had been great company and with her insisting that she paid, he felt humble to accept, as he hadn't carried any cash on him that evening. Zeta kindly dropped him off at the farm, which had been a great consideration too.

As he passed the farmer's cottage the old man's wizened face peered at him from the window, but William felt great power within him, so he made sure hid did not to lift his head. Instead he turned his back on the old man and waved to Zeta as she drove away.

The following afternoon after milking, William made a special effort to clean himself up and head for Phaedra's cottage. He even stopped at the cliff edge to pick a bunch of wild flowers called 'sea pink' which grew in abundance near to the cliff edge, the same place where he had rescued the nanny goat and her kid.

He knocked on her front door, with more confidence this time. Phaedra opened the door and was flabbergasted when she saw him with wild flowers in hand. He had never tasted dandelion tea before, and her attempt at cakes made him smile.

'Now William, tell me what is on your mind, and how can I help you.' She asked smiling.

The Woodman's Quest

He felt a bit like a little boy at first, as he had never been in such company before, but somehow Phaedra seemed to be the right person he could talk to. He began by telling her everything he knew about his life in children's homes and orphanages. It had been a tough upbringing without any knowledge of who his parents were, but as he grew up he had soon accepted that. With his disabilities, it seemed to him that there would be no chance that they would want to be found.

At this point Phaedra seemed quite upset, knowing that she had never experienced such loneliness in her life, but did her best to imagine what this poor man must have gone through. William then decided to skip much of the time he had spent in London; he considered that this could have not served much of a purpose.

'Phaedra I want to ask you for some advice. I have been saving money since working on the farm, and by now I have close to two thousand pounds which is currently stashed away in the old caravan that I'm living in. I had a close shave with three strangers the other night who, in my opinion were up to no good. What shall I do with the money?' He looked a little desperate when he asked her.

A strange thing happened as he waited for her response. She stood up and pulled the chain around her neck, and retrieved some sort of crystal, which glowed when she held it. Within a few moments there was four loud knocks on the door, and William went to open it. The great raven flew into the room and landed on the oak dresser which was greatly scratched on the top, presumably made by his fearsome claws. William assumed that the dresser was the bird's favourite perch.

The Woodman's Quest

Phaedra beckoned to the huge bird, that immediately flew onto her shoulder and nodded its head furiously. She spoke quietly and quickly to the bird in a strange language, after which the raven flew back onto its perch.

She explained that her pet had understood her second language which was Russian and that she had consulted it with his problem.

After a few minutes of tense silence, the raven looked up to the ceiling, opened its great beak and uttered the following words;

 'Bury in a box and plant a flower.'

 'There, you have your answer, from the wisest Bopoh in the world.' Phaedra smiled at her pet visitor, and then asked William to open the door and in a flash Bopoh was gone.

Time had flown by at the cottage, and William knew that if he was to tell anyone what had happened that afternoon, no one would have believed him accept of course, his other friend Zeta. So, back at the farm, as he performed the evening milking he considered the advice he was given, and knew then just what he had to do.

The Woodman's Quest

Chapter 6

The impossible task

Adelaide Columbine had smoked her third cigarette by the time that Josephus had laid down the silver salver on her silk eiderdown. Breakfast was predictable; a lightly boiled egg, brown toast cut into strips, that she annoyingly called 'soldiers' and a strong cup of Java coffee.

She was a faded film star keeping up appearances with only the faithful butler, for an audience. The long cigarette holder, the Chinese silk dressing gown and an affected manner depicted her once high station in life. In the fifties she had acted opposite some of the best actors such as Niven, Bogart, and Gable, three of many, who often would vie to be her leading man in the next big screen epic.

This morning after a visit by her old friend, Dr. Nigel Beeton, she had been finally told of the malignant tumour that was soon to pull down the final curtain of her life. The fantasy that had kept her going in the twenty first century was in tatters. Most of the friends and acquaintances had already left to that 'concert hall in the sky' or if still living were by now tucked up in one of the many nursing homes for retired actors, out of sight and out of mind.

At the now lowest point in her colourful life, it was time to look back, and maybe regret some of the things she had done. Perhaps just one thing had forever been with her, for the past thirty years or so had come to the front of her mind once again.

The Woodman's Quest

Adelaide had secretly married Solomon Qirk, a renowned film producer in London England. Her career was already in decline, yet up to that point she had resisted numerous offers of marriage from a raft of famous men. She always resisted them, as it seemed to her just a sham marriage for the insatiable Hollywood publicity machine.

Solomon was a very complex character, a short and powerful man but with a devastating temper. She was soon to find this out in the first week of their marriage. London's famous club land seemed irresistible to her new husband, and he would often return to their Claridge's suite worse for wear, having consumed great deal to drink. She soon learned never to confront him in that state, as this would enrage the man, having once left her with a bruised jaw and put her into hospital.

At the advanced age of forty five Adelaide was shocked to find she was pregnant by a man she had grown to hate, in such a short time too. Adelaide had decided that she would give birth to the child in London, particularly as she wanted the whole affair to be kept secret.

Solomon was not by her bedside when their child was born; in fact he was in North Africa working with the cast of a war film. He was so wrapped up in his work; Adelaide had not received anything from him, no telegram, no flowers and she wondered if he actually knew what was happening over there in England. This made hate just about the only feeling she could muster, when she thought of him.

What she was unaware of however, that at the time of her confinement her secret husband was already dead. He had

The Woodman's Quest

been frequenting a whore house in Tunis, when he got involved in an altercation with three local men. She later heard that he had put up a terrific fight, where two of his adversaries lost their lives, but one stab in his heart had been enough to end it all.

The greatest decision of her life had been made. She had signed the appropriate papers to the effect that the new-born child was to be given up for adoption. She was assured that the private hotel would deal with all of the details for her. She even made it clear, to them that she had no intention of seeing the child, based on her belief that she would best able to recover mentally from the confinement. What made the decision even more final, was that she already had plans to fly back to Los Angeles as soon as she was fit enough to leave the Portland Hospital.

After taking breakfast she rose and showered in her usual way eventually dressing as if she was about to go on set at her beloved Universal Studios, and glided down the sweeping staircase heading for her favourite leather couch in her huge lounge. After dismissing the butler with an impressive wave of her hand she began to open her sharp mind and once again thought of the child she had never seen. Was it a boy like Solomon, or a graceful girl looking like herself at that age?

She pondered that the child's age would be about thirty three, and in the prime of life, no doubt. The more that the subject crossed her mind, the more that she wanted to solve the enigma of what had she left behind that June the second in London?

The Woodman's Quest

About three in the afternoon Adelaide was insisting that the firm of lawyers, who had always represented her, send an experienced female lawyer that very day, and would accept no excuses. At six o'clock on the dot, a rather young attractive lawyer who introduced herself as Wilomena Ruzinski was presenting her credentials to the aged actress and was finally accepted with a brief smile from Adelaide.

'I'll come straight to the point my dear, I want you to find someone, but there are three things you need to know. The first, is that the person lives, I think, in London England, the second is that you have very little information to go on. The third one is the most important one, there is very little time to do it in.' Adelaide outlined.

'I see that you want us to start the search forthwith, so please give me as much detail as you can, and then I'll report back to you tomorrow when I have discussed the matter with one of the partners.' Wilomena placed her tape player on the coffee table and her client told her everything she knew.

The next day the young lawyer returned to the old mansion door with her briefcase packed with a proposal for Adelaide, fully expecting her to reject the very large fee that the partner had quoted for her. Her sceptical senior also hoped that if the huge fee was to be rejected, it would free Wilomena to get on with her already full schedule.

He couldn't have been more wrong. Adelaide had taken a real liking to the young plucky lawyer and even proposed that she pay fifty percent of the fee up front, as long as Wilomena could get over to London and start her search right away.

The Woodman's Quest

Wilomena asked permission to ring her boss with the client's proposal, and it was reluctantly accepted by the partner.

This was the biggest challenge to date that Wilomena had embarked on and as she sat in her seat in the American Airways flight heading for London, she opened her laptop and looked at the very brief clues that she had to go on;

Subject was born on June 2nd 1978 in the Portland Private Hospital in Great Portland Street Central London.

No knowledge of sex of the child as it was given up for adoption at the time of birth.

The child's father died at the time of birth in Tunisia.

Client has been diagnosed with terminal cancer so time is at a premium.

She stared at the very short list and her heart sank, realising the enormity of the task ahead.

The next morning after she had checked into her modest hotel, Wilomena began her search by calling into the hospital on Portland Street and was very impressed with the entrance hall. She boldly approached the receptionist and asked to speak to the records manager.

The young woman looked at her quizzically at first, but regained her composure and suggested the Hospital Administrator so the young American lawyer nodded and waited in a nearby seat. She had started getting a little impatient, and was about to speak to the receptionist again

The Woodman's Quest

when a large man in a pinstripe suit walked into the reception area.

'Good morning I'm Howard, how can I help you?' His voice was somewhat stuffy and pretentious, but Wilomena ignored that and introduced herself, and then asked if it was possible to speak in private.

She followed him through a large oak door to their left which opened up into a bright white corridor with at least six doors on each side. The third door on the right was his office. As she walked by the other doors, each had a small brass plate with only a number on them.

It seemed quite obvious that he was a manager of something as there were no filing cabinets as such in his office, just a desk, several chairs and a glass cabinet with a few odd ornaments in it.

'I'll come straight to the point Howard; my client is trying to locate her child that was born here in 1978, not long after this hospital was formed. I hope that you can help me by turning up the records of a specific birth to a specific mother.'

Howard remained silent for a while, but then his brows furrowed.

'I'm reading between the lines here miss, I think that your request for information is more complicated than just that, am I right?' He asked.

Wilomena nodded slowly, realising that the man was no fool, so she had to explain to him that her client had left her child for adoption without even seeing it. She had left it in the

The Woodman's Quest

hospital's good hands to clear the whole mess up for her, and returned to Los Angeles soon after the birth.

'Did your client sign a confidentiality agreement Miss Ruzinski? Howard asked.

'This was not mentioned in our meeting two days ago.' Wilomena replied.

'I think she may have, and if this is the case, there is nothing to be done. Those files are destroyed after a period of ten years, so I think that you have come here on a wild goose chase, sorry.' He looked quite smug and superior at the young lawyer.

Wilomena told him that she would ring her client that evening and ascertain if any document was signed, and requested that she had another meeting with him the following day. She wasn't going to be fobbed off as easily as that, but deep down she felt the first door of opportunity had been slammed in her face.

The Woodman's Quest

Chapter 7

Good intentions

Zeta was pleased to welcome an old friend into her shop in Tintagel. She was looking for a special birthstone for her daughter. Her friend Catherine was the wife of an egg farmer Kieran, their large farm was on the outskirts of Truro, in the centre of Cornwall. On this visit Catherine had brought a gift of a pack of freshly laid eggs for Zeta, as well as a manor house cake that she had baked the previous day. Zeta closed the shop for a while so they could catch up on any news.

'Tell me about the young girl that was rescued from under the bay horse on the High Street, it all over the news at the moment.' Catherine asked, as she picked up her tea cup.

After hearing the whole story, all Catherine wanted to talk about was the mystery man hoping that Zeta had an angle on him. Zeta knew, or perhaps suspected the William had a part to play in the saga, but if she was right she knew that Catherine would certainly be the last one she would tell. She decided to change the subject as an idea had passed through her mind.

'What happens to the chickens that retire from their egg-laying on your farm Catherine?' Zeta asked nonchalantly.

Catherine told her that recently they had been able to supply a demand for these birds where people had wanted to rescue them for pets. As they were no longer any use to the farmer, they were happy to give them away, especially to those who would give them a good home. She had paid follow up visits

The Woodman's Quest

to the older birds, and she had often seen that both people and their new pets had flourished beyond recognition.

After Catherine had left her shop, having purchased a ruby pendant and an expensive crystal reference book, Zeta's mind was turned to thinking of her new friend William. He could most certainly benefit from having a few chickens for company at his little caravan, so when she had closed her shop, she drove to the cliff top to Phaedra's cottage.

Zeta had interrupted Phaedra and Bopoh having their fish tea, although those days nothing would surprise her, Phaedra was certainly a one-off and she loved her for it.

'Do you think that William might be a bit lonely in that old caravan?' Zeta asked out of the blue.

'Why do you ask me that Zeta?' Phaedra mused.

Zeta explained her idea to her friend, and then asked her give an opinion. She watched as Phaedra grasped the little stone that glowed in her hand and then thought for a minute.

'William told me that old George is getting grumpier by the day. He never gives William a day off from the milking, and yet since William had overslept one morning George seemed to have got worse. It was as if he was trying to get rid of his 'slave" Phaedra explained.

Phaedra added that before broaching the subject with William, Zeta's first course of action would be to get old George on board. She also promised that if the idea got both of their agreements, she would help to construct the chicken

The Woodman's Quest

run and use her Land Rover to pick up the birds from the farm in Truro for him.

As she drove back into Tintagel that night, Zeta realised that the simple idea of helping her friend with the chickens was going to be more difficult than she first envisaged. Phaedra was of course quite right. Even if she had got the agreement from William, he was only a tenant at the miserable caravan, and there was no doubt that his employer would have taken a dim view of not being consulted. However she did go to bed with a warm feeling in her heart.

She had to think carefully about her approach to George. Going straight to the farmer and asking him certainly would not work; she would have to think of some other way. She thought of threats, perhaps a trade, or maybe an offer that he couldn't refuse. She certainly had some thinking to do that night as she drove to her little house on the edge of Tintagel.

The next morning Zeta made her way to George's farm somewhat nervously. No clear plan of action was forthcoming overnight, but when she got out of her car parked in the farmer's yard, she was greeted by a smiling George, who seemed very happy to see her. She shook his gnarled hand and followed him into his ram shackled parlour. An idea quickly came to her as she spoke.

'Just popped around to see how you are getting on with your tenant.' She asked.

At first he wasn't quite sure what she had meant, and then the penny dropped when he realised that it was William she was talking about. To her relief the response was very

The Woodman's Quest

positive. His impression as a tenant was good, but as a herdsman he was full of praise for him. In turn Zeta explained that William had made a very good impression on her and her friends too.

'George, I have a friend who can let William have some chicken for free, and I wondered, if it was ok with you, to let him have a chicken run up there. They will make nice pets and company for him.' Zeta waited for his response with baited breath.

'Does he know of what you intend my dear?' He replied.

'I intend to ask him if you agree first.' She cleverly responded.

'As long as Bill does his job and pays the rent, I've no truck with it.'

As Zeta made her way up the short path leading to William's caravan, she wondered what his reaction was to being called 'Bill' was. It wouldn't have surprised her, if old George called him that on purpose just to rile him. Her friend was sitting in front of the open door of his caravan and concentrating on carving something with his little red penknife and had not noticed her approaching

'Hello Bill' she said sweetly.

The man looked up without a smile, and she instantly had her guess about George confirmed.

The Woodman's Quest

'Sorry, William, but old George called you 'Bill' just now, but I'm guessing that you aren't too pleased about it.' She said apologetically.

William smiled and nodded at his friend and stood up to shake her hand. They were soon in friendly conversation where William revealed that he wasn't sure whether or not his employer was still happy that he was still there on the farm. Zeta fortunately had some good news for him by explaining that she had just seen George and he had said categorically that he was very welcome there and happy with his work as a herdsman.

The relief on William's face was evident, and when he offered her a mug of tea she took the opportunity to talk to him about the reason for her visit. He listened intently and had many questions; mainly to do with building a good fence; making a good 'run' and how in heavens name could he get any chickens on George's farm without him knowing.

She was at that point confident that William was interested in acquiring the chickens so she told him that George was very happy about the whole thing, with one proviso; that his duties on his employer's farm would not suffer.

William asked just one more question; did anyone she knew, know how to build a chicken run or teach him to look after them? After more discussion, they agreed to meet up with Phaedra two days hence and all three of them go to her friend Catherine's farm in Truro and get the best advice possible.

The Woodman's Quest

William told Zeta that he had just less than six hours between milking sessions at the farm, so he would make his way to Phaedra's cottage at around eleven, but to let him know if there was any change of plan. They parted on the note that Zeta had left a very happy man, pondering the first time that no one in his lifetime had ever been so kind to him.

William sat in the back seat of Phaedra's Land Rover, being escorted to Truro to meet even more new friends. Zeta had rung Catherine the day before ensuring that they got the best reception at the large egg farm. William had worked on several farms but had never been to an egg laying one before, so was very pleased to be shown around by Catherine's husband Kieran.

He explained that the eggs were totally free range and were regularly inspected in order that they could claim that status to their customers. He also explained that there were many specialist people in William's area who, for a price, would erect a secure home for his chickens and advise on looking after them. He reminded them that although they become good pets eventually, they would need time to acclimatise from the very different way of life they had had previously.

It was a very interesting day out for the three of them, Catherine had treated her guests with a huge homemade quiche made with their own eggs, but soon William was becoming nervous about his cows and getting back for milking, so they said their goodbyes and headed back to Tintagel.

As William sat in his little mobile home, he pondered about all the things he was shown to him, he was torn between the

The Woodman's Quest

extra work that would be most definitely needed to look after the chickens, and the obvious benefits for the birds, living in a much smaller and stress-free environment.

Chapter 8

A digestive break

'It's Miss Ruzinski on the phone from England sir.' The receptionist put the call through to Conrad Richmond.

He was the senior partner in an uptown Los Angeles law firm. Very much full of his self-importance, however unless he had lawyers like Wilomena doing such sterling work, his position would have been in jeopardy. Instead of praising them he often treated them badly, only to get the plaudits of their success for himself. He was the one with the fat pay check and profit shares from the partnership, but as usual did the least to earn it.

'I'm in a bit of a hole over here Conrad; apparently all the records of the births from that period have been destroyed, as the client had signed a confidentiality agreement at the point of birth of the child.' Wilomena explained.

'Can't help you old girl, I'm a bit busy right now, just use your initiative ok?' Conrad said as he placed the phone on its cradle, and then got back to reading the L. A. Times.

The next morning Wilomena walked into the hospital reception not nearly as confident as she felt the previous day, but as she approached the desk she noticed that the girl had been replaced by an older woman, much older in fact. She explained she had visited that the previous day, to see Howard and told her quietly that he wasn't very helpful to her.

The Woodman's Quest

'Why am I not surprised dear? No one likes him here.' The woman smiled knowingly.

Wilomena's mind was extremely sharp, and knew in an instant that this lady may be able to help her. She asked her outright if she would like to join her for lunch as she had some questions to ask. It was a long shot, and she was expecting to be abruptly rebuffed, but no, they made arrangements to meet at 1pm in a little restaurant opposite the hospital.

The young lawyer had a spring in her step as she left the hospital foyer, she turned and waved to Edna indicating 'one' with her finger and the woman nodded silently. There now was no need to seek a further interview with that stuffy Howard and she really felt at last that this was a positive opportunity that she was not going to miss.

Wilomena had an A to Z street map in her coat pocket and as she opened it on Great Portland street, she noticed a very large green area very close to it; Regent's Park. She was determined to stay as near as she could, so a leisurely walk around the park, away from the busy roads fitted the bill perfectly.

Wilomena had never been late for a meeting, it was her utmost fear, especially if it was her fault, but this time she was late, and it was her fault. In Regents Park, at the far end there was the famous London Zoo and ever since being a child in Chicago she loved zoos, there was always a surprise around every corner.

The Woodman's Quest

She was in fact only five minutes late after running back all the way to Portland Street and what a relief, Edna was waiting outside of the little restaurant for her. Wilomena was so happy, she could have kissed her.

'I'll bet you've been to the park, am I right?' Edna smiled at the young lady.

Wilomena apologised profusely and had to admit to her that zoos were her weakness which made the older woman laugh. It did however serve as a good ice breaker, and this would be very useful as the lunch proceeded.

She outlined her problem to Edna, and when she told her that Adelaide had terminal cancer and had little time left, it seemed to stir Edna's compassion for her. The young lawyer however, was very careful not to push the friendly receptionist, as any action that might compromise the hospitals confidentiality code could be very dangerous, so she let her guest lead the conversation. Edna had been at the hotel for twenty years, starting as a ward orderly, and had made several friends on the wards, especially to some of the resident midwives.

Time was running out for the receptionist and she had to leave the restaurant, however Wilomena knew that there was still something there to pursue, but continued to leave the onus on her friend. She had promised to call the young American woman as soon as she was able to come up with a way to solve her problem. The number that the American had left with Edna was her private mobile number and so all she needed to do was wait for the call.

The Woodman's Quest

The following night at the hotel, was most disturbing for Wilomena. She had enjoyed the British people's favourite meal of fish and chips, after the receptionist had recommended a local 'chip shop'. He told her that it was customary to eat the meal wrapped up in newspaper and doused with plenty of salt and vinegar. The whole thing was most enjoyable, if not a little too many chips.

Of course this was a recipe for indigestion to the first timer, and subsequently the result was a very disturbed sleep. It must have been two am before she had finally got to sleep and for the first time she was shaken by a dream that was imprinted on her mind. Two people had entered her room in the dream, one was an old lady who called herself Aggie, and she was holding the hand of a bulky man dressed in rough clothing with a hood over his head. Then the old woman pulled the dark figure close enough that she could see his face. The face smiled at her, but it was greatly disfigured, but when she saw his mouth, part of his teeth was visible though his deformed lip. Nothing was said, but in the final part of her dream, the old woman pointed a crooked figure at the deformed man and nodded her head. That was the point when Wilomena woke out of the dream shocked and terrified.

She spent the next day walking along the Thames Embankment accompanied by a host of tourists. She marvelled at the Cutty Sark, an old three mast tea clipper that was moored alongside the great river. The she spent a long time at Cleopatra's needle looking at the hieroglyphs carved on all of its sides. At about lunchtime, she treated herself to a light salad served on a floating restaurant, no more fish and chips for her, she promised.

The Woodman's Quest

Having eaten she glanced along the embankment and a large red bus was approaching which had a destination for Trafalgar Square, so she flagged it down and alighted. It was most satisfying to be among the thousands of excited tourists and it was fun being so anonymous, as she melted into the throng.

She didn't head for the square with its statues, colourful fountains and thousands of hungry pigeons. Instead she headed across the square, admiring the huge statue of Nelson atop of the tall plinth and then walked into the National Portrait gallery. Next to visiting zoos, this was her other favourite pastime. Although most of the subject matter was alien to her, there were ones like the 'Sampson and Delilah' by Rubens, that took her breath away.

As always happens when you are enjoying yourself, a mobile phone rings and to her dismay it was hers. She quickly made a retreat into the square and to her utmost delight, the unrecognised number that was displayed, was Edna.

'Can't talk on the phone Wilomena, but would you like to meet somewhere to chat?' She asked.

Wilomena said that her hotel did a very nice meal, and so would she like to join her at say seven that night as her guest? That confirmed, the young lawyer looked at her watch and was pleased that it was only three in the afternoon, still time to indulge her passion for art.

Spot on time, Edna arrived at her hotel dressed in a long dress in crushed velvet and a dark blue colour, greatly outshining anything that Wilomena could muster.

The Woodman's Quest

'I don't get invited for dinner very often, so I thought that I would make an effort.' The older woman proclaimed self-consciously.

Four delicious courses were presented to them and to Wilomena's surprise they had chosen the same meal for the first three, only the sweet course differed. They found a quiet spot in the hotel lounge for their coffees, which was less exposed and so that they could not be overheard.

It transpired that Edna had a special acquaintance who used to be the senior midwife in the hospital at the time of the confinement of the lawyer's client; June 2nd 1978. She had taken the opportunity to ring her retired friend who lived in some flats in Kensington and Hermione was willing to meet, and promised to give Wilomena as much help as she could. The only proviso for the meeting was that the old lady wanted her friend Edna to be there too.

Two days later Wilomena waited outside the block of flats called Beauregard Mansions in a quiet cul-de-sac in Kensington, probably built in the fifties, but still in excellent condition on the outside. This time the American lawyer decided to make sure that she wasn't late for her meeting with Edna. Spot on 10am Edna turned the corner and the ladies hugged each other in greeting. It was Edna's day off that day, so time was not at a premium for either of them.

Hermione opened her flat door and welcomed them in. The flat was beautifully furnished, in mostly dark oak furniture and she ushered her guests into a well-appointed lounge. Edna had to remind her about the reason for their visit, which immediately lowered Wilomena's expectations. Edna however,

The Woodman's Quest

cleverly commented that Hermione's long term memory was extremely sharp. She did mention however, that sometimes events recalled from the day before were hit and miss and reminded her friend that that was normal for an eighty three year old. Edna began questioning Hermione in a gentle way;

'Hermione dear, can you recall when you used to be at the Portland hospital?'

'Oh yes, I was in charge of six midwives then.' She answered without delay.

'Can you remember 1978 when you were there?' Edna asked.

'Oh yes, it was the year that the hospital had opened, we had many famous people there.'

'I'm going to ask you about one of your ladies who went into labour in June 1978, can you concentrate it is quite important.' Edna asked the old lady.

'Do you mean that American film star dear? It was very hush hush; we were not allowed to talk to anyone about her, some scandal or other I think.'

'You can tell us about that dear, it's ok to talk after so many years have passed. What was her name, can you recall her name Hermione?'

The old lady stalled for a minute, as if that question had hit a blank. At this point Wilomena asked if she could make them all some tea and the smile reappeared on the old lady's face.

The Woodman's Quest

The American remembered that the English do not like tea to be made in the cup, but in a teapot. In Chicago she often visited her grandmother on the north side of the city and recalled how she made her granddaughter learn to make tea 'the right way'. Her family originated from Yorkshire and many of the customs from that area of England still survived to that day. She was just pouring out the tea from the teapot when Edna shouted for her to return to the lounge.

'She's remembered a name Wilomena, now tell my friend the woman's name dear.'

'It was Adelaide, but I can't remember her last name, no, just a minute it was Adelaide Columbine the American actress. Yes that's it, and she wasn't young either, mid-forties I would say, at least.' It all had tumbled out of the dear old ladies' head. Wilomena was utterly amazed and went back for the tea that she had made for them.

Over tea, Wilomena asked Hermione if she remembered the child that Adelaide gave birth to. The old lady looked first to Edna for a kind of approval before she answered. The young lawyer held her breath.

'She didn't hold her child you know, but I often wondered what her reaction would have been if she had.' Still Wilomena held her breath. 'The boy was quite deformed you know.'

Wilomena gave no reaction to the last statement from the retired matron, outwardly she looked as calm as could be, but her mind was racing, really racing! Only the night before, she had had the most vivid dream about just that, a deformed

The Woodman's Quest

man who was smiling at her. Was it a coincidence, or something else?

The Woodman's Quest

Chapter 9

Changes a' plenty

In the two weeks that had followed the trip to the chicken farm, William had suspected there was something different about old George. Usually when milking was in progress there was often a short visit from the farmer. He would not speak, but a faint smile and a grunt was enough for William to be assured all was well with him. He had probably seen the old man about twice in that time and the second time had been at least five days ago.

As he cleaned up after the last cow had been milked, he decided to just look in on George to make sure, so to speak. The front door of the little stone cottage was unlocked, but that was not unusual, so he walked in shouting; 'Hello! Is there anyone home?' The house seemed really quiet for the time of day. He knew that George often had his TV on and blasting out, even if he rarely sat and watched it, considering that it was probably just for company.

All the downstairs rooms were empty so he went back to the disordered living room at looked at the opposite door which he assumed led to the stairs. As he approached the door and reached for the latch, it was already slightly ajar. He looked down at the base of the open door and froze. Three gnarled fingers were just visible and William touched them gently, they were cold, stone cold.

The Woodman's Quest

He could visualise what was behind the door at that moment and his stomach turned over. Instinctively he knew not to disturb anything but instead picked up the house phone and dialled '999'. The ambulance arrived with a cacophony of ringing followed by a police car doing the same.

The police sergeant asked William to leave the cottage and stand in the yard whilst the policeman and his colleague interviewed him. Although he had answered all their questions truthfully, he could feel by the tone of their voices that they were harbouring a suspicious attitude towards him. He accompanied the two policemen to his little caravan where, without his permission they meticulously searched his van.

The constable trod on the flowering fuchsia near the caravan, flattening it without an apology, making no effort to repair the damage he had caused, but William just smiled at him. He had to explain about his life in orphanages and children's homes but neither of them showed any compassion. In fact he thought that they reacted even harder towards him.

He returned to the cottage with the policemen, pleased with himself that they had found nothing incriminating. The two ambulance men were just coming out of old George's cottage and just nodded solemnly to the three men standing outside.

'Do you know if he had a next of kin sir?' One of policemen asked William.

'I don't but a shopkeeper I know in the High Street might. The shop is called 'Mystique' and her name is Zeta' He answered, so they asked him to accompany them to the shop.

The Woodman's Quest

Zeta was tidying in the back room when she heard the voice of William shouting her name. What a surprise when two large uniformed policemen towered behind the bent form of her friend.

'Bad news Zeta, its George he's... well, er... he's not here anymore.' William stuttered the words out unsure of her reaction.

'You mean he's dead don't you?' Then she looked at his face. 'Oh no, it's not old George is it!' She exclaimed and tears were beginning to run down her face.

The policeman asked her if she knew that George had any close relatives, and she told them that he talked about a son John Creswell who lived in Lansing in Sussex, but they weren't close. She offered to help to find his address in the cottage and was pleased when they accepted. William felt much better when he was in Zeta's little car instead of that police car, as they made their journey back to the farm house.

'How are you William, was it you that found him?' Zeta asked as they drove the short distance.

William had just enough time to nod to her as they had arrived at the farmyard. The police let Zeta look in and old bureau and she easily found some letters from George's son with an address and phone number on them. The police then promptly drove away, promising to return in a few days, and as an afterthought they asked William not to leave the area until they said so.

The Woodman's Quest

Zeta placed an arm around William's broad shoulder and offered to make some tea in George's now deserted cottage, so that he could get his breath back after such a harrowing ordeal. They talked for about an hour before she left, promising to return the next day with her friend Phaedra. Once again, he felt so grateful that there were at least two people who were willing to stand by him in his time of need.

As he made his way back to his caravan after locking the cottage door, there seemed very little to smile about. That was until he noticed the crumpled fuchsia bush, with most of its crimson red flowers detached from its little branches. He did his best to repair as much of the plant as possible whilst thinking how fortunate he had been that he had buried his savings there. How could he have explained nearly two thousand pounds to the policemen?

William realised that whilst the police were getting in touch with George's son, he felt that it was his duty to stay and look after the stock and ensure that the milk tanker collections were completed correctly. The driver asked about George, but he made a point of being vague in his answer, coupled with the fact that these milk tanker drivers don't have a great deal of time to chat.

On the third day after his sad discovery, William awoke as normal but not with the sound of the cows but with a sharp knocking on the caravan door. Two well-dressed men waited patiently to see him. The one in front introduced himself as John Creswell and reached out his hand to shake in greeting. He then introduced Noel Simpkins his lawyer and then they departed to the cottage, and asked William to join them there, when he was ready.

The Woodman's Quest

The cows were already at their stalls waiting to be milked, with the queue of the rest of the herd patiently waiting and making their soft lowing sounds. He was always amazed that each cow knew where to go and when, with the least amount of fuss. How unlike the humans, he thought to himself.

The two visitors came out into the milking parlour partway through the milking process, obviously unaware of the farm routine. John was particularly impressed with the efficient way that William had performed his duties and as he was spraying the water to clean the stalls, they stood back, not wanting to soil their suits and shiny shoes.

Soon after the completed milking process, the three men were seated in the cramped living room, where George's son outlined his plans for the farm. In the preceding three days he had already secured a buyer for the little farm, 'lock stock and barrel' and was in a hurry to get back to Sussex. He told William that his services would be no longer required, as of that day and the herd was to be picked up in the afternoon by the new owner. John then passed the loyal worker an envelope, and at the same time asked him to collect his things and leave the farm forthwith.

The two men stood up indicating that the conversation was over, so without shaking hands they left the cottage, waited for William to join them in the yard and then John ceremoniously locked his father's cottage and drove away with his lawyer. William just stood outside the cottage stunned. In a matter of fifteen minutes the job that he had grown to love had been wrenched from his hands.

The Woodman's Quest

~ 68 ~

He wearily made his way up the hill to the caravan, with the unopened letter in his hand. He looked around to make sure that no one was watching, pulled up the damaged fuchsia and retrieved the plastic bag that was secreted underneath it. In the caravan he looked around the little room, scanning it for any belongings, which he carefully filled into his knapsack. Before he zipped it up, he smiled to himself, it wasn't even half full, but that was in fact the sum total of his whole worldly belongings.

He pushed the folded notes, still in the original protective plastic bag, into the smaller zipped area at the front of the army-styled knapsack, along with the unopened envelope from George's son.

Before leaving the farm, he walked among the herd; each one came up to him in turn nuzzling him with their wet noses. He loved them as much as they obviously loved him, but it was time to be strong, and the loud bellowing from the beasts continued to echo from the grassy hill, long after they were out of his sight.

He decided to head to the next hillside to visit Phaedra, he had a great respect for this young woman, in a way she had turned her back on society and had become totally self-sufficient. Her little cottage had its own power supply courtesy of a wind powered generator and this also pumped up the water from her nearby well. Added to this attribute, she was wiser that her years, although he had an apprehension that she dabbled in the 'dark arts' particularly when the thought of that raven, although that bird seemed to be her constant companion.

The Woodman's Quest

There was one other gift that she seemed unaware of, she had the most beautiful voice, and yet she refused to talk about it. He waited at her door, hoping to hear her singing again, but it was silent. He took a quick look around the back of the cottage and was disappointed to see that the Land Rover was not there.

Having waited for about half an hour there was no sign of Phaedra, William made his way to Tintagel and to look up his other friend Zeta; she would know what he should do next. Where normally he would solve his own problems in this case, the whole episode had somehow been a little too much for him so he knew that this time he needed some help.

The Woodman's Quest

Chapter 10

News for Adelaide

Edna could sense the tension between Wilomena and Hermione, as the three of them sat in her flat in London; however she was pleased to see that the old lady had not yet finished in her recollections to the young lawyer, so Edna asked the next question.

'Hermione, whilst we are thinking about the baby can you remember what happened to it when the mother had left the hospital?' She tentatively asked.

'Yes dear, I do recall that there was a great fuss about the baby, being as it was quite deformed with a crooked back, but most alarming was the boy's upper lip. I think that it needed some surgery, but the agency had found a foster couple waiting for him, so there wasn't time to do it.'

Amazingly, the frail old lady had even recalled the couple's name 'Gilpin' and that they had come to London from Filey in North Yorkshire to collect him. At that point the old lady sat back in her armchair looking rather drained, but she had done a wonderful job for them. Wilomena kissed her forehead in gratefulness; she raised a tired smile and waved her arm, already drifting off to sleep.

The two visitors quietly let themselves out of her flat and dropped the latch. Edna promised to call in to see her friend the next day to make sure that their visit had not taken too much out of her.

The Woodman's Quest

They had been just one hour at the flat but it seemed more like three. Edna told her friend that she would like to take a walk in Hyde Park which was a short distance from the block of flats and so they headed in that direction. In the park, they took the path that crossed it diagonally and about halfway along it they spied an empty wooden bench underneath a large sweet chestnut tree.

Edna looked down to see her American friend rewinding her hand held recorder, and they listened again to the momentous interview with the graceful Hermione.

'I think I should like to ring my client and tell her some of the news, what do you think Edna?' Wilomena asked.

'I don't know about that my dear; much of the news is not good is it?' Edna was thinking that giving her details of the physical condition of the baby would be very hard to take, especially thinking about the state of Adelaide's own poor health.

'How about you omit the bad news, but tell her that the baby was a boy and his last name was Gilpin? You aren't exactly lying to her and it may do some good.' Edna was a great source of wisdom at that point.

The young American lawyer nodded and gave it a go. After explaining to Josephus that she had a very important call for his mistress, he reluctantly put her though to Adelaide. After apologising for her early call she told the old film star that she was sitting in a sunny Hyde Park under a tree, with a friend who worked at the Portman Hospital.

The Woodman's Quest

The line went very quiet after Wilomena had given her the sparse details, just as Edna had suggested. Adelaide was just taking the information in, as the shock of hearing those details about her long-lost son would have been a shock to anyone. However, she now knew that she'd had a boy and his surname was Gilpin.

'Have you anymore facts for me dear? Where does he live? What does he look like? Does he want to see me?' She asked breathlessly.

Wilomena gently told her client that she was still at the beginning of the search and at that time had no idea how long it would take to get answers for her questions. She wanted to tell her that her brief was for only a few more days in London, but didn't want to spoil the exuberance that her client must have been feeling at that moment.

As she listened to the 'click' of Adelaide's receiver, she waited as a second 'click' happened before the phone line went dead. She smiled to herself as she realised that the second one was Josephus discreetly listening in to their conversation.

Wilomena tried to visualise just what Adelaide was going through after that phone call, who never even knew that she had given birth to a boy or a girl, and now she knew, as well as his surname. Her life could not be the same again, of that there was no doubt. The next step in her quest would be to get to Filey and that had to take some planning.

Her boss had called that evening in her hotel who, out of the blue, told her that she must wrap up what she was doing and return to Los Angeles by the end of the week. Another case

The Woodman's Quest

had materialised and only she could deal with over there, and the case meeting would begin the following Monday at 9 am.

That had left her only two days to get up to Filey and begin her search all over again. She tried vehemently to persuade Conrad that the scent was getting stronger, but he wouldn't budge. There was only one thing to do, ring Adelaide right away.

The Woodman's Quest

Chapter 11

William's secret

Zeta's shop was unusually busy that morning and so she hadn't noticed William enter, but it was soon evident that something had changed. Gradually most of the customers began to drift outside virtually at the same time.

It was somewhat unusual that the gentle chit chat had stopped too. As she looked around the shop, in the far corner, leaning over one of the glass-topped counters was a small thickly set man with a crooked back and carrying a rucksack. If she hadn't known him, the sight of such a character, would have been somewhat menacing to her too.

'William, what are you doing over there, and why aren't you at the farm?' She asked.

One sad look from the man said everything to her, and her compassion was raised towards him. She closed the shop for lunch and they went into the little back room where the séance was held and sat opposite each other at the small round table.

He told her the sad story of the treatment he had received from George's son and his lawyer, and that he was planning to catch the first bus to Wadebridge and hopefully find some lodgings there. He had just come to say goodbye. She made him stay where he was, whilst she made some tea and offered him to share some of the sandwiches she had made that morning.

The Woodman's Quest

'Look William, I don't want you to leave Tintagel and I know that Phaedra would be devastated if you had left, having not said goodbye.' Zeta became quite tearful and sad; realising that this man had no other friends and his future looked bleak.

She then asked him to follow her outside and climb an iron staircase at the back of the shop to a door on the first floor. They entered a spacious room which was a little dark and somewhat damp smelling, and there was some furniture in the room which was covered in dust sheets. It looked to William that there had been no one up there for quite some time.

'I used to live here for several years, after I had taken the shop, but now I have a home of my own. Would you like to stay here for a while, at least for as long as you decide what you are going to do?' Zeta asked.

'Yes that would be great Zeta, but I must insist that I pay rent.' William replied, opened up his bag and showed her the dirty plastic bag full of notes.

As he pulled the bag out of the small pocket, a white envelope came out with it, and fluttered to the floor. Zeta picked the envelope up to pass it to him and noticed it just had his name hand-written on the front and it hadn't been opened. He indicated to Zeta that she should read it for him.

'*Dear William, please accept this cheque as full and final settlement for your dismissal from Home Farm. I wish you well in the future.*

The Woodman's Quest

John Creswell'

She looked at the cheque made out to William Gilpin and told him that it was for *'Two thousand five hundred pounds'* He looked at the cheque in disbelief.

'Well you deserve every penny of this William, you never had a day off all summer' She retorted.

'I loved those animals Zeta, and they loved me, the hardest thing I have ever done, was to leave them.' As he told her, a single tear ran down his face, but not as much as what had streamed down Zeta's.

They settled on £150 per month for the flat which had a bedroom, a living room with a little annex for cooking and a small bathroom. He had stayed in hotel rooms since he left London, but never in a flat of his own. All the rooms were basically furnished but clean, and Zeta promised to supply some bedding later that day for him.

As they walked back to the shop to open up, William asked about Phaedra, and mentioned that he had been past her cottage and noticed that her car was not parked in its usual place. Zeta told him that she had gone back home to visit her folks in the New Forest.

She had received a letter addressed to the shop as 'care of' that looked quite important, and when Phaedra had read it, left the same day. William thought about how she sang on the occasion of his last visit to her cottage, and hoped that perhaps his comments had made her think again about her future.

The Woodman's Quest

News travelled very fast in Tintagel, so fast that the old woman who owned the rescued goat was soon calling on Zeta to tell her the news about the sale of Home Farm. Aggie of course realised that Zeta would have known that, but she used that news as a disguise to ask what had happened to William.

Knowing that it was Saturday, and meeting day, Zeta parried Aggies questions for the time being, but to Aggie, her friend's smile had not fooled her in the least.

The two other regulars were not able to make the meeting, so it was just Zeta and Aggie seated around the little table in the backroom of the shop. Aggie couldn't wait any longer for the news about William and was just about to ask her again when William himself appeared, asking to join them.

He re-told the story of his layoff at the farm to Aggie, but he could tell that she was not showing a great deal of interest, and so he asked her if there was something she wanted to tell him.

'I have a message for you William; it is a very important one.' Aggie said in a sort of disembodied voice. 'There is someone looking for you and I have visited her through spirit world.'

Initially he thought about the old score that hadn't been settled by the money lenders in London, but when Aggie said 'she' he lifted his guard and asked Aggie who was this 'she'?

She told him that it was a young woman who had come from afar, and she was just the agent for someone very important

The Woodman's Quest

to him. This made William think deeply about all the people that he had met in his life, but couldn't think of anyone in his past that he could call 'important'. He tried to change the subject with the old woman but she was not going to be moved.

'I watched the young woman in my dream last night William, and she has told this person, many thousands of miles away, that she has made some progress in her quest to find you. The signs are not good though my boy, as she may well have to leave and return without completing her mission.'

William was utterly dumbfounded by all these jumbled messages but, he did ask Aggie one question;

'Tell me who you think this very important person is, if you can Aggie?' William asked trying to humour the old woman.

'Don't scoff at my words William, but I do know that it is very important that you are found, she has something that could alter your life, but I don't know what it is yet.' Aggie seemed a stressed by his question.

'What do you mean by 'yet'? He probed.

'Maybe we should take a break, who's for a cup of tea?' Zeta asked, trying to break the tension in the room.

The meeting had broken up early with Aggie leaving the shop wishing that she hadn't mentioned about the situation with William, but it had to be said whether he liked it or not. She had felt very strongly that this 'important' person was something to do with his birth, maybe even his mother, but to say that to him at such an early stage could have been a

The Woodman's Quest

disaster for William, as there was no substantiation, only a dream.

The next day, William decided to go back to the community notice board in the main car park in the town, to see if there was any chance of some work. As he scrutinised the cards that were pinned there, he couldn't see anything that resembled any suitable opportunity for his skills so he reluctantly made his way back to the little flat.

The shop was open and he could hear talking so as he stepped into the shop, he nearly tripped over the wheel of a wheelchair. Zeta was describing the duties of the shop assistant to a young girl, who turned her chair around and greeted William rather hesitatingly.

'William, this is Hannah, I may have told you about her. She was going to work here at the weekends but she had had a nasty accident with her horse on the High Street and has damaged her spine.' Zeta said.

'I still want to work here at Mystique even like this.' Hanna said bravely pointing to her wheelchair.

'Are you the girl that was rescued by someone who lifted the horse away from you?' William asked innocently.

'Yes that's right, my Dad said that he saved my life that day, I would love to meet that man and thank him, and do you know him William?' She asked.

William shook his head and left to go to his flat. He did feel happy inside that she had made some recovery from the horrific accident, but he knew that no one must learn about

The Woodman's Quest

what he had done, consequences would then get out of control and that must never happen.

In the following week Zeta had convinced William that he needed to get a bank account of some sort, in order that he could put the cheque to some use. He had explained that in his past he had not has any permanent address, and that was why he had to insist on cash payments for any work that he did.

They agreed to open an account in the local Building Society with a passbook. Not only would he be able to see at any time what his balance was, but if he was to travel in any part of the country, there would always be somewhere to access his cash.

The bank accepted Zeta as the proposer and character reference and in a very short time he had banked the cheque and most of the cash that he had saved, the whole amount came to four thousand pounds. The figures printed out on the first page on his bank book did not fill him with enthusiasm, as it would have other people, money had never been the biggest part of his life.

Zeta had also convinced William that as he now had a permanent address, it would be a very good idea that he should also apply for his passport. She told him it would always be something that would prove his identity, even if he hadn't any need to go abroad. William took this on board and with her help they soon had the form filled in and had his photograph authenticated. Zeta thought again about the message from Aggie about the person who was looking for him, but at the time didn't share it with William.

The Woodman's Quest

Chapter 12

The invitation

Phaedra was somewhat surprised and a little disappointed to receive that letter, which was delivered to her by Zeta. The postmark was Philadelphia USA and it was obviously a stiff card inside, and so before opening it, her heart sank. Mikhail did know that she had turned her back on society, and things like wedding invitations were probably the last thing she wanted to consider.

Slowly she opened it up, and of course her guess was right, it was from her only brother and as much as she tried to put it at the back of her mind, she again recalled how he had played a very big part in saving her life a few years before. He had written a special message inside of the card that had touched her greatly;

`Dear Fay I have made a bet with Marcy that you would come to our wedding. She thinks that you are too headstrong to consider this invite, but I know you!*

I remember when we sat locked up in that room, both looking death in the face, and it had taken all that time to make me realise how much I loved you. If you ask Bopoh the raven, he will tell you to come over here and witness the biggest day of my life.

The Woodman's Quest

If you don't make it Fay, I shall be heartbroken, and anyway Teddy is coming from L.A. surely that's enough 'ain't it?

Please come.

Mickey'

The date of the wedding on the card was only five days hence so she gave Zeta her parent's telephone number in Lyndhurst to let them know that she would be arriving that evening.

Before she left her little cottage she had to turn off the generator connection to the windmill, and then after a thorough check that all was secure inside, she locked the front door and fired up the engine in the Land Rover, thanks to the new battery.

Five hours later Phaedra was pulling into the Gables' gravel drive, and even before she had time to get out of her car, her parents were there to receive her. It was by far the best homecoming she had ever had.

All their travel plans had been arranged by her brother Mikhail. They were booked in the Hilton at Penn, right next to the University as well as close to the Penn Museum where he worked as assistant curator. Even the International Airport was only twenty minutes away, he'd thought of everything. Their American Airways flight was a midday departure and they had arranged a taxi to take them there.

In all the excitement, Phaedra couldn't remember where she had left her passport, not thinking that she would ever need it again. After some panicky searching in the house, it was finally found in the glove box of her father's Lexus. She

The Woodman's Quest

remembered that the last time she had used her passport was when she and her brother went to France to visit their grandmother.

Theo and Helen Spiros stood at the top of the white marble steps flanked by pink marble columns that supported a portico. This was the example of a wealthy Greek family and Victor was highly impressed. As he looked at his wife Lydiya, who just managed a thin smile, her Russian upbringing was always to give the opinion that this sort of portrayal of wealth was a little on the crude side.

Marcia's parents were quick to explain that Mikhail was at work at the Museum and that Marcia was upstairs on her room. They sat in the library waiting to see their son's future wife, but they didn't have to wait long. She burst into their presence like a whirlwind full of excitement, going first to Phaedra to give her a hug.

Marcia's mother Helen, asked the two young women to stand together for a moment. Although Phaedra was a little taller and she had black hair instead of deep red, their features could very easily be mistaken for sisters she exclaimed.

'But Mom, in two days' time we will be, don't you get it?' Marcy was quick to respond and that caused great mirth to all assembled.

They only had to wait an hour before they were joined by Mikhail, who was so pleased to see his sister at the house of his prospective in-laws.

'How much did you bet me Marcy? A million I think you said!'

The Woodman's Quest

He explained to Marcia's parents that they had had a bet to see whether his sister would have joined them, and that bet Marcy had lost.

'Well Mickey, let me show Marcy what you wrote on my invitation shall I?' Phaedra smiled as she dodged her brother's hand and passed the invitation card to her. 'I think he cheated, don't you, how could I have turned him down when I read this?' She asked.

Marcia asked if she could show the card to her parents and Phaedra nodded. Helen burst into tears after reading it, asking Phaedra to perhaps tell her what really happened. As she took the card back from Helen, she whispered to her that it was still too painful a memory, but promised that one day she would write to her explaining why.

Mikhail had started his vacation from work on that day so he and Marcy spent the next two days in the city showing Phaedra around. Marcia had quickly grown attached to Mickey's sister and although they were very different characters, there seemed to be a deep connection between them, almost transcendental.

Phaedra's favourite location in the city was the place where they took a leisurely stroll alongside the Schuylkill River, and eventually arrived at the East Park Reservoir in the middle of Fairmount Park.

'This is where we met, right on this bench here.' Marcia said, and looked lovingly at her betrothed.

The Woodman's Quest

Mikhail seemed to be a little embarrassed because he knew what was coming next. Marcy told his sister that he was crying when she met him and he had even called her by her name, even though he had never met her before.

Mikhail looked at Phaedra, appealing for her not to get involved, and she knew exactly what he was referring to. Less than a year before he had met Marcy, Mikhail had had a torrid affair with a French woman called Marcella and amazingly she had the same copper coloured hair as his future wife, although his French lover was about twice her age. At that time, he was suffering a great loss of Marcella, who had disappeared in strange circumstances.

Quickly Phaedra changed the subject by asking where they were to get married, and Marcy did not seem too happy that it was going to be at her home. She particularly wanted a church wedding, but had given in to her parent's request. Apparently the wedding was going to a 'no expense spared affair' but the look on the couple's faces proved to Phaedra that it was not their preference at all.

 'I guess there are some things we just have to let our folks have, don't you agree?' Phaedra said, hoping to diffuse the obvious tension.

 'Mickey, you mentioned in your card that Teddy was coming from L.A., when would that be?' Phaedra asked.

Mickey put his arms around Marcia's waist lovingly and smiled as he realised that this was his moment to get back at his sister, and he wasn't going to 'spare the horses'. He carefully explained to Marcy that Teddy was a very old friend of the

The Woodman's Quest

siblings from when they were very young, it looked as if Phaedra might have got married to Teddy before his own wedding.

'He just wasn't my type Marcy, we tried but I couldn't cope with the guy jetting off to all parts on bloody concerts, leaving me in his boring flat most of the time.' She countered her brother's jibe, just as she always was able to do, with ease.

Mikhail gave in once again and said that Teddy would be arriving the next day and was to stay at Marcia's home. Her mother had prepared a special room made up for him, even with a grand piano in it if he got lonely.

Whilst the young ones were enjoying their walk around the city, Phaedra's parents Victor and Lydiya were being entertained by Theo and Helen at the mansion. After a sumptuous lunch they separated for a while and the two women had left the men in the study. Helen detailed the arrangements for the wedding to her guest, as she escorted her around the many rooms that they had.

After a protracted time of listening to all of the details, Lydiya sat on one of the nearest armchairs and asked Helen to do the same. When Helen sat opposite her, Lydiya soon noticed how tired she looked.

'Just be still now Helen, and gather your thoughts for a moment, I want to ask you something personal, do you mind?' Lydiya asked boldly. Helen seemed to get smaller in the chair as if the wind had been taken from her.

The Woodman's Quest

'I think that you can see right through me can't you?' Helen asked meekly.

'Helen, you are not happy, and you haven't been happy for a long time have you?' Lydiya passed her a Kleenex tissue that was on the table nearby.

The Woodman's Quest

Chapter 13

The Greek Wedding

Wilomena tried her utmost to convince her boss Conrad, to give her more time in order that she might complete her task of finding the child. She explained to him that the search had taken a new twist and in the first instance she needed to get to a northern part of the country called Yorkshire. With only two days to achieve her goal, would be impossible for her to achieve any closure on the task.

As usual, Conrad became utterly intransigent on the matter and eventually, she had to admit that his word was law. Her big problem was what was she going to say to Adelaide? She had retired early but was unable to sleep, at around 2am her mobile phone rang and she recognised the Southern drawl of Josephus the faithful butler.

Adelaide, had taken a turn for the worse and she had to be rushed in to the Saint Vincent's Hospital in Los Angeles for some tests. He told her to halt the searching for the time being, until they knew if she was going to stabilise. Wilomena had to make a show of sadness to the caller, but deep down was relieved somewhat.

The clerk at the check in desk at Heathrow airport told her that there was a spare seat on the L A flight that night at 9pm, which gave her plenty of time to make a final call on Edna at the Portman Hospital to let her know that she was returning to America earlier than planned, and to thank her

The Woodman's Quest

for all the help she had given. After that day with Hermione, there was definitely a very good chance that she would have been able to find the lost son of Adelaide's but at that moment it seemed that it was not to be.

Wilomena arrived at the hospital just in time to catch Edna leaving, but asked if she could take her to lunch at the restaurant across the road, to which Edna gladly accepted.

'I was hoping to involve you on a little trip to Filey this week, partly to help with the journey and partly that you might like to find out more information on Mr. Gilpin.' Wilomena said.

'I would have loved to join you because I am owed some days off and I could have joined you on your trip, but still maybe next time that you are over here eh?' The hospital receptionist tried not to show her disappointment, and Wilomena held her hand in a comforting gesture.

'Please text me if you have anything, anything further that Hermione remembers, or anyone else for that matter. I'm determined to get back on the case, except I was given some worrying news about my client. She has been taken into hospital, the future is uncertain at the moment.' Wilomena explained.

As she sat in the American Airways flight lounge, her mobile rang. She quickly answered it thinking about her meeting that she had that day with Edna, but no, it was from John Spiros. There was a sort of relationship going on with the sports editor of the L.A. Times, but pressure of work was the reason that they never became serious.

The Woodman's Quest

'Hi Mena, where are you right now?' John asked.

'Well, I'm sitting in the departure lounge in Heathrow Airport at the moment' She answered a little coldly.

'Is that London England? What are you doing over there hun?'

She told him some brief details and said that she was called back to the States and would be at home early the next morning. In reply, he told her that in two days there was going to be the biggest Greek wedding that Philadelphia had ever seen. His sister Marcy is marrying this English guy. John told her that he worked at the Penn Museum but was not that complimentary about that.

'Meet me at the airport Johnny and I'll let you know, ok?' She answered with her arrival time and then disconnected.

As she checked in at the departure desk she shook her head, as she was thinking about flying half way around the world to the East Coast one day, and then flying again to the West Coast on the next – crazy! One thing in her favour though, was that the eight hour flight would be only five hours on the clock! John seemed to have no concept about the distance involved, or the damage to her brain cells, but on reflexion she would like to be cheered up at a big wedding.

'Look Johnny, I hope you realise that I've got a client meeting at the offices at 9am on Monday, and you know what that boss of mine is like.' Wilomena said in a mock protest to the six foot Greek Adonis who hugged her as if she was a rag doll.

The Woodman's Quest

'No worries hun, it will be a piece of cake, I've got work to do back in L A too you know.' His smile could melt the polar ice cap, but she was never going to let him know that.

Wilomena had been to his parents' house in Philadelphia once before, and who could forget that. A house it wasn't, more like a mansion on one of those old cotton plantations, but in this case bigger and even more palatial, virtually built in marble. His father seemed formidable and cheerless, but John knew how to handle him, just shout back even louder!

As the plane touched down at Philadelphia she had a few misgivings, hoping that Hugo Spiros would be a little friendlier towards her than she had experienced on her last visit.

Fortunately they had both slept virtually all of the flight, she because of all that travelling and he, well he liked sleeping, especially with a beautiful lawyer's head on his chest.

After a five hour flight their taxi dropped them outside of John's parents' house and the first person to greet them was Marcy. She gave them traditional hugs and then introduced Wilomena and John to Mickey and Phaedra explaining that they were brother and sister and their folks were inside with Hugo and Helen.

'I expect that I am the Koumbaro for the wedding is that right Marcy?' John asked.

John explained to Wilomena, that a Koumbaro is a Greek styled 'best man' but in traditional Greek weddings it is much more than that. Of course, being as he had just flown in from L.A., his mother had arranged everything for him. They also

The Woodman's Quest

needed a Koumbara which is the female counterpart and that role was to be played by a first cousin Alyssa, flown in from Athens.

They were all sitting down to a grand dinner when they heard the front door chime and within ten minutes a tall thin man in a white suit and black fedora hat entered the dining room. He took off his hat to reveal shoulder length blonde hair. Mikhail and Phaedra rose up together to greet the man, but Phaedra was there first, hugging and kissing him.

'This is Teddy, everyone!' Phaedra shouted to all assembled.

She was overjoyed that he had arrived at such an opportune moment, as in a strange way she was feeling a little out of it, at the time. Mikhail kindly moved chairs to the other side of Marcia so that Teddy could be beside Phaedra. For once she seemed to have blossomed in her heart, as if she had been waiting just for that moment to arrive.

Phaedra had spent much of that year alone in her little cottage in North Cornwall with little or no company. One of the few visitors she had was that William. He was of course a very interesting character and she had an underlying feeling that he was quite a bit more than he made out to be. He had a fine mind and did appreciate the finer things in life, at least when he was exposed to them. There was something in her mind told her that he had several secrets in his past that he seemed unwilling to talk about.

It was strange therefore, that in the midst of the chatter at the dinner table, did she think about him at all. She unconsciously pulled the snake chain necklace out of her

The Woodman's Quest

dress exposing the pale orange stone that was fixed on it. Unknown to her she was being watched intensely by Wilomena who was sitting opposite her at the dinner table.

'What's that you've got there, Fay? Is it your birthstone?' She asked nonchalantly.

Phaedra was very deep in her thoughts and didn't answer her at first, but Teddy came to her rescue.

'I gave it to Fay, it used to belong to my mother and before that, my grandfather used to keep it in his pocket. It's very old and has some strange properties attached to it. Perhaps you'd like to hear about it sometime Wilomena?' Teddy answered and Phaedra gave him a look of tender thanks and squeezed his hand. She knew that he still held a torch for her, but her own feelings were still in the clouds.

In the fading light of the extensive gardens, Wilomena made an effort to catch Phaedra and try to get to know her better. Mysteries were her weakness and there was no doubt Mikhail's sister was a real enigma. What was it about this tall black-haired woman? She had got to know.

'There's so much I want to ask you Fay, but before I do, I would like to tell you a bit about me, is that ok?' She linked her arm in hers in a friendly manner and met with no resistance.

'Ok, then here goes. I'm a lawyer in a L.A. practice and up until recently I was covering rather boring cases. So boring in fact that I was thinking about giving it up altogether, but just recently something amazing happened to me.'

The Woodman's Quest

Wilomena told her about the aged old actress in Los Angeles who recruited her to try and find someone. She had just made a breakthrough and had to be recalled to start a new case back at home.

'Back home? Where did you have to go to find this person Wilomena?' Phaedra asked.

She told her new friend that only the day before, she had flown back from London and was most disappointed that having made the first breakthrough in her most difficult case; she then had to abort it.

'I had just got the surname of the person I was looking for Fay; I know it would have been very tough, but that with some more luck, I'm sure Mr. Gilpin would be found.'

Phaedra stiffened a little when she heard that name 'Gilpin'. She had just been thinking about him, only an hour ago at the table. Wilomena felt the stiffening of her friend's arm and perceived that she was a little cold, so she suggested that they return to the house.

Back at their hotel, just before her parents retired for bed, her mother asked Phaedra if she was well and she replied that she felt that she needed to go to the bar and have a drink before bed, stating that the whole day had been a little overwhelming.

She ordered a milky drink in the hotel lounge and sat in a deep comfortable chair to collect her thoughts. Did the stone she was wearing warn her about what was to come? Who was the 'old actress' and what had she to do with William?

The Woodman's Quest

~ 95 ~

She decided that in the small amount of time left, she would prize more information out of Wilomena if it was the last thing she did.

The Woodman's Quest

Chapter 14

Phaedra finds her voice

As they say in America; 'It sure was a swell affair'. The wedding ceremony and the following reception was a fantastic pageant that could only happen in such a place as the mansion of the Spiro's. Phaedra looked at her father Victor, and she could read the weak smile that he gave her. She knew that he'd just about had enough, large gatherings gave him a headache, but the excitement did not have the same effect on her mother, oh no!

Lydiya was holding court amongst the Greek guests. They seemed fascinated by the way she spoke, alternating in English, French and of course Russian. She had always been the show off of the family and that moment it seemed to be her turn to shine once again.

Greek wedding receptions were high on music and dancing, but low on the quieter side of the enjoyment scale. Phaedra felt some relief as she could easily spot Teddy coming towards her with a big smile on his face.

'Fay, how do you feel about letting these people know what you're about?' He asked, and pointed to the white Yamaha baby grand in the corner of the vast room.

She reluctantly nodded and followed him through the dancing, screaming throng. Teddy checked first with the Koumbaro, and as soon as John saw them heading his way he

The Woodman's Quest

produced the loudest shout they had ever heard. The room fell silent and all looked towards the bride's brother.

'Ladies and Gentlemen, tonight for your enjoyment, two of our guests will play and sing for you, and put a little class into this gig! He shouted.

Phaedra stood at the side of the piano whilst Teddy started the performance off with a couple of bagatelles from Franz Liszt and Beethoven called the 'Leibestraum' and 'Fur Elise'. He then cued to Fay that it was her turn.

On the way over to the piano with Teddy, Phaedra had suggested she would sing a piece from West Side Story called 'There's a place for us' and then her own interpretation of Stevie Wonder's 'Lately'.

Teddy finished the little concert with a piece of Jazz from pen of Cole Porter and made famous by the legendary Art Tatum, called 'Night and Day'

When they had finished, the room was silent for about twenty seconds and then the floor simply erupted! No one was expecting such a performance from the couple, not even Victor and Lydiya, who rushed over to her daughter and hugged her so hard she could hardly breathe.

'Darling, your voice is back, your voice is back! Her mother screamed as tears ran down her face in relief.

Fortunately the guests had soon returned to their merriment, bent on getting that Greek legendary wedding and reception to be the greatest on record. Teddy ushered Phaedra outside

The Woodman's Quest

to the garden to talk, but they had been spotted by Mikhail and Marcy and had unfortunately caught them in an embrace.

'Sorry about this you two, you must let me congratulate you 'sis' for a wonderful recovery, you are now going to fulfil your early promise aren't you Fay. Please say that you are going to use that voice again.' Mikhail pulled her from Teddy and hugged her.

'This is my best wedding present Fay, hearing you sing. I hope you don't mind, but Mickey has told me what you went through to get to this point, and I'm truly humbled.' Marcia just stood in front of the tall dark woman and burst out crying. She was still sobbing as Mikhail led her back into the house.

'I remember when you came to my granddad's flat on my sixth birthday party in a beautiful black and gold dress and sang 'Happy Birthday' to me in Russian and do you know what Fay, I still haven't got over that. I loved you then and I love you even more now.' Teddy looked down into her dark eyes as he spoke, looking for a response.

'Teddy, please don't ask me, please don't. I'm still very confused.' Phaedra knew that he was about to pop the question and she didn't want to break his heart again.

She did agree however, to go to Los Angeles after the wedding was over, for a short stay with him and see what he was doing there. She also told him that at that point, she had no intention of taking up singing again, as her confidence was still in tatters. On the other hand, she secretly felt the warm glow of the rapturous appreciation that the guests had made

The Woodman's Quest

after her performance, and that certainly did something to her deep inside.

At midnight most of the wedding guests had reluctantly gone home, leaving only the closest members of the family together. Victor was already asleep in Hugo's favourite arm chair and Helen suggested that the maid make up a bed for him and Lydiya at the house.

Over breakfast the next morning, Phaedra announced that she was going to Los Angeles with Teddy for a while, which came as a very pleasant surprise to John and Wilomena who had booked their flights back that morning. Teddy tried to book the same flight, but was unable to get any seats, so Phaedra promised to look up Wilomena later on the next week for lunch. Wilomena gave her a business card to make sure that she called, reminding her that they had never got the chance to talk that much at the reception.

Hugo had to leave the table on a pretext that an urgent business call had to be dealt with. Victor on the other hand needed some peace and quiet and left the room to commute with the flowers in the mansion's extensive garden. This left Helen and Lydiya alone at the breakfast table as the newlyweds had jetted off to Hawaii for their honeymoon.

They resumed the conversation that they had started sometime before the wedding. Lydiya remembered that Helen seemed sad about something and reminded her of it. It had been quite obvious to Lydiya that Helen had had to take a 'backseat' in her relationship with Hugo and she didn't need to be reminded of his forthright manner when he discussed anything.

The Woodman's Quest

'How do you cope with someone who is always overbearing and refuses to accept that he might be wrong sometimes?' Helen asked.

Lydiya thought for a moment before answering her. She had to be very careful because that question could have easily been directed at her own husband, because that description of Hugo's character could have easily been referring to her own.

'It would be easy to answer you with a comment like; 'stand up to him', but in your case that would not produce any success.' Lydiya opened. I think that the best answer I can think of Helen is not too clever. You've been married a long time just like Victor and I have, so in the end it is all about what you want out of your marriage.'

'Would you both could consider staying here as our guests for a while, so that I could get to know you both more?' Helen pleaded.

For once Lydiya could not answer Helen directly as her question needed Victor's input. She knew that he was already missing his quiet country style living in the New Forest. Big city life did not attract him at all, also his health was getting more delicate and his stamina was nothing like it used to be.

Helen could see that a big question like that had caused her new friend some concern and her intuition told her not to pursue that thought.

'I have an idea Helen that perhaps would suit us much better. We live in a large house in the middle of a forest. It's

The Woodman's Quest

very peaceful there with nature all around us. Why not try and persuade Hugo to agree for you both to come visit us in Hampshire, you can stay as long as you like. You can also use our place as a base for touring the country if you wish to. Or if that is too much for Hugo with his work commitments, why not come on your own. We would certainly look after you.'

This was all a little too much for the hostess, as she broke down in tears, and then suddenly rushed out of the room having spotted Hugo returning after his phone call. Just as Lydiya had expected, Hugo hadn't noticed his wife's distress. Certainly that was Lydiya's view anyway.

The Woodman's Quest

Chapter 15

The downfall

William lay on his bed in the flat considering what he might do in his quest to find some work. He had taken his shirt off and felt a twinge on his shoulder. He began to rub where the pain was, and as he felt further down his arm, his had brushed over the deep scar that ran from just below his shoulder to his elbow. The edges at each side of the scar were still red, indicating that the wound had been inflicted quite recently.

The memory had been a constant source of anguish for the man as he lay there, so he averted his eyes further down his arm to his open right hand. The empty hand had triggered memories further back in his childhood. It had been the third children's home that he had been moved to in the three years after he had become a teenager.

He was classed as 'disruptive' and once anyone has a label, it tends to stick with them. He may have been disruptive but only because he had always been the butt of jokes and jibes that were incessantly aimed at him because of his physical appearance. Very few of the people who took charge of the classes in the children's homes, tended to be of a compassionate nature, and often turned a blind eye to his suffering.

He quickly learned that the only defence for such treatment was attack. Usually the boys of his age were less aggressive than the much older ones. Bullies tended to be bigger than him and they always had a sadistic attitude, and at that time for young William, the attacks had become more and more difficult to ignore.

The Woodman's Quest

One morning after breakfast, which he invariably ate alone, he happened to be leading the line of children to their first class when an apple hit him hard on his back. When he managed to turn around it was obvious to him who the culprit was. Three of the taller boys guffawed loudly, and each congratulated the other on such an accurate throw.

William felt a red mist form behind his eyes and he picked the green Granny Smiths apple and instead of throwing it back at them, held it up over his head and squeezed it. In seconds the fruit had been crushed to a pulp, and only then did he throw the mashed apple at them. They ducked and the remains of the green fruit ran down the white wall of the corridor. For a moment, William stood and blocked the older boys' path saying nothing, but he just hoped that they might try to get by.

'The next time it will be one of your heads that gets it!' He shouted, noticing immediately their silly smirks had been wiped off their ugly faces.

After that incident he knew that they would still be making fun of him, but from the crushed apple incident, it would always be out of earshot. He continued to be moved from one children's home to another, right up to his eighteenth birthday, when finally he was told that he had to leave the institution to find his own way in life. One thing he had learnt on his journey, that adversity was the mother of invention and so he told himself to aim low in his target for employment, and he'd always get by.

At the age of twenty five, his philosophy of aiming low in the job world was at least working. A kitchen porter in a small Italian restaurant was his lot. The other staff would leave him alone as long as he did his job. On occasions there would be

The Woodman's Quest

a fellow worker in the wash house that was probably out of prison or off the streets, but soon they would move on, unable to tolerate the mundane conditions. One those men commented to him that it was better where he came from – Wormwood Scrubs.

Next door to the restaurant was a small betting shop and he was soon making a habit of standing idly at the TV screen watching the races. One shady character came over and asked him if he had a tip for the next race, and showed him the list on a newspaper; Newmarket 3 o'clock. William looked at the list and without thinking pointed half way down the list.

The man screwed up his face and shook his head saying that selection would never win. He then left, to place a bet and then soon returned to stand next to William. Together they watched the progress of the race, and he watched the stranger getting more and more excited, even the commentator was shouting.

'I don't believe it pal; your horse came in first. Just wait here will you and I'll collect my winnings.' He exclaimed with a big smile on his face.

He returned with a handful of notes, and waved them in Williams face. He had backed the horse that William had chosen on the paper, and had won over one hundred pounds. William tried to explain to him that he had no idea about horses, but the stranger would hear none of it.

He introduced himself as Harry Smith and William did the same. It seemed to him the Harry wasn't at all interested how he looked, and not being treated as a freak was highly refreshing. Harry laid the list of runners for the next race on

The Woodman's Quest

the table in front of William, and asked him to pick a winner again. As much as William protested, the stranger just smiled at him and pointed to the list again.

William shrugged his shoulders and peered at the list again. The harder he looked at it the more difficult it got for him to choose a horse's name. He looked at the man's face, who seemed to have faith in him but what if it lost this time? Hesitatingly he pointed to the name that was next to the top and Harry rushed to the window to place his bet.

This time William didn't wait for the outcome, as soon as the man was instructing the teller and his back was turned, he beat a swift retreat out of the shop. A few days later, he was tempted again to return, and as the TV screen was near the entrance, he stood against the table opposite, and watched the action. No sooner had he began to relax, when Harry Smith came up to him again brandishing the newspaper with the new runners' lists on them.

'Hey Bill, glad you're in again mate, that horse you tipped made me a hatful of money, here's your share.' The man forced some twenty pound notes in his hand and then proceeded to offer him the next list of horses. William looked sternly at his new friend and decided to tell him the truth.

'Now look here Harry. I am no tipster, in fact that was the first time I had ever been in a betting shop. You must have mistaken me for someone else.' William said firmly, and then handed the notes back to him.

As he walked back to his little bedsit a few streets away he realised that Harry was being rather generous to offer him

The Woodman's Quest

part of his winnings. The gesture of the man had gone deep in him, so he turned on his heels and returned to the betting shop.

Harry was standing with his back to him at the teller, obviously laying another bet, so he went up to him and apologised for his rudeness. The smile he received from Harry told him that it was alright. They sat together on a chair in the middle of the room and discussed the races, and William had underlined the fact that he was truly a novice at the sport, but even when he had said it, he really didn't think that his new racing companion believed it.

That afternoon William had predicted three winners, one second and a third place out of a total of six selections. In the end he reluctantly accepted twenty-five percent of Harry's winnings which amounted to fifty five pounds. That was William's introduction into racing, but just like all gambling, the entertainment factor soon descends into obsession, the young man soon frittered away his meagre earnings just to get onto that 'winning streak' again.

He had resorted to borrowing from local loan sharks to fuel his addiction and finally he knew that there was going to be a reckoning to pay. He knew that not repaying a loan to these people was dicing with danger and one night it came to pass.

He was careful not to leave work at the same time, or take the same route back to his room but one late evening he was just about to walk up the steps of the old converted tenement when someone came out of the shadows from behind. He had a steely grip around his neck and in the other hand was brandishing a cut throat razor.

The Woodman's Quest

The thug's companion was a mountain of a man who immediately punched William in the solar plexus which made him double up in pain. A red mist clouded William's eyes as he grabbed the knife hand of his assailant and at the same time lifted him over his shoulder as in a fireman's lift. The big man ran to stop him but he was too slow, William physically threw the knifeman into the chest of the other man without making a sound.

The young man stood for a few moments, waiting for them to get up, but neither did. He separated the prone bodies and gasped as her saw the result of the altercation. The razor, held by one of them had plunged into the throat of the other. Not only that, he saw that when the two bodies had collided, they had staggered backwards, towards an old style low iron fence. One of the spear-shaped spars had pierced through the first man's back and then impaled itself through the chest of the other. Blood was everywhere!

During the altercation, he had received a flesh wound in his shoulder, but fortunately they hadn't cut an artery. When he got into his room, with great dexterity he was able to sew the open wound with a needle and thread, and by the next morning, the bleeding had stopped.

That was at the time that William decided that he had to escape from London and its dangers. He headed out of town westwards, hoping to find work on the way, but had no idea where that was going to be.

The Woodman's Quest

Chapter 16

:

The city of angels

Teddy was overjoyed that Phaedra was able to join him in L.A after the wedding of her brother. He lived in a high rise bock in the centre of town and on a clear day there was a glimpse of the ocean. He worked as the principal piano at the Los Angeles Philadelphia Orchestra whose home was the Walt Disney Concert Hall in the Hollywood Bowl.

The first day in town was spent showing her around the usual sights that the entire tourist fraternity frequented, but she did not seem that impressed, particularly when he asked her to look on the floor to identify the impressions of famous people from the past embedded in the concrete.

They headed for the Hollywood Bowl, he had his own entry pass, so he was able to gain access to the place that he worked, and to let her see for herself the stunning auditorium of the concert hall. Just as they were about to enter the side door, a man was just leaving, and Teddy had said that he dearly wanted her to meet him.

'Hi Lewis, how are you? Let me introduce you to Phaedra.' He said.

The man looked familiar to her in a strange way, but he seemed rather aloof and in a hurry, so after a brief conversation with Teddy, the man left in his car. As they entered the hall he explained that Lewis was the son of Louis Owen. Only a few years before, they had both received a generous income from his father in his will.

The Woodman's Quest

Mickey also told her that the house her parents were currently living in, was the same house that Louis Owen used to live in. This information had made her realise that was why she vaguely recognised Lewis, as he would have had a strong resemblance to his father whom she knew well.

Phaedra asked why the man seemed so aloof, but Teddy shook his head, and seemed just as surprised as she was at his attitude on meeting her. He explained that he was the resident conductor of the orchestra, and before that, he was the lead violinist.

Something said to her that the man was troubled in some way, because she remembered that her brother said that although he was invited to the reading of his father's will, he did not attend for some reason. She had mentioned that fact to Teddy too, but said that the man was not that approachable by anyone, but he was unable to get the chance to talk about it to him.

Phaedra thought that she would try to get to the bottom of the enigma that was Lewis Owen, and perhaps she could help him come out of his shell. When they used to live together in the apartment in Southbourne, she rarely saw him so it was not surprising that here in Los Angeles, Teddy had to attend the intense rehearsals for the next programme of events, so she was free to roam the city on her own.

She did however, take heed of Teddy's warning to avoid the areas where a woman alone might be in danger. City life was beginning to wear thin for her after a short time, and so she seemed drawn to the more open spaces, of which there were many in that great city.

Her heart was uplifted when she walked along Palisades Park, and strolled along the path overlooking the ocean, with the

The Woodman's Quest

pale blue outline of the Santa Monica Mountains in the far distance, which completed the magnificent vista. Each side of the track that she strolled on, was flanked by Eucalyptus and Palm trees and in the warm breeze the smell was utterly intoxicating for her. The sun was out that day, and the wind was coming off the ocean. She had never seen such beauty, and indeed it was the first time in America that any one place had pulled her heart strings and cleansed her soul.

Towards the north end of her walk she saw that the beach was deserted, apart from a couple of dog walkers and a few people like her, who thought very little about the hustle and bustle of the city life. She decided to leave the path and took her shoes off and let the golden sand get between her toes. The biggest difference between her home in Cornwall and there, was of course the sunshine. The pace of life was the same, and she was grateful that in the vastness of the State of California there was still the space to find one self.

She had made good progress along the wide stretch of golden sand and had covered at least two kilometres before having to avoid two teenagers rushing out of the sea, racing towards an older woman that she presumed to be their mother. They kicked the sand up in their exuberance not even noticing Phaedra. She stood and watched as they collected their towels from their mother who surprisingly waved at Phaedra to join them.

'Really sorry miss, they are so full of energy, I do hope that they didn't splash you.' The woman said.

'That accent sounds familiar, are you English at all?' Phaedra asked politely.

The Woodman's Quest

The two girls chimed in saying that they came from Buxton in Derbyshire and that they had lived in Santa Monica for the past ten years. The woman introduced herself as Sarah and the girls were Rowena and Sara.

She had laid out a beautiful picnic and what a surprise, Sarah invited their visitor to join them. They sat on a crimson Scottish-checked rug and there was a lovely array of sandwiches and a potato salad bowl. Phaedra reached for a sandwich and looked at it before she tried.

Sarah smiled, asking if she had ever eaten any Jewish food before. She explained that they were Tuna Nicoise sandwiches and Hummus and Vegetable sandwiches. Phaedra observed that the twins attack them with gusto, so she tucked in and enjoyed every mouthful.

Phaedra told them a little of her background and where she lived, and then said that she was visiting a close friend Teddy who played piano with the L.A. Philharmonic Orchestra. She looked and smiled at Sarah, but was concerned when her face dropped after mentioning Teddy.

'Our Daddy is the Conductor there.' The girls said in unison.

'You're not Lewis's wife are you Sarah? You can't be!' Phaedra shouted, and Sarah nodded and smiled disarmingly.

After their meal, Sarah asked Phaedra if she would care to join them at their home, the girl's mother instinctively knew that there was much more that this young black-haired stranger had to say, and she eagerly wanted to find out as much as she could from her. Meeting someone who was

The Woodman's Quest

connected to her husband and from home, was an opportunity she didn't want to miss.

The journey to their house in Santa Monica was short distance from the beach. The Volvo glided up San Vicente Boulevard and then turned into 26th Street. A large ranch-styled bungalow awaited them. The girls were very excited to be visited by someone who came all the way from England.

'I knew Lewis's father you know Sarah, and at this moment my mother and father are living in his old house in Lyndhurst in the New Forest.' Phaedra opened with a bang; she knew that that statement would shock Sarah to her roots.

The response was earth shattering to her hostess, she just about held on to the coffee cup that she was holding, and had to sit on the couch for a moment as the wind had certainly been blown out of her sails. A chance meeting on Santa Monica beach had resulted in opening a can of worms that she thought had been buried for years.

After a short time, she went to a large oak bookcase behind her, and rummaged for a while until she found a letter and passed it to Phaedra for her to open. After protesting at first the young woman opened the letter, and recognized the heading immediately. It was from Mark Bussell in Southampton, inviting Lewis to attend the reading of his father's will. Phaedra was very careful not to speak about what she had read in the letter, she knew instinctively it was a very delicate subject for Sarah.

After a few minutes of heavy silence, Sarah asked Phaedra if she had attended the will reading. Phaedra shook her head,

The Woodman's Quest

but told her that both Teddy and her brother Mikhail had. Once again she avoided telling Lewis's wife that her brother had told her that Mark had tried many times to contact Louis's son but had received no response.

Sarah finally got up out of her seat and sat alongside her visitor and told her that the relationship between his father and Lewis was a very strange one. There had been a mix-up when he was born and his father wasn't aware of his existence for forty years. In fact his mother told him that his father was dead. She said that her husband was a very proud man and for some reason known only to him, he couldn't seem to forgive his father for all those years of absence.

It seemed to Phaedra after such an emotional speech by Helen to what could only be described as a total stranger, proved to her that her husband's actions were not agreeable to his wife. Phaedra pulled out the necklace around her neck and gripped the glowing stone in her palm, and suddenly she decided that she had to do something to help this man whose anger was consuming him. The only time that she had met Lewis, was when he was coming out of the auditorium door and even then, she could see a deep suffering in him.

'I wonder if you and Lewis would like to join us for dinner. I hope to be in Los Angeles for at least a week longer, because Teddy has invited me to see the first concert in the new season, Rachmaninoff, I think it is. Do you think you could arrange it Sarah?' Phaedra asked.

The relief on her hostess's face was clear to see, as she was soon hugging her visitor. They exchanged phone numbers

The Woodman's Quest

and she promised to ring Phaedra the moment that she had spoken to her husband.

'Please call me Fay, that's what my friends call me.' Phaedra answered.

Sarah and the girls drove the young woman back to Teddy's apartment in downtown L.A. and reiterated that she would call soon.

At first Teddy was not pleased that she had invited Lewis and Sarah to dinner, without checking with him first. He told her that at that point it was impossible to ascertain when they would be able to find the time. Lewis very often called a practice at short notice and it could be at any time of the day.

He was of course unaware that Phaedra had an ulterior motive. She was aware of Teddy's excuses but it seemed to her that those excuses didn't hold much water. Lewis, his boss seemed to her to be a bit of a tyrant based on her very short knowledge of him. She felt also that unless someone got to the bottom of his inaction regarding his late father, Lewis would continue down the path where no one would be able to challenge his misguided thinking. In fact she felt strongly that only a stranger like her could have the power to make him think differently about it.

Phaedra tried to explain this to Teddy, but his reaction, like most men in his position was looking at it as a risk to his job, he didn't want to be seen as party to some crack-pot psychoanalysis challenge to his boss's character. They continued to discuss the pros and cons of her idea, when her phone rang.

The Woodman's Quest

'Hi Sarah, it's great to hear from you. Yes we would be able to make it to your home tomorrow, just one thing Teddy is concerned about the concert practise. Well, that would be no problem then, see you tomorrow, bye.' Phaedra' mobile went into disconnect mode.

Teddy just stood in the middle of the lounge of his flat and stared at her with is mouth open in amazement; she had only met Sarah once, and had already made quite an impact. He had never persuaded Lewis's wife to get him to cancel the evening practice so that the four of them could have dinner together, and in his view that was a great achievement.

The fact was, he had never been to Lewis's house, never mind been to dinner with him. Fay told him their address was on 26th Street in the district of Santa Monica and although she couldn't remember the house number, she would be able to recognise it when they got there.

'I hope that you don't get too controversial with him Phaedra, he's got quite a temper you know.' Teddy remarked.

'Look Teddy, will you stop being a wimp, if the guy doesn't like to hear the truth, what reason could you have to continue working for him anyway? Start being a man Teddy, what's the worst he can do to you, kill you?' Phaedra shook her head.

The Woodman's Quest

Chapter 17

Big decisions

It had been only two days since Wilomena had returned to Los Angeles from the Greek wedding in Philadelphia, yet she had much on her mind. Firstly the problem of John, he was certainly something big in her life and on the flight back home, he started hinting about moving in together. Worst of all, he had said that he loved her, although to put it bluntly, pretty well full of drink at the time.

Another question had come to mind, what about this Phaedra? She remembered that having just explained her mission in England finding the last name of Adelaide's lost son, Phaedra's response had looked like it had touched a nerve or something, and she suddenly reacted strangely the moment Wilomena had mentioned 'Gilpin'. Did she know him? At that stage it was impossible to ascertain.

Next problem was Conrad, her boss and senior partner. Although he had taken her off the Adelaide case, he had proposed that she represent a large corporation who were involved in some major fraud. This was the sort of case that would drag on for ages, dealing with boring accountants and even more boring spreadsheets.

With those and other more minor challengers in her life, it seemed to her that she would like to 'stop the world' and jump off, but how, when and where? These were the biggest questions for her at that time.

The Woodman's Quest

She duly attended the recently arranged board meeting at the corporate headquarters, but she was totally bored in just fifteen minutes after she had been introduced to its members. Her mind wandered to Adelaide's situation as soon as the CEO began to speak, and he droned on in a monotone fashion so badly, that she finally had to excuse herself and get out of that horrible place. Outside of the skyscraper building, she was relieved to see that there was a taxi waiting for a fare.

'Saint Vincent's Hospital please, it's urgent.' Wilomena was in no mood to see the sights of L.A., she just wanted to see Adelaide and get the 'lowdown' on her situation.

She easily found the old actress's room on the third floor in a private wing, the last door along a narrow corridor. Just before she opened the door she held her breath, desperately wondering what she would find in there. It was only nine thirty in the morning, and perhaps Adelaide may not be in a good enough state to receive visitors, none the less, she took a deep breath and pushed the door open.

Adelaide was not in bed, but standing at the window looking out. She turned around to greet her visitor with a broad smile on her face and held out her thin arms to give Wilomena a hug.

'It's so nice to see you young lady. I think you have made a wonderful start, so please sit on this chair and tell me all about it. I hope that I can call you a friend.

Wilomena told her every detail about her search in London for her son including the conversation that she had with

The Woodman's Quest

Hermione the retired midwife who attended Adelaide in her confinement. She thought very carefully about omitting the information concerning the baby's deformity, but Adelaide was very perceptive and insisted that Wilomena come clean. Saved by the bell, her mobile chirped and she excused herself to answer it in the hallway.

'What the hell are you doing Wilomena? Why did you leave the board meeting? They are awaiting your return!' Conrad was shouting.

'Sorry Conrad I had to check in at St. Vincent's I think I have picked up a virus when I was in London, and I didn't want to pass it on to them. Will you come to visit me when they have cleared me from the isolation ward?' Wilomena again portrayed a very clever response.

'No, no it's ok, just get yourself better, I guess I will have to get over there and 'wing' it.' Let me know when you can get back here.' He stammered.

'Does this mean that you can't visit me here? She asked, but the phone went dead, and she smiled at herself and knew that he wouldn't come within a mile of the hospital, game set and match.

The young lawyer went back into the private room to apologise to Adelaide, but she was getting into bed and apologised for being suddenly tired with all the excitement.

'Will you return this afternoon, Wilomena? There is something I want you to do for me.' Adelaide wouldn't let go of her arm until she had agreed to return a few hours later.

The Woodman's Quest

On the first floor of the Medical Centre was the cafeteria and at 11am had just started to serve luncheon. Macaroni cheese was on the board so she had chosen that with a large fruit salad to follow. As she ate her meal, she thought about how she would tell Adelaide about the severe disablement of her son. At the same time she had also to tell her about being taken off the case.

It was around 3pm when Wilomena carefully opened the door to get into Adelaide's room, and was pleasantly surprised that she was not only up but it looked as though she was leaving the hospital, being discharged.

'The Cancer has gone into remission according to the doctor, and I'm going home Wilomena. I've got a car coming in half an hour will you come back with me please.' She stood up out of her chair and reached for the young woman who gladly took her thin arm.

Josephus came into the room immaculately dressed, pushing a hospital wheelchair. Adelaide smiled sweetly and with a little help lowered herself into it, and they were off. The formalities were duly completed at the reception and in less than an hour the wheelchair was entering her private elevator in the mansion, on her way to her bedroom.

Josephus had been instructed to tell Mildred the maid to prepare a room for Wilomena as she was to be staying for a while as Adelaide's own companion, without of course being consulted. Wilomena did not protest, as at it happened it suited her purpose well. It was the ideal opportunity for her to gather her thoughts and make plans for her own future, as now there was no going back for her.

The Woodman's Quest

~ 120 ~

In the late afternoon Wilomena accompanied Josephus in the old pink Cadillac to pick up some of her things from her flat and she was soon unpacking them in her ornate but comfortable room in Adelaide's mansion. Dinner was served in Adelaide's room and Wilomena was told to dress and attend her. It was like being in a time warp, but in its simplicity, for the young woman, a welcome relief.

'I think that I ought to finish the conversation about your son Adelaide, is it convenient to talk now?' She asked.

As the old, but sprightly woman sat up in bed with her tray, she beckoned for Wilomena to remove it and then gestured for her to continue.

'I'm afraid it is not good news Adelaide. The old midwife had remembered that your son was, well, quite disabled. She also remembered that he had been adopted by a couple who lived in the Northern part of England, whose name was Gilpin.'

'Why are you not still searching for him then, is it that despicable boss of yours?' The old lady asked knowingly.

Wilomena was quite upset with that direct question, and was a little unprepared for it. She had to agree that she had been forcibly taken off the case and was at that time absent without leave from her job and in fact had lied about being poorly to Conrad.

Adelaide was still as sharp as ever, she knew that the young woman was unhappy with her lot and asked her to consider her offer of an alternative employment. She told her that because Conrad had cut short her search for her son, she

The Woodman's Quest

asked that for an unspecified time that Wilomena could work directly for her, matching her current salary and as soon as they had agreed the terms, Adelaide wanted her to fly back to England to resume her search.

This proposal was like manna from heaven for Wilomena, but after a short period of thinking she became quiet and did not answer the old lady.

'I know what you are thinking my dear, what if I should leave this mortal coil before you have completed your task? Well, I've already thought of that.' With that she rang the bell at the side of her bed and Josephus appeared in a flash.

She had instructed him to bring in a draft proposal so that the young lawyer could look at it as some late night reading. Wilomena took the hint and retired after a sweet little kiss on the cheek of her new possible benefactor.

There was certainly a great deal to think about for Wilomena. It would have been a very big decision for her. Resigning as a junior partner in a respected firm in the city could be suicide for her future, but just lately she had to ask herself was that the sort of future for her? The alternative, to put it coldly, was to be associated with an old woman who was in the advance stage of cancer, even though at that time in some sort of remission.

The document was clearly put together by someone who knew the latest US employment law and was particularly clear concerning Adelaide's demise should it happen during the time she would be working for her. In short she was tasked to

The Woodman's Quest

complete her mission and it specified that there were two particular aims that Adelaide wanted to be clear on.

Firstly, that her only son would inherit her estate subject to the usual identification safeguards, and secondly that he must come to Los Angeles himself to claim it.

This clause in the document was rather earth shattering and would put most people off taking it on in the first place, but to Wilomena it was as a 'red rag to a bull' and she had no doubt in her mind that she would complete the task come 'hell or high water'.

She awoke in the very early hours of the morning in her room at Adelaide's mansion by a warbling sound and sleepily looked at the recognition name on the screen of her phone, it was Edna from England.

The Woodman's Quest

Chapter 18

Aggie and the woodsman

Saturday night had arrived without William having being aware of it. He was still struggling to find work in the little town of Tintagel, so that all days of the week seemed the same. The summer was drawing to a close, and there was little chance of any seasonal work. Even Zeta's little crystal shop had begun to wind down somewhat. Very often at this time of the year the mornings would be interspersed with low level sunshine and heavy cloud cover. The latter would often descend into sharp rain which could lash into the face if anyone ventured onto the cliff top.

At six in the evening one Saturday, it was already dark and he needed the lights on in his little flat earlier and earlier. He had become a member of the mobile library and spent much of his time with his favourite classical poets. A sharp bang on his door broke his concentration and it made him jump a little.

'Aggie wants you to join us at our little meeting downstairs William, would you care to come?' Zeta shouted through the door, he opened it and reluctantly agreed to join them.

The old lady had come up with several 'dream' episodes during the previous meetings he had attended that seemed to star William in. Considering some of the events that he would rather not be reminded of, he did sometimes find it a bit of intrusion, but he came down his steps and entered the shop anyway.

The Woodman's Quest

Four shadowy figures sat around the circular oak table huddled around a dim candle light, their faces barely visible. He noticed they had left a space opposite the old woman Aggie so in silence he sat down and smiled to them all individually.

'They are still searching for you William.' Aggie spoke slightly in a disembodied way.

'Oh yes, and who might they be then?' William asked, trying not to be too condescending.

Aggie then explained another of her dreams to all of them, saying that she had travelled halfway across the world this time, and she had met a very famous person who was very old but she had a very important message for him. The old goatherd seemed to be going into a trance and her voice seemed to waver as she spoke.

William tried not to laugh at her performance, but he looked around at the other listeners to see that they were deadly serious. He looked again at Aggie, who in turn seemed to be staring at the ceiling. She told him that the old woman that she had met in her dream was dying and that there wasn't much time left.

'Can you give me any more information Aggie?' William asked, but then he started to laugh out loud.

Zeta held his arm as he asked, because Aggie wasn't in any fit state to answer him. The old woman made a strange gurgling sound and without another word dropped her head sharply onto the table with a bang that surprised everyone. The other

The Woodman's Quest

three women occupants on the table sat stock still for what seemed an age. Bertha finally shook her on the shoulder but she did not move.

William rushed around to her and gently pulled her up into a sitting position and Zeta put the electric light on. They thought initially that she had knocked herself out as she banged her head on the table, but William's eyes grew wider as he gently felt for a pulse on the side of her scrawny neck, but there was no response.

In ten minutes the ambulance had arrived at the shop but after a short attempt of a defibrillator, she was sadly pronounced dead. The shock to her friends had been immense, but the paramedics declared that she had had a massive heart attack and had died on the spot where she sat.

The local police man had called to see each one of the séance attendees individually and had declared that poor old Aggie had died of natural causes. The next day Zeta closed her shop in respect and gave William the task of contacting her new wheelchair bound assistant to tell her that she had no need of her services at such short notice. She was too upset to do it herself.

It was raining that Sunday morning but that was of no consequence to William, he knew where Hannah Deville lived, it was about three miles north of the shop, but at least it was on a road. He had reached a wooden signpost for 'Heron's Roost' and was soon banging on the double oak doors.

The woman that answered the door was not that friendly. In fact quite hostile at first, but as soon as he mentioned where

The Woodman's Quest

he was from, she quickly warmed and asked him inside away from the inclement weather.

'Hello William.' A young voice came from behind the woman that he recognised instantly as Hannah.

'Really sorry Hannah, but Zeta's shop will be closed today.' William said. He then explained that a good friend of Zeta's had died the previous night, and she had taken the news badly.

He was made to feel at home in the great wood panelled room, and he was quick to admire its qualities. He said that he had spent some time in forestry, and had recognised the type of wood that the panelling in the room had been made from, being Scots pine.

Hannah's father Alex came into the room just as William had spoken and was greatly impressed it the visitor's knowledge and promptly asked William what he was doing for work at that time. When William shook his head, Alex asked whether he would be able to take a walk around the land surrounding the house.

They got into the Land Rover Discovery and drove about two miles north on an unmade road until they came to an enclosure in a broad-leafed wood badly in need of some forestry management. As they walked through the trees, William noticed the main problem; the trees were in need of a serious thinning to allow for new growth. Also that there were many examples of non-British species that were blocking out the natural habitat, for instance the rhododendron bushes

The Woodman's Quest

were in great abundance and yet beneath them the land was bare.

When William had made the comments to Alex, he offered his visitor the stewardship of the woods starting immediately. William said that he didn't own a driver's license yet and Alex responded that it was not a proviso for the job, although he offered to help in that area. To the west of the woods there was a small woodsman's cottage not unlike the one that Phaedra lived in, on the cliff top. The cottage had a lean-to shed which contained all the tools he would need, including petrol driven chainsaws with adequate protective gear.

They agreed a salary on the spot and William told his new employer that his offer was just what he was hoping for all his life, and promised that Alex would not regret giving him that opportunity.

He refused the offer of a lift back to town, as he wanted so much to contemplate how fortunate he was to get this chance. He also, for the first time, thought about old Aggie and the last message that she had for him. He weighed it up in his mind and decided that the detail of her message was so vague that it would be best for him not to dwell on it. However in the memory of dear Aggie, he decided that his motto from that moment on was; 'whatever will be, will be'.

The next morning being Monday, Zeta was in for a surprise. William told her the exciting news that he had, and remarked that she could not be happier for him and assured him that he would always have the little flat above the shop should he need it.

The Woodman's Quest

She also told him that Phaedra had rung her from Los Angeles in America, and said that she was heading back to Tintagel in the next few days, and like Zeta was devastated about the news of Aggie. Wisely she did not tell William about another matter of when Phaedra had met a lawyer called Wilomena, and she had mentioned about looking for someone called 'Gilpin' and felt that she didn't want to muddy the waters for him, at that time.

He was about to leave for his new job and had called in to the tiny shop to say goodbye and return the keys of the flat to her, when Zeta passed him a little parcel. He opened it and was puzzled to see a small mobile phone.

'This is a 'pay as you go' phone William. I have loaded a few numbers on it for you including mine. When you get the time, ask Hannah up at the big house to teach you how to use it will you?' Zeta said and turned away from him, hiding the tears in her eyes.

When he arrived at Heron's Roost, he was let in by Hannah who showed him around the back area of the house to the garages and outbuildings where she showed him an old Massey Ferguson tractor. Hannah told him that it had been topped up with fuel, and her father had told her to tell him that it was for his use, to hitch up the trailer and load in anything that he would need. Previously, when he had been working in some of the other jobs on farms, it was necessary that he knew how to handle a tractor, but for this job it was an absolute must.

Before he drove it away he asked Hanna to look at his new mobile phone, and explained to her that he needed to be trained on it, having never owned one before. As she fiddled

The Woodman's Quest

with the phone for him he smiled to himself, but of course, said nothing. She then told him that the battery on the phone needed charging and so he asked if her father could bring her to his forester's cottage the next day, when she had charged it.

William had an excellent memory; he easily found the route to the cottage, drove the tractor and trailer around the back, and he was pleased to see the front door key of the cottage was attached to the tractor keys, they had thought of everything. In only one day, the Deville family had stocked up the larder with food and a clean set of bedding had been laid out on top of his little truckle bed.

The light was fading fast, so he lit a fire in the wood burner and settled down for the night. His mind was still active though, thinking about what to do with that stand of trees. A long inspection on foot was the first thing he planned for the next day.

The Woodman's Quest

Chapter 19

The error of his ways

Sarah was flabbergasted with the reply from her husband Lewis when she first broached the subject of meeting Teddy and Phaedra for a meal. Normally, his usual response for any suggestion like that would have been a straight 'no' and then he would always make the excuse of work, or tiredness. That time however he seemed quite enthusiastic about the prospect. He even went so far as to ask his wife if she would like them to come for dinner at their home.

In all of their stay in America, this would have been the first time that anyone connected with his work would be entertained at their home. Initially she was in a sort of shock with his reply, but soon recovered and rang Phaedra with the good news. She looked at Lewis again after ringing, and he was still smiling with the prospect. What had happened she pondered to herself, and shook her head in amazement?

On his way from the auditorium, Lewis had felt really bad as he drove home after he had met Teddy, his principal piano in the orchestra. Teddy had introduced his companion as Phaedra, but as usual, he had blanked her off with a brief handshake and offered no conversation with the young woman.

He tried in his mind, to make the usual excuses for his bad behaviour but this time there weren't any. He was a talented man, at the top of his career and doing the things that most

The Woodman's Quest

people involved in his field would give their 'eye teeth' for, so why was he so unhappy? Suddenly on impulse, instead of going straight home he changed direction and headed for the ocean shoreline. He parked his car and walked onto the beach.

The sea air filled his lungs, and as he looked down he saw a big friendly dog sitting at his feet with a wet stick in his mouth hoping for Lewis to throw it for him.

'Brucie, come back here will you!' Lewis could just ascertain a distant shout.

Further down the sandy beach he could make out a man and boy waving his way, so he took the stick and threw it towards them. Of course, the big wet dog didn't go back to its owners; instead he returned the stick for Lewis to throw again, the dog had obviously found a new friend. Lewis had thrown the stick for Brucie two further times before the boy arrived and grabbed the enthusiastic dog.

'Sorry sir, he's a real nuisance ain't he, but we love him just the same.' The boy said.

His father arrived and also apologised for the dog, but Lewis would have none of it, in fact he laughed for the first time in ages. The two men shook hands and introduced themselves. The man's name was Walter and his son was Joe. They were taking a few days off from his work in the city, and he made a joke of his job as a plumber. Walter asked what Lewis did for a living and he just answered that he played in a small orchestra as a violinist.

The Woodman's Quest

He looked at the father and son as they rushed their goodbyes to him and was soon engrossed in the fun they were having with their dog. For once he was deeply moved and somewhat jealous of the father and son having such a great time without any sort of pretence. Suddenly his heart became full and began to cry, he cried so hard that somehow he couldn't stop. That chance meeting, as so many are, was a catalyst for Lewis as he examined his own life.

Before he and his family had moved to the USA, his life was simpler and less of a rushed merry go round. His talent lay as a virtuoso violinist which although meant lots of travel, it was more predictable.

At the age of forty, something big happened to him and his whole family. His father had come into his life; a father that his mother had said was dead. Getting to know his father at such a late stage in his life was not an easy one and as he got to know him, he very soon had to realise that he had Jewish blood in his veins.

His wife Sarah had accepted this knowledge much easier than he did, as both of her parents were of the Hebrew faith. The whole thing had been further complicated, as the person whom he thought was his mother, was in fact his half sister, and his birth mother was the one that he thought was his grandmother. She had died with that secret, without telling him.

Lewis, from the moment he had met his father, had looked at his life, not as a new one, but as one where his whole identity had been taken away. What made it worse for him was that there were no rules to help him re-adjust to his altered past.

The Woodman's Quest

He had a father, who apparently had no idea of his son's existence having left to France before he was born, and the two women in his young life had lied to him blatantly for whatever reason. The whole thing was a mess and the result was that he felt betrayed by everyone in his life.

He had always been a sensitive person in the past and this seismic change had resulted in him receding into himself, and so to the outsider, he had become rude and unfeeling. He gave no one, outside of his family circle, any opportunity to reach his deep hurt and confusion, not until the day he had met Phaedra.

Not long after he had moved his young family from England, enticed by the wonderful opportunity of resident violinist at the famed L.A. Philharmonic Orchestra, his baby son Zachary had contracted hepatitis and had passed away only months after they had settled in their new life. His wife was devastated and yet extremely brave, having opted to stay in America for her husband's sake. She probably had hoped that at long last Lewis's work in an orchestra would mean that he would not be travelling around the world, but have a base in Los Angeles.

As he trudged alone in the sand, he thought about Sarah and the twins, and for once he realised that they had been dragged halfway around the world, into a beautiful area and yet they had endured such bad treatment by him. From that moment he vowed that there would be a change in his attitude, and even if it meant that he was to leave his work, he would do so for the sake of his family.

The Woodman's Quest

The next day after another gruelling practice, Lewis announced to all assembled that the following day would be a holiday. As the surprised and yet happy members of the orchestra were leaving the auditorium, Lewis waved to Teddy as he sat at the piano, and shouted that he looked forward to seeing him and Phaedra at his home the next day. Teddy looked back in amazement too shocked to speak, so he just nodded back to the conductor in agreement.

Phaedra was waiting for Teddy back at his flat and she noticed that he was still looking a little confused and even shook his head after he had kissed the dark beauty.

'I've got the day off tomorrow Fay, the first one we've have had when we were practicing, what do you think has happened to him?' Teddy asked.

'I've been thinking about the man in the last 24 hours, and at the same time I've had this stone in my hand. I can't explain it Teddy, but we'll find out tomorrow at Lewis's home.' Phaedra had an air of confidence in her voice.

Santa Monica was one of the best areas to be living at the time and it was no effort to find the Lewis residence. The ranch-styled bungalow was built in yellow sandstone and the bright sunshine had bought out the soft colour. Phaedra felt an aura of peace as they entered the thick carpeted hall.

Rowena and Sara were the first to greet them with a polite 'Shalom' and then ran off screaming with excitement. Lewis and his wife Sarah came to greet them and they both received a hug from Sarah and were relieved at last that they were looking at a broad welcoming smile from Lewis. They

The Woodman's Quest

were asked to go there as early as they could, because their plan was to have the starters for the meal set on the house's patio in the sunshine, as Sarah wanted to show Phaedra her attempt at a Japanese garden.

'I know that you were probably surprised to be here Teddy, but I want to be the first to apologise for the way I've been treating you and all the other members of the orchestra, but during your time with us today, I hope to make amends for that.' Lewis stood up out of his chair and indicated that he would like to embrace his fellow Englishman.

Around the dining table, in front of his wife and children, Lewis told them all what he had experienced two days before, when he had walked on the beach and had met a stranger, his son and a dog called Brucie. When he had finished the story, all four of the adults were reduced to profuse tears. However the twins were in for a greater surprise when he told them, that subject to their mother's agreement, he was willing for them to get a dog, but it had to look like Brucie. That went down a storm with Rowena and Sara particularly when their mother quickly agreed with Lewis's proposal.

Just before they were leaving the Lewis's, Teddy went to his car but Phaedra held back and Lewis whispered in her ear.

'You are not aware of this Phaedra, but it was because of meeting you, that I have not only come to my senses, but I've also put my life back on track. Thank you.' He said, and he held his wife closely.

Phaedra just smiled at him and shook both of their hosts' hands and then went to join Teddy, knowing it wasn't her but

The Woodman's Quest

the glowing stone that was around her neck that did that to him.

The Woodman's Quest

Chapter 20

More than she bargained for

'Hello Edna she said sleepily, do you know what time it is over here?' Wilomena asked.

Her caller apologised profusely saying that it was lunchtime over there in London. She then asked if Wilomena was still on the case of looking for her client's son. Wilomena answered quite cagily, as there had not been any agreement on the proposal she was reading from Adelaide. Edna however took no notice of her vague comment by telling her that her friend Hermione had remembered some other important things about the boy.

Wilomena asked if she could tell her just one of Hermione's memories and then promised to call her back later in the day.

'I now know what his Christian name is now Wilomena, it's William.' Edna said and rung off quickly

At around ten in the morning Wilomena asked Josephus if she could see Adelaide and he replied that it was ok to go right in, with his southern drawl. Adelaide sat up in her bed, propped up with her silk pillows and gave the young woman a bright smile, which lifted her up.

'His name is William, Adelaide. I've had a phone call early this morning from my contact in London.' Wilomena said, and waited for the response.

The Woodman's Quest

'William Gilpin! Now we can get to work, what do you say Wilomena? Have you read the document? What is your answer? When can you take a flight to London?' Adelaide unconsciously tried to get out of bed but her strength was not there so she rang the bell for her butler, to find the times of the flights to London Heathrow.

'Adelaide, will you wait a moment, you are like a whirlwind. I haven't said that I will take the job yet, and I haven't let my boss know.

'Tittle tattle, I'll have no tittle tattle, are you going or not Wilomena?' Adelaide asked as Josephus arrived. Wilomena nodded with a broad smile and Josephus shook her hand in relief.

There was a thick silence on the other end of her phone for at least twenty seconds when Wilomena broke the news to Conrad. The tone of her conversation was firm and final, so before he had chance to speak, she topped her statement with the stonewall addition.

'There will be no changing of my mind Conrad. I cannot work with you any longer, so please send me my final pay check to the following address.' Wilomena barked.

Conrad had recognised Adelaide's address in Hollywood and was immediately aware of what his ex-colleague was up to, so he meekly agreed to her terms and hung up without another word.

She had rung him on her mobile in Adelaide's bedroom so when she turned to Adelaide, all she got was an old fashioned

The Woodman's Quest

thumbs-up. Wilomena walked over to her new benefactor, who hugged her in deep appreciation.

'Go and find my son Wilomena, and keep me informed every step of the way.'

This time when she arrived in London, it was with a much improved status. In line with the Hollywood star's generosity, she was booked in a suite in Claridge's indefinitely, and Adelaide had set up a line of credit with Harrods for her, it had an embarrassing ceiling of two thousand pounds per week.

Wilomena had been raised in Chicago in an environment with modest means and therefore was not mentally prepared for that sort of luxury. However she made sure that any expenditure she did make in that world famous shopping emporium, would always be kept at a sensible level.

Edna had been contacted on the following day of her arrival in London, and Wilomena asked if she and Hermione would be able to join her for tea at Claridge's. Edna asked her to repeat her request, because she had never been there before and pointed out the very high costs that would be incurred. When Wilomena had explained that she had a suite there, Edna nearly collapsed in shock!

The next day Wilomena was at Hermione's address in a taxi, waiting for her two friends to appear and then whisked them away for an afternoon that they would never forget. The delight on her guests' faces as they sat at their table was worth every penny that was spent on them. She said to the two English ladies that the special tea was a gesture of thanks

The Woodman's Quest

by her benefactor Adelaide for what they had done to give her hope in finding her long-lost son.

Hermione's memory had been jogged to the further extent that she remembered that the foster father had returned William to the agency in a very short time, because he was unable to cope with the boy. Apparently the man's wife had been killed in a car accident shortly after they had finalised William's adoption, which had left him as a lone parent clearly unable to cope with the situation of caring for a disabled baby.

Now that she had no need got to go to Filey in Yorkshire to search for him, Wilomena knew that the next step would be to try and trace William Gilpin's movements between any children's homes or orphanages in the vicinity of London.

She had brought the most important tool of a laptop computer with her and began to troll through all the related places that would have taken an orphaned baby in the late seventies, and initially was disappointed to find that many had been closed down forcibly by the local authorities. Stricter controls had been put into place on the way that children were looked after in the nineties, and many were closed as the result of such legislation, and along with the disappearing schools went their records.

The borough of Streatham in the East side had come up with the name of Gilpin, but his details were to say the least sketchy, but she did find out that he had moved around quite a number of times even before the age of ten.

The Woodman's Quest

In a period of two weeks she had not got very far, and was surprised how difficult it was to get clear answers from any local authorities, who generally showed little concern about those youngsters who had passed through their hands.

She had never thought about checking with the police before, but because she had not been at all successful in any other channels, it was time to ask if they had anything on their missing person's files. Surprisingly, soon after her first enquiry at the desk of the local station in Clapham, she was surprised to be asked to join two officers in an interview room.

Wilomena was initially subject to a rather harsh interview and made to feel that she was being investigated. Her expertise as a lawyer soon kicked in, and was soon bringing her knowledge of the law to the fore. After insisting on an apology from the senior member of the police team, she had finally insisted on their grudging apology before she would answer any further questions.

One of the police officers had a manila folder in front of him and had kept his hand firmly on top of it. Wilomena looked at the officer and then at the folder and immediately sensed that this was a file on William. They had the information she was looking for, but how was she going to get him to open it?

She had told them the reason she was looking for William, and had also briefly outlined what she had done to try and trace him, but because of the officer's intransigence she considered that there was no reason why she should speak further on the matter.

The Woodman's Quest

'I can see that you have no intention of answering my questions concerning Mr. Gilpin, so I shall not bother you further on this matter.' Wilomena said indignantly.

She had taken a distinct disliking to both of the surly officers and decided that this was then the best course of action. She stood up to leave and the officer holding the folder gestured that she sit down again for a moment.

'The information we have on Mr. Gilpin is confidential of course, but in this case it may be to both our advantage that we outline some of the information in this file to you.' The officer opened the file and read a short passage from it.

'William Gilpin is wanted in relation to two deaths in this parish, from an incident in the early morning of 10th December 2012'

The officers cautioned Wilomena that should she find out any clues to the whereabouts of William, then she was duty bound to report that information to them right away.

Wilomena sat alone at dinner in her hotel with a very complex problem on her mind. This young man had had a very difficult upbringing and more than likely just as difficult a life in the outside world too. Every door would have been closed to him and he would have been ridiculed and put down at every step. This new information from the police was even worse, now he was on the run with the suspicion of involvement in two murders.

Directly after her visit to the police station, she visited the local library and asked to see newspaper reports for the local

The Woodman's Quest

area of Clapham around the 10th December 2012. She was shown every publication for two weeks following that date, including all the nationals. Having spent a great deal of time scouring the records there was no mention of the two deaths at all. She lay on her bed and asked herself what Adelaide would do in her place, and there was only one answer she could have come up with; find him, no matter what!

Over breakfast, Wilomena's mobile phone rang and the name recognition said 'unknown' so she ignored it. It rang for the second time and she hurriedly opened the line with a sharp 'hello'.

'Is that Wilomena, its Phaedra here, would you like to meet up, I heard that you have finished at your job and was told that you're in London. I'm at Heathrow, can we meet?'

'How about that we meet under Nelson's Column in Trafalgar Square at eleven Phaedra?'

The Woodman's Quest

Chapter 21

Starting afresh

For two weeks, William had spent surveying the whole area of his woodland, and was determined not to rush into making any quick decisions on how to manage the area. He had decided that the first task was to clear as much of the dead trunks that were getting in the way of new growth. Before attempting this task however, he had to make some clearings and tracks, to enable him to get the debris out by tractor.

The southern part of the wood, near to the cottage was the first area that he tackled, and he stopped at the clearing work about two hundred metres into the forest, and at the same time made sure that the path that was cut in, was wide enough for the tractor. Each fallen trunk was secured by heavy chains attached to the tractor and dragged out into a grassy clearing. In the first two weeks he had a very large area with over ninety large pieces of timber that were primarily oak, beech, elm and a smaller amount of chestnut.

They were all in various forms of decay; he estimated that they had fallen between one and ten years ago. On one of his infrequent visits Alex Deville was shown the assembled timber. William pointed out to his employer that some of the trunks were in very good condition, and there would definitely be a market for them. He suggested that he invite would be customers from furniture makers, as they would arrange for transport to the saw mill, as well as offer the best prices for them.

The Woodman's Quest

Alex was impressed by his employee's ingenuity, but said to him that he had called for a different reason.

'I have a question for you William, and I hope that you can answer it truthfully.' Alex looked very serious as he asked the woodsman.

William immediately thought again about the events in his recent past, and the unfortunate incident of the two gangsters that had been killed. He looked again at Alex before he answered him, and was relieved that he was smiling this time.

'We have two friends of ours, who live above the Post Office on Tintagel High Street, right opposite where Hannah was thrown off her horse. They came to visit us at the house today and they said that had seen all the events after she fell. In fact they watched this man lift the horse's hindquarters up and let my daughter get free.

'They told us that it was definitely you that they saw, William was it? I understand that you didn't want to advertise the fact, and I promise that I will take it no further, but I really would like to know.' Alex just stood and looked at William as he just stood expressionless and didn't speak.

Finally the woodsman told him that he had done it on the spur of the moment, and that anyone else would have done the same as he had. Alex knew the implications of the actions of William, and he knew that he had no need to explain them to him. Instead he went to the man and hugged him. They agreed that Hannah didn't need to know about the incident as

The Woodman's Quest

she was happy for that person to remain anonymous. Alex also promised that his wife would keep their secret too.

Only a week had passed since Alex's visit to the cottage, but his employer had returned just before dusk, and knocked on the cottage door. The woodsman was around the back of the cottage having a strip wash in the water butt. Alex asked if he could speak to him inside and followed William into the darkened room. The storm lamp was lit and William proceeded to light the stove.

'I would like to leave you some printing matter that I've printed from the internet, and I want you to read them and then come to see me tomorrow with your views.' Alex said and quickly left.

The first set of papers were a technical review if a private hospital called Spire Bushey in Hertfordshire that specialised in a procedure called 'kyphoplasty' it covered the operation to correct problems with the vertebrae in the back area. The other set of papers were from Frenchay Hospital in Bristol who specialised in correcting cleft palates.

Initially William was somewhat upset when he had digested the papers, but after he had time to think about it, there was a feeling of relief that Alex had gone to such trouble for him. He also realised that it was Alex's way of thanking him for his part in helping his own daughter, without making it obvious. So he calmly decided to let Alex know that he was happy for him to arrange both procedures.

Only ten days after the insertion of a 'balloon type' instrument into his vertebrae, his stoop had virtually disappeared and he

The Woodman's Quest

had been given the correct exercises to do which further improved his stature. William had been booked into Frenchay only a week later for work on his cleft lip, and amazingly he had been discharged from the hospital the next day.

Battered and bruised he accepted a room at Heron's Roost to recuperate, and with all the help from Alex and his wife they were to witness an amazing change in the man. Alex continued to take William personally to the Bristol hospital for follow up speech therapy and several trips to Wadebridge for regular physiotherapy sessions. Alex never mentioned the horse accident with his daughter, but William knew that he had been deeply moved by his woodman's selfless action.

William was getting ready to continue his work in the forest, but just as he was leaving in the tractor, Hannah shouted from the front door that there was a phone call for him.

The Woodman's Quest

Chapter 22

Wilomena is close

Wilomena and Phaedra decided to visit the nearest Neros coffee shop to Trafalgar Square, and swap all their news that they had, since they had met each other at Mikhail and Marcia's wedding in Philadelphia. Wilomena apologised that she had promised to catch up with her new friend in Los Angeles, so she took time to explain the reasons why.

Phaedra was amazed about the wonderful hotel she was staying at in London, and her eyes lit up when Wilomena told her about the charge card she was given by her benefactor.

'Do you mean that you have two thousand pounds per week to spend at Harrods?' Phaedra exclaimed. 'It's positively obscene!' She shouted. Then they both laughed so much that the other customers stared at them.

After coffee they both decided to visit the Natural History Museum in Knightsbridge and as they walked through the great hall, they passed the towering skeleton of the brontosaurus. Wilomena suddenly looked serious at Phaedra and asked her companion directly if she had ever known someone called William Gilpin.

'Why are you asking me Wilomena?' Phaedra tried to procrastinate over her answer.

The Woodman's Quest

'When I first mentioned that I was looking for him, you suddenly went very quiet, as if you knew something. Was I right Fay?' Wilomena asked pleadingly.

Phaedra knew that for whatever reason, William was escaping from something, and if she was to betray him, it would have been a betrayal of their friendship, so she used the next ploy to delay.

'Why are you looking for him Wilomena?' She asked.

They headed for the cafeteria through the museum gift shop and when they were seated somewhere quiet, Wilomena told the full story of why Adelaide was looking for him, as well as what she had found out to date, from the state of the baby's severe disability to the latest information about him from the local police.

Wilomena had observed that during her description, she guessed that Phaedra knew him, but had obviously not known until that moment, what he was hiding from.

'I will tell you what I know when I've talked to my mother and father, they are sure to help me with this problem I have. Will you accompany me to their house in the New Forest and then I promise to decide for you. Is that acceptable Wilomena?' Phaedra asked seriously.

Wilomena agreed that any help from her parents to make her decision, would be the right one. Phaedra accepted her friend's offer to take the spare room in her suite at Claridge's for the night, and then to set off to Lyndhurst the next day.

The Woodman's Quest

They taxied to Kings Cross Station the next morning and headed for Brockenhurst Station, in Hampshire. This of course was the first time that Wilomena had been outside of London, and Phaedra had described the area well, especially the New Forest town of Lyndhurst where her parents lived. Phaedra wisely telephoned her parents with the train arrival date.

The Lexus belonging to Victor and Lydiya was waiting in the station car park for them as they crossed the pedestrian bridge. Instead of returning directly to their house, Victor drove them to the village of Burley, where the Norman family had lived previously. The plan was to visit the Queen's Head pub for lunch and then take a two minute guided tour around the village.

Wilomena breathed in the clean air as they walked, and as Phaedra explained to her father the reason for their visit whilst her mother was pointing out the quaint shops that abounded there to Wilomena. The one thing that baffled the American was the abundance of New Forest ponies and donkeys that were allowed to roam the main street, without hindrance.

Wilomena asked if the animals were at risk from the traffic, but she was reassured that all the car owners were aware of the four-legged residents, and made allowances for them.

On return to Lyndhurst, they sat around the large oak dining table at 'The Gables' with their coffees and Victor took advantage to speak to both of his visitors.

'I should like to thank you Wilomena for coming to see us, and I hope that you have enjoyed your little visit. Phaedra

The Woodman's Quest

has updated me on the quandary she seems to be in respect of William. Lydiya and I have talked at length and this is how I see it.' Victor said.

Firstly he had mentioned that William hadn't directly asked Phaedra not to reveal his identity to anyone specifically, but knowing his daughter, she would have sensed that fact and wanted to be honourable to that. He also considered that William ought to have the opportunity to contact his birth mother and make his own decision what to do about it. He then discussed the incident of William and the two dead people, but at that point was unsure what to do about that problem, but thought it best to leave that to Wilomena.

'Are you saying that Phaedra should take me to meet him Mr. Norman?' Wilomena asked.

Victor and Lydiya both nodded in unison and then said however, it was still up to Phaedra whether or not to disclose the information to her.

When Phaedra had flown to Philadelphia to attend her brother's wedding, she had driven to her parents from her cottage, and left her car in the garage, so the next day her old Land Rover was winging its way with two excited passengers to North Cornwall and Wilomena's next amazing adventure.

Before they left, Victor had pulled out a large map which depicted the whole of the South of England. He pointed out London in the east, Lyndhurst in the centre and then their next destination Tintagel in the far west. This Victor hoped, would give Wilomena some idea of the relationship of where

The Woodman's Quest

London, Lyndurst and Tintagel were to Wilomena. Phaedra had rung the Castle Hotel in Tintagel and had reserved a sea view room for Wilomena and promised her that she had never seen anything like that hotel before.

Four hours later that day, they had pulled up outside the little crystal shop in Tintagel, belonging to her friend Zeta, who promptly closed her shop, there being no customers, and took them next door to the little cafe called 'Arthur's'. Zeta gave a potted history of the legend of Tintagel to Wilomena who was fascinated, having seen several films depicting King Arthur in her own country.

Phaedra told Zeta that they were looking for William, and asked if he was still in the upstairs flat, above the shop. Before she answered, Zeta looked a little edgy at Wilomena, as she felt that William was not particularly used to strangers, but Phaedra had reassured her that all was well.

Wilomena in turn reacted to Zeta's reticence, so she explained the reason for her search for William and what she had uncovered in London, however, she omitted to mention the facts that she had uncovered with the London police officers. The young lawyer considered at the time, Zeta didn't really need to know too much of the negative facts involved.

The three young women agreed that whatever his future might hold, it was a very delicate matter to introduce his birth mother to him, especially at a time when he wasn't actually looking for her.

Zeta actually recalled to the other two that her recently departed friend Aggie had said to William that there was

The Woodman's Quest

someone looking for him, and that they came from across the sea, but had sadly died before he could get any further from her. As she mentioned that, Wilomena recalled the nightmare of the old woman and the disfigured man, and went cold for a moment.

Wilomena was relieved that perhaps William may not be too surprised with the news that she could bring to him, but it could only serve to reinforce the words previously said by Aggie's dream. This then made the decision to go ahead and meet William much easier, so at that point, Zeta picked up her mobile phone and made the call, one that perhaps may change his whole life.

Wilomena then asked if Phaedra would take her to the Castle Hotel, as she was getting a little tired from all of their recent travelling. It was a very short road to the hotel but Wilomena was staggered at what she saw. It was the only visible building on the cliff top. Nothing hindered it from having such magnificent views eastwards of the ruined church perched on the top of the next cliff, or westwards to the ruins of the old castle famed to once housed the legendary King Arthur. Those lovely views were even bettered by an unhindered panorama of the sparkling sea and the crashing rocks of the North Cornwall coastline.

Zeta and Phaedra were invited for dinner at the hotel, as guests of their American friend and they took advantage of that time together, to discuss further how they were going to break the news to William Gilpin.

The Woodman's Quest

Chapter 23

The invitation

'Hello, who is calling?' William asked, as Hannah passed the receiver of their house telephone to him.

'Hi William, its Zeta here, I wondered if Phaedra and I could come up there to see you. Phaedra has got some information that you might find of interest.'

William told her that he could not meet them for some days, as he had just started back 'in the saddle' at his work and needed to get acclimatised before he could take time off. They agreed to meet on the following Sunday at Phaedra's cottage. Just before she rang off, she told him that there was another person with Phaedra called Wilomena, and she had come a long way to see him.

He sensed that she was hanging a carrot in front of him, so he did the same by intimating that they could be in for a little surprise themselves when they saw him, and then put the phone down.

Zeta had told Wilomena that she would have to be at the hotel for at least four days and before she had finished her call, suggested that perhaps it would give her the opportunity to explore the area.

On her first night at the Castle Hotel, Wilomena took the opportunity to call in with Adelaide in Los Angeles, firstly to check on her health, and secondly to bring her up to date on

The Woodman's Quest

her progress with the search. She checked her watch before going to bed and saw that ten pm would be early afternoon at Adelaide's mansion.

It had been over two weeks since she had spoken to Adelaide. There had not been a great deal to say until then, however a great deal had now changed, which hopefully the old lady would be pleased with.

Although she had signs of tiredness when she spoke, the information that came over the line was inspiring for her. The details that Adelaide was receiving was life changing for her, especially when Wilomena told her that within a matter of a few days Wilomena would at last meet William Gilpin face to face.

To Adelaide, it was the confirmation of her confidence in her young lawyer. In fact that young woman meant more to her at that time, than anyone had ever achieved in all her life. She knew that in her heart, soon she would see her son for herself, and so she made it her goal to keep alive until then.

Wilomena had felt a warm glow after the call and had congratulated herself having made the impossible possible for someone she had grown to love, Adelaide Columbine the forgotten Hollywood star.

The following morning Phaedra had arranged to pick Wilomena up from the hotel and take her to see the little cottage where she lived. Fay was very proud of her little cottage, and when she had moved in, with Zeta's help, they were able to furnish the rooms of the cottage very similar to a

The Woodman's Quest

traditional Cornish fisherman's home, by sourcing each item from local shops and auctions.

Far away from the city life, Wilomena was enthralled that someone like her new friend Fay, who although not brought up in the area, should be perfectly suited to the isolation and self-sufficient way of life. As the two young women sat in front of the small wood burner, after the two minute guide of Fay's cottage, Wilomena began to cry unashamedly.

'I have never experienced such beauty in this area, and I'm utterly blown away by it.' Wilomena said through her tears.

'Do you scare easily Wilomena, because I may be receiving a call from a friend of mine, but he is not quite what you might expect, shall I call him?' Phaedra asked.

Wilomena had remembered that Zeta had briefly warned Wilomena about Phaedra's 'familiar' as well as her having special powers in the stone she wore around her neck. The young American woman was a little apprehensive about Phaedra's question, but trustingly she nodded to tell her to go ahead.

The young American watched Phaedra as she pulled the necklace from around her neck and revealed that mystical orange stone which seemed to be glowing slightly. She then held the stone in her left palm and looked pensively towards the ceiling of the room. In a very short time she smiled and looked at Wilomena as she replaced the stone beneath her denim shirt.

The Woodman's Quest

'In a few minutes you will hear knocking on my door four times, please open it and then let him in, his name is Bopoh and he is a large raven. I've asked him to bring me my tea.' Phaedra said as if in a dream.

In less than thirty seconds there was a sharp 'rap' on the door and Wilomena did as she was told. She opened the latch, swung the door open wide and then stood back. A very large black bird flew into the room and unceremoniously landed on the bare table where it deposited a large live silver fish, still alive as it continued to writhe around.

She watched transfixed as Phaedra killed the fish professionally and dropped its body onto the draining board, its tail still thrashing. The head, which she swiftly detached, threw over to the raven that had by then perched on an old oak cabinet. The bird caught the fish's head and swallowed it whole with a loud deep 'croak'.

Wilomena cautiously made her way back to her chair which was not four feet away from the cabinet and the bird watched her with large coal-black eyes. Phaedra stood up in the middle of the room and said something to the bird, which immediately perched on her shoulder nodding its head furiously. Phaedra then pointed to the open door and in a heartbeat he was gone. Wilomena visibly shuddered as she could hear the feint rasping cry of the bird as it disappeared from sight.

The two young women did not speak for what seemed an age and the visitor was struck dumb with the whole episode that she had just witnessed. There were no words she could find in her mind to say to her hostess, but she thought that

The Woodman's Quest

perhaps Fay was somehow possessed. What sort of person, who had sung so beautifully a few weeks before with Teddy, at her own brother's wedding, could have such a dark side?

'Do you remember when Zeta had spoken about Aggie yesterday? When I first arrived here she foretold that I would have a 'familiar' and initially it scared me a bit. When I lived at my home in Burley, there was a legend that told of a witch who had a jackdaw as a familiar. She used to walk around the village with the bird on her shoulder and woman and bird talked to each other all the time.'

'You spoke in a strange language to the bird, what was it? Wilomena asked.

Phaedra told her that it was her mother's tongue and the raven fully understood any command that she had said to it. She said that she was half Russian and her father was English. She invited Wilomena for a fish tea, but she declined the invitation, giving her host the excuse that she had to get back to her hotel in order to ring Adelaide in Los Angeles and keep her updated.

She was sitting in Fay's Land Rover as they returned to the Castle Hotel, and Wilomena could not understand how such a strikingly beautiful young woman, with long black curls in her hair should live as a recluse with only the company of a black fearsome raven.

One day, she vowed to find out much more about that enigma she called Phaedra, but at that moment she did not like what she had just witnessed in that little cottage. Secretly she hoped that one day she might have an opportunity to

The Woodman's Quest

persuade Phaedra that the life she was currently leading was no good for her.

The Woodman's Quest

Chapter 24

Serious moments

Zeta was just preparing to close her little shop for lunch, when a large brightly painted vehicle drew up just outside of her door. The chequer board colouring could only be one thing, the police. The passenger of the vehicle donned his peaked cap just as she came out of her shop to see why they had parked outside it.

The policeman gruffly asked if she could return into the shop, and the driver had also alighted and followed them in. She had no reason to fear, yet the off-hand manner that they maintained did disturb her somewhat, so she immediately put up her guard.

They told her that they were looking for someone and asked if perhaps she might help them. Of all people they were looking for was William Gilpin, and when she asked why, she got the usual reply of none of her business. Her mind was racing as she considered how to answer their question.

'What does he look like' She asked with an innocent air.

The policemen looked at each other as if they were unprepared for that question. It was obvious by their lack of response that they had no idea what he looked like. This posed further questions by Zeta, but she refrained from answering any, instead she just waited for their response to her initial question.

The Woodman's Quest

'We heard that this man is in this area and I wondered if you had come across this name anywhere, perhaps he may have come into your shop?' The driver asked in a little more persuasive manner this time to Zeta.

'He may have been here officer, but I'm not in the habit of asking everyone's name when they come in, so if you were to give me a rough description and perhaps his age I might be able to help you.' Zeta began to gain confidence knowing that they again seemed to be wrong-footed as they stood in front of her.

They finally told her that he was short in stature, perhaps disabled in some way and his age was early thirties. Zeta made a show of thinking and then, looked as if she had remembered something, and they looked at her in anticipation of her answer.

'Yes I do remember, a man fitting that description was looking for a place to stay, here in Tintagel, and I think that he stayed for a while on old George's farm in a little caravan. There's the farm over yonder.' She said, and pointed towards the green hills on the other side of the road.

They thanked her and jumped into the big car and were soon gone. Zeta urgently dialled William's mobile phone to warn him of the latest developments, but at first received no answer, so she tried again and this time she let it ring longer.

'Hello, this is Hannah; you must have the wrong number, because this isn't my phone.' The girl seemed a little harassed when she answered.

The Woodman's Quest

'Hello Hannah this is Zeta, can you find William for me? I need to speak to him urgently.

'He's up in the woods Zeta, his phone is here at the house because there's no signal up there!' Hannah shouted.

Zeta realised that was something she hadn't bargained for, so she asked if either of her parents were in, but the girl was home alone at the time. Zeta then promised Hannah that she would ring back later so as not to worry her.

She had to think quickly. Would the police return to her shop when they had found out that William had left the farm, and then want more information? She decided to take a chance and drove up to Heron's Roost, and collect Hannah so she could show her where William was. In less than half an hour the little Peugeot 205 had arrived at the front door of the big house, but Zeta was alarmed to see Hannah's wheelchair empty in front of the main door, where was she?

She got out of her car and ran around the house shouting the girl's name, then suddenly stopped when she looked along a narrow unmade road that meandered up a large field. About halfway up the incline she could make out a person struggling on crutches. Hannah was trying to find William. Zeta rang the mobile phone, and watched as the figure stopped to answer it.

'Stay there Hannah, I'm coming darling!' Zeta shouted, and the girl turned around waving that she had understood.

Hannah hadn't mentioned to her parents that she was beginning the transition between wheelchair and walking she

The Woodman's Quest

explained, as she had struggled to get herself in the little Peugeot. It was only the fact that there seemed some urgency in the phone call that she forced herself to use the crutches.

Hannah piloted Zeta over the brow of one grassy hill and headed straight to the edge of the woodlands which was perched on the next one. They followed the track to the right, skirted the edge of the trees until the chimney of his cottage came into view.

Zeta held her breath, frantically thinking about the words she would say to him as Hanna jumped out of the passenger door and fell clumsily on the grass. She refused help and reached for the crutches instead. Even then she had reached the cottage door before Zeta had, but only to find that the little house was empty. Hannah asked her companion to check if the tractor was at the back.

'He must be working in the woods Zeta, so you'll have to leave a note for him.' Hannah insisted.

Zeta reached in the glove compartment and found a used envelope and just scribbled on it;

'William, call me urgently – very important. Go to Heron's Nest to get a signal. Zeta.'

She wrote her own number on the envelope for reference.

When she had dropped Hannah off at her home, Zeta kissed the young girl and congratulated her on her fortitude and then made her way back into the town. All the way she was trying to figure out what William had done to attract the

The Woodman's Quest

police, and in the end had decided that it must have been something in his past. He certainly hadn't done anything since he had lived in Tintagel, which would have caused the police to call in that manner.

On the spur of the moment she turned around and headed for the cottage belonging to Phaedra, hoping that she might be able to help. As they sat in the tiny cottage, Zeta unfolded the drama that had occurred at lunchtime and then asked Phaedra if perhaps she could throw some light on the problem.

She sat in the cottage with her mouth open as Phaedra reluctantly had to tell her what Wilomena had discovered more about him, when she had been at the London police station. Fay reluctantly said to her friend that he was wanted in connection with two men's deaths some years before.

They both decided to visit the hotel where Wilomena was staying in the hope that she hadn't gone anywhere. Fortunately they found her in the great lounge looking at the numerous paintings on the walls. She ordered coffees and they went to an empty corner table where Zeta retold the story of the police visit to her shop. She also told them that she had sent the police on a sort of 'wild goose chase', which could possibly look bad on her.

Phaedra asked Wilomena if she knew how the police might have, of all places chosen Tintagel to look for William and the American looked at her resignedly.

'The guy that interviewed me in London took all of my details including my mobile phone. They had also cautioned me to

The Woodman's Quest

keep them informed if I had discovered his whereabouts.' She then assumed that they could have pinpointed her whereabouts through their tracking system, it seemed the only explanation.

Zeta then suggested that whilst they were drinking their coffees, she would try and ring William's mobile phone that she had left on the table of his cottage. She had hoped that there was a signal and he had returned from the woods. At last he answered his phone, it was intermittent, but she was able to speak just a few words to him.

'William, are you in your cottage?' She asked.

'Yes' He answered.

'Please don't move from where you are, we're coming to see you!' She shouted and rung off.

The Woodman's Quest

Chapter 25

Connections

Now and again Adelaide would get a visit on a Sunday morning from a young black man called Rufus Brown. He was the leader of a group of teachers and professionals who had given up their well paid jobs to focus on the education and support of young teenagers who had suffered from abuse and neglect in one of the roughest inner city areas of Los Angeles.

Their operation was in a rather run down shop, which looked from the outside like a squat, but to these young people it was a lifeline. For many years Adelaide had provided a large regular donation which kept everyone's dream alive at the little centre. Rufus, in his spare time would visit the mansion and keep her up to date with everything.

There was a special reason for liking her young visitor and it went back before Rufus was even born. His father Peter Brown was working as an extra on a film the Adelaide was starring with Spencer Tracy. The film was set in Texas and between shoots; Adelaide would often join the cast for coffee or even eat lunch with them in the makeshift canteen.

She spotted Peter one day and was struck by his resemblance to Harry Belafonte. She regularly chatted with the extra, and found out that he was working to pay for his studies at a Dallas Law school. By the end of shooting they had become great friends and Adelaide promised that she would support him through his studies if he made a promise to her.

The Woodman's Quest

He made that promise, and passed with the highest honours for that year and was given a junior partnership with a then new law firm in New York, called Spiros and Partners. He had not only become the first black full partner in the firm, but also the first non-Greek one. He never forgot the bargain that he had made with that movie star Adelaide Columbine, and only ten years from the start of his stellar career he became a member of the US Congress representing the east side of New York.

His son Rufus didn't follow in his father's footsteps, after graduating he left the city and headed west to California. He tried teaching in the usual State schools but found no satisfaction with the system imposed on him. He was not as ambitious as his father; his energies were focussed on the more compassionate side of life. 'Charity work with a meaning' was his life's motto.

He met like-minded people who were also fed up with the rat race and its continual striving for material wealth. Instead they began to form an ambitious idea of helping the helpless, and the consensus of opinion of that new group was that many children in L.A. needed a better deal. Their biggest problem was to get sponsors, and one day after a brainstorming meeting everyone was asked to name one person who the group could contact, Adelaide's name just jumped out of his head. His father was always talking about this actress who gave him a helping hand, but it was so long ago and he feared that she was no longer around so to speak.

The main thing that he inherited from his father was his tenacity, so he persevered against the odds, and in only two
The Woodman's Quest

weeks of persistence, had unearthed an address on the swankiest boulevard in Los Angeles, and the rest as they say was history!

That particular visit by Rufus had coincided with the first breakthrough telephone call from Wilomena in the UK. For once as they sat sipping their tea, Adelaide had something to tell Rufus. He by then had become extremely interested in William, her long lost son. She had to admit to Rufus that William had been born without any knowledge of a mother or father, just as some of the kids he helped, had.

From that time Adelaide, had become a real person to him and not an old faded film star and her dusty old grey demeanour, had transformed into a beautiful coloured flower in his eyes.

The Woodman's Quest

Chapter 26

The little fawn

William had left the Herons Roost to head back to the woodman's cottage for the first time in three weeks. Still a little battered and bruised from his two operations, one on his back to remove the hump and the other on his cleft palette which had still had a large scar between his nose and his lip. The wonderful thing from all the work done was that he had become a thoroughly transformed person.

As he sat upright in the cab of the tractor, his smile was a real confident one especially he looked at his own image in the rear view mirror. The confident woodsman was so looking forward to getting back to his task of managing the woodlands, that he hadn't noticed that the cottage door was wide open.

He jumped out of the tractor and as he walked to the cottage, his mirth had receded very quickly as the gaping door came into view. He breathed in deeply as he gently pushed it open further, trying to be as quiet as he could. The gloomy room revealed nothing as he searched with his eyes from the entrance.

A soft rustling sound came from the far corner of the room and he instinctively stiffened and stared into the gloom as hard as he could. Suddenly the sun appeared from the clouds and streamed through the window landing on the floor in the place where the sound came from. Looking up at him was

The Woodman's Quest

two of the most beautiful eyes he had ever seen. A roe deer kid was curled up on the old rag rug that he had placed in front of the wood burner.

He slowly crept to his chair hoping not to frighten the animal, but at the same time he had left the door ajar for its escape. He spoke softly and in gentle tones to the deer and he could hear his own heart beating as the fawn stood up on its gangly legs and tottered towards him. Unknowingly he had his hand held open as he sat, the fawn pushed its nose in it and he could feel that it smelt him.

For an absolute age, which was probably about fifteen minutes, he sat stroking the soft downy fur and soon the kid was almost snuggling against him. He was so scared that if he rose out of his chair it would run away, but eventually he did, and the fawn followed him out of the door, without a sound.

William got into the cab of his tractor and started the noisy engine up, and looked down to see the kid still looking up at him unafraid. As he looked back to the cottage, and before he was out of sight, the little roe kid was still standing the cottage door unmoving.

After a morning's work of clearing rhododendrons in the centre section of the wood, he was just unable to get the roe kid out of his mind, and to satisfy his curiosity, he had to return to the cottage. He stopped to pick up some bramble shoots and leaves for the animal, just in case it was there. He had turned the engine off and as it went silent William looked towards the cottage doorway, which he had left open, as he approached, a small brown head peered out towards him.

The Woodman's Quest

As he ate the sandwiches that he had prepared earlier, he watched the roe deer munching on the brambles and stroked the black spotted back of his new friend.

On the second day of his return to the woods, another amazing thing happened. He was about to get into the cab of his tractor and the kid seemed to push him aside and tried to get into the cab with him.

He lifted the little deer into the cab and it curled up by his feet, not flinching as he started the engine up and bumped his way towards the woods. He began to clear the rhododendrons again after lifting the little kid out of the cab and watching as it bounded in and out of the trees perfectly happy. William regularly glanced over, here and there between the trees to see glimpses of the animal as he continued his work.

On the third day he returned to the cottage feeling like a new man. The work was rewarding and he had a new friend who seemed to be happy with his friendship. As he passed the cottage he noticed that there was a white envelope pinned to the door. When he retrieved it and read the message from Zeta, his heart sank. He tried to ring the number she had left him but there was no signal from where he was standing.

A million things went through his mind as he went indoors; even the closeness of the roe deer kid could not raise the dark clouds that had gathered around him. For some unknown reason he felt that the two lines scribbled message on that envelope would be the beginning of the end of his dreams. His mobile phone then jumped into life, and made the kid jump too.

The Woodman's Quest

'Don't move we're coming to see you!' Zeta screamed.

He sat in his chair and waited patiently; the little deer came to him and muzzled his nose in William's hand. It seemed to know that something had changed in the new friendship that they had found.

'I think that this could be goodbye little friend.' William said as he stroked the soft head which had rested on his knee.

Half an hour after he had received the call from Zeta a Land Rover pulled up outside and so as not to disturb the sleeping kid he rose carefully from his chair and went to the door. He was amazed to see three young women get out of the car and walk towards him. As soon as they saw him they stopped and stared at him as if they had been struck down. Zeta ran to him and hugged him really tightly and then Phaedra came up and smiled disarmingly and then she introduced the third woman to him.

'This is Wilomena, William; she has come all the way from Los Angeles in America to see you.'

She then stood back to let her visitor step forward. Wilomena came up to the man and without speaking hugged him softly and then stood back with a smile on her face. 'I told you that I had a surprise for you didn't I?' he said.

They surveyed a man who was at least six inches taller and straight-backed. His tanned face was not showing that gash in his lip, instead a slight mark where the surgeon had expertly rebuilt the deformity.

The Woodman's Quest

'You even talk differently William, how did this happen?' Zeta asked, and couldn't resist another hug, and this time he hugged her back.

He told them that there was another surprise for them inside the cottage but warned them not to make a sound until he told them. They followed him inside on tiptoe and all gave out a stifled scream to see the little 'Bambi' deer looking up at them. William had christened him 'Butch' as he explained that it was everything the name wasn't.

He stood with the women and called his name, and the little kid got up somewhat clumsily and then tottered over to the waiting women. They were all bowled over by such a wonderful surprise; all three were reduced to blubbering girls once they had each taken their turn to stroke and cuddle him.

He found three little stools for the ladies and explained that Alex Deville had found out about the horse incident with his daughter and instead of broadcasting the deed, he insisted that William undergo some corrective treatment which he had paid for privately. It had been performed by surgeons in Hertford and Bristol. Phaedra was going to explain to the American what he looked like before, but there was no need as she was already aware of his birth situation.

'William, I'm now going to tell you something that you may want to sit down, before you hear it.' Wilomena said.

Zeta stood up and held his large rough hand as she told him gently that his birth mother was trying to contact him. She then waited for his response.

The Woodman's Quest

'You are telling me that I have a mother?' William asked as the words pierced his heart.

He looked at Zeta, who had always been so very kind to him and she got on her toes, reached up and kissed the big tears that rolled down his cheek. At this point, Wilomena asked him if she could take a photograph of him, which considering his new stature, he was happy to agree to.

'William, before Wilomena tells you anymore, I have to be the bearer of some worrying news to break this lovely spell.' She said.

'Don't worry Zeta I know already, is it about the police?' He asked, but his smile had disappeared.

He took the rest of their visit to tell them the circumstances around the deaths of the two thugs in London, who attacked him in the course of recovering a debt, but of course they had come off worse than they had expected.

Suddenly a strange bell ringing cut his speech to them, and he looked at the floor in silence. He knew that the noise could only be one thing, they had found him and the reckoning had to be paid. Firstly he nodded to Phaedra, who opened the door and little Butch flew outside; even the little roe deer kid knew that the bad news had begun.

Just before William went to the door, Wilomena told him that she was a lawyer and said to him that from that moment she would be representing him if that was acceptable. William just squeezed her hand and smiled at her in gratitude.

The Woodman's Quest

Zeta, Wilomena and Phaedra went back to the Castle Hotel for dinner, it had felt like the last supper, considering the atmosphere that their visit to William had been. The only compensation for all the disturbing news from William was Wilomena's determination to defend the case with all of her body and soul.

Chapter 27

Good news, bad news

William sat in the cell at the Truro police station having been charged for the murder of the two men in Clapham and was awaiting transfer to the appropriate police station in the capital. He lay on the hard bed and tried to take in the earth shattering news about his mother. That American lawyer had just enough time to tell him what her name was; Adelaide Columbine, who lived in Los Angeles in California.

A myriad of questions arose in his head, some had revolved around how on earth could his birth mother live in California, and what was her connection to London? At least he somehow knew that this young American was there to help him and he looked again at her calling card she gave him.

His mind then wandered the way Zeta was to him; she seemed so different at his cottage. He thought back to the time that whilst Wilomena had told him the news about his mother; Zeta had held his hand and kissed his tears as they fell. He was unable to make the connection that she wanted to be more than just good friends; even so it gave him a warm glow in his heart. Could someone really care for him? That thought alone was to keep him sane as he stood on the brink of hell.

Back in Tintagel the three young women were still talking about William and it didn't go unnoticed that Zeta was looking not unlike a lovesick school girl. Phaedra had seen that look

The Woodman's Quest

before when her brother Mikhail had visited Tintagel and had met Zeta, so she wrapped her arm around her friend's shoulder for comfort.

'Do you love him Zeta' Phaedra asked softly.

The tears would not let her answer, except for a nodding of her head. Wilomena looked at Fay who seemed just as emotional and reiterated that she would move heaven and earth to get William free especially now, for her new found friends' sake.

As Phaedra looked at her friend, she was distracted for a moment as she noticed a man who was sitting alone on a table in the middle of the hotel dining room, and he was smiling directly at her. His smile seemed to penetrate her mind but not in a controlling way, more in a warm and friendly way.

'If it's the last thing I do, I will get him free for you to love Zeta, I promise.' Wilomena said, as the tears welled up in her too.

Having been distracted for that moment, Phaedra looked back to the middle of the room to see the man again, but sadly he had left. She sighed unconsciously as if she had missed meeting someone she knew.

When finally Wilomena had been left alone in the hotel, she had another dilemma on her mind; Adelaide would be awaiting her update on William. The problem was a big one. Should she just tell her the good news, or both the good and the bad news about her son. At least now she didn't have to

The Woodman's Quest

tell her about his severe disability, as that was thankfully gone, but what about his arrest? How would dear Adelaide take that? Her brain ached with the weight of the decision.

Josephus, Adelaide's butler had with her help, got connected to the internet by purchasing a small laptop and she even equipped him with an email address. She had decided to only transmit the good news, for the time being.

She telephoned the mansion, and thank goodness Josephus had answered the telephone. Whilst on the line she instructed him how to power up the machine, and step by step opened up the new email address for him. Before calling she had transferred the picture from her phone that she had taken in William's cottage, to her computer and with this photo as an attachment, sent a short message to him.

He told her that he had read the waiting message from her, so she then told him how to open the photo attachment. Within a few seconds he had a picture of Adelaide's son taken the same day, in front of him. He was utterly amazed at the technology. Wilomena then asked him to take the machine to Adelaide's room, but not to show her until she had talked to the old lady.

'Wilomena dear how lovely to hear from you, have you got any news for me?' As Adelaide answered her call, she had looked quizzically at her butler as he held on to that 'shiny object' at the side of the bed.

'I've seen him Adelaide, and he is so nice! She shouted.

'How nice is he darling?'

The Woodman's Quest

Josephus took the hint and passed her the shiny silver machine and opened the top of it in order to reveal the picture.

'Yes Adelaide, that's him.' Wilomena said, and was so proud that she had achieved the thing that Adelaide could have only dreamed about.

'Hmmm quite good looking, but what is he dressed in my dear?' Adelaide asked.

Wilomena explained that he worked with his hands; in fact he was a forester. Adelaide had no idea what a forester was, so she explained about taking care of woodland. It was no good trying to explain though, as Adelaide came back with the question why couldn't the woodland take care of itself?

Adelaide was getting tired of those questions, so she and asked her young friend directly, when was he going to be coming over to see her. This question was the one that Wilomena dreaded, as she knew the only excuse for not taking him there would be the truth, but how would she take it? The wily old actress could sense from her extended pause on the telephone, that it was not all good news so she made it easier for her.

'Now my dear, you must remember that I'm not in a position to play with words, so come out with it and tell me why he can't come to see me.' She asked bluntly.

'Adelaide you mustn't get upset with what I'm going to tell you, but he was involved in a very serious incident three

The Woodman's Quest

years ago, to which he has now got to answer for in court in the UK.' She tried to soften the blow for her but to no avail.

'Please don't make me angry dear, I don't like these legal terms, just give it to me straight, I won't break!' Adelaide was not amused this time.

Wilomena swallowed hard and told her the full story of how her son had been attacked by two men in the night when he lived in London and by a freak accident, whilst he was acting in self-defence, the two attackers were killed. For a moment she had remembered her husband, William's father, who died in that fight in Africa all those years before.

Adelaide responded, and came to her son's aid by asking why his case hadn't been dismissed. Wilomena told her there were two reasons; firstly there were no apparent witnesses and secondly, that he absconded out of the city, and that was why it had only just come to light. The police had in fact, only that day found him and what made it so heart breaking, it had coincided with the same day that she had found her long lost son.

Their conversation ended with Adelaide instructing her young lawyer to keep a close watch on all the events concerning her son and to keep her updated with a daily phone call, and in the meantime she would pull a few strings from over there.

After her call to America, Wilomena decided that she would return to London as soon as she had heard that William was to be moved there. The next morning she received a courtesy call from the desk sergeant at to say that the person in custody at Truro was to be moved that afternoon, so she

The Woodman's Quest

immediately rang Zeta to ask her to drive her to Truro so that she might catch a train to Paddington.

As they stood on the platform, Wilomena could see how much Zeta felt, but knew that it wasn't the time for talking, but did promise to ring her as soon as she had any information. About half way into her journey, her mobile phone rang. The voice on the other end of the line introduced himself as Harry Sinclair and asked politely if she would accompany him to the American Embassy. He seemed to know that she was travelling to the capital, so trustingly she told him of her arrival time at Paddington Station and described her attire.

She smiled to herself as she already knew that Adelaide had been pulling a few strings, or in this case large ropes. As promised, a long Mercedes limousine with blacked out windows was waiting for her at the kerb outside the station and a tall man in a dark suit opened the passenger door for her to get in. She did not move, and waited for him to offer some identification which she took from him and scrutinised very carefully.

Satisfied that it was the same person that had called her on her phone earlier, she cautiously got in the car and they were soon on their way. He told her that the Ambassador no less, was granting her an interview at 5pm, and he casually asked what she thought it might be about, but she looked coldly at the agent as she considered her answer.

'What the Ambassador and I have to speak about buddy, quite frankly is none of your business.' She said curtly and turned to look out of the car window.

The Woodman's Quest

The Limo whisked them into Grosvenor Square in a matter of minutes, and in a few minutes more Wilomena was sitting in an empty waiting room awaiting the call. She glanced at her watch, it was 4.30. She then looked at her mobile phone, hoping to call someone, anyone, but the signal was blocked and smiled knowingly that this was the real deal. Harrison Letts was surprisingly genial when he shook Wilomena's hand and after a brief introduction, he opened the conversation.

'Do you know Peter Brown Miss Ruzinski?' The Ambassador asked, and then smiled at her. 'I didn't think you would, but I've had a rather animated call from him today asking that I get my, er... Well you get the drift don't you?' He then smiled a little shyly to her.

She asked him what was Mr. Brown's status and he answered in a whisper that it was Senator Brown from New York. He had been asked in no uncertain terms that he was to accustom himself with the details of William Gilpin's case forthwith and then, with Wilomena's help to 'get the guy off.'

She gave him a detailed account of the plight of William and afterwards and the ambassador did seem interested enough, to ask her what he could do to help her. Being a lawyer, she told him that they needed the best defence brief they could afford and that she might need some help in gathering evidence to prove William's claim of self-defence.

'You are probably aware that money to pay for a lawyer is not the problem here, but I have no knowledge of who to appoint so I will leave that to you Miss Ruzinski, or may I call you Wilomena as we are both on the same side?' He stood up and shook her hand; it was the end of the audience, for now.

The Woodman's Quest

Outside of the Ambassador's office, Harry Sinclair was waiting patiently for her and he told the Ambassador that he was taking it from there. The two of them went into a nearby office and they passed a receptionist who gave Wilomena a broad welcoming smile. Harry's office was just down a well-lit passage to the right. He had obviously been briefed beforehand and asked her what she needed to get things going for Mr. Gilpin.

She had only been in the Embassy for one hour, but was quite amazed how the wheels had turned. She had received a direct contact number from Harry and he promised the best backup 24/7 until the case had been finalised. In her short taxi journey to Claridge's she made some plans for the next day. First call would be a visit to the police station to see William and tell him how things were moving.

After dinner alone, she made a call to Adelaide, but had to leave a message with Josephus, as she was resting. She then rang Zeta and told her all the amazing developments since she had seen her on the station platform and that she was planning to see William the next day. Zeta couldn't believe that a US Senator had instructed the American Ambassador for the UK to look into William's case. Wilomena said it was not what you know, but who you know that makes things happen, and said that she suspected that his mother Adelaide had pulled those 'strings' for him.

The Woodman's Quest

Chapter 28

Powerful helpers

William decided that he must speak to Wilomena and find out what was happening, as there seemed to him, to be no one who was offering any help. Sitting in a windowless cell with a steel door, was beginning to get to him. The small window in the door slid open to reveal a pair of eyes, and then a voice informed him that the prisoner had as visit from his lawyer. The echoing sound of the door being unlocked was deafening to him but as the door opened he was relieved to see that same young woman who broke the news to him about his birth mother.

He sat on the bed and Wilomena sat on the plastic chair. She firstly told him the good news she had received from the American Embassy, although he didn't understand why they should be involved. She realised that his knowledge of the history behind his parentage was lacking considerably, so she took on the task to fill in as many of the gaps as she could for him.

Wilomena explained to him that both his mother and father were American citizens, which had helped him to realise the reason why this particular embassy was so interested in him. That part over, Wilomena began to interview him in more detail about the three year old incident, as she told him that this would help her to determine what chances there could be in tracing any witnesses, or even the person who ordered the attack on him.

The Woodman's Quest

He gave her the full address where the attack had occurred and the name of the person who had lent him the money in the first place; there was no doubt in her mind that that name would be crucial. Zeta had told him that William loved poetry, so after the first interview, she left him with a large volume of selected verses from nineteenth century poets and saw his face light up in thanks.

She also told William that when she took the picture of him at the cottage, the same day she sent it to his mother who was delighted when she saw it. Sadly she had to tell him due to the gravity of the charges, that bail would not be considered in his case, but he did understand that.

William asked if she had spoken to Zeta recently and asked if he could be remembered to her. Wilomena was very careful not to give away the feelings that Zeta had for him, as she knew it wasn't her place to do so. She did, however agree to pass on his wishes to her.

Wilomena's next place to visit was the Middle Temple, which was the old home of the finest barristers in London. She had read up on the internet in order to reference what barristers were currently the most successful Q.C.'s that would give William the best chance of acquittal. Three names kept occurring in the registers and because she herself had the right qualifications, she was able to breach the usual protocol and get their timetables.

Sir Charles McLeish QC had recently been working in Australia where he had defended three high profile employees of a large mining organisation on a very complex international

The Woodman's Quest

fraud case, and in his usual manner had gained full exoneration for them.

At that point Wilomena rang Harry Sinclair at the embassy, and told him that his boss was waiting for information concerning Mr. Gilpin's defence lawyer. She gave him the appropriate legal reference numbers for his case and asked if Mr. Sinclair could use his office, as American Ambassador for the UK, to get Sir Charles on their side. She also told Harry that speed was critical as the QC would not be available for long, and she knew the great man liked a challenge.

The following day she received a telephone call from a man with a very deep voice and she guessed correctly that it was Sir Charles, so she took the initiative and invited him to dinner at Claridge's where she was staying. It was a very good move as that particular invitation had impressed him greatly, and so he readily accepted her offer.

A large portly man in a dark suit and a bright red waistcoat arrived at the appointed hour of 7pm and the head waiter graciously guided him to the waiting Wilomena.

'I see that you have some friends in high places Miss Ruzinski, so over dinner I want you to give me as much information as you can.' He said with a broad smile.

From all the information that Wilomena had supplied, he was particularly interested in William's disability and how he had recently made some amazing recovery from it. He told her that he had found out that the Crown Prosecution Service had felt that they had a case to answer and had set the trial just

The Woodman's Quest

four weeks hence. He also had work for her to do before the hearing.

'I want you to get the names of the consultants who did the work on Mr Gilpin; I need that quickly so that they will provide me with appropriate medical records. You will see why later my dear.' He smiled.

He also asked her to find out if anyone in the area had seen anything on that night, no matter how small. He told her that the key person in the case would be the loan shark, and said that he planned to subpoena him to go on the stand. He had already put into motion three private detectives to investigate the past dealings of this man as he felt that it had a considerable bearing on the whole case.

Wilomena took the advantage of having the leader of William's defence team wanting to hear any other suggestions and so she told him that she would like to offer him character references from the time that William had been in North Cornwall, including the time when he had saved a young girl from certain death having fallen from a horse. Sir Charles responded by taking her hand and kissed it, as if to say that it would strengthen William's case immensely.

If Wilomena had thought that this meal was going to be a nice social meeting she would have been disappointed, but on the contrary she was ecstatic that he had obviously worked so hard since that call from the ambassador. From that first meeting she held this man in great awe, and was so happy that he had considered her as part of his team.

The Woodman's Quest

The young American lawyer knew that she had only a month to get as much information for Sir Charles as soon as she possibly could. Some of the work could be done over the phone, but most of the other work would mean that she had to return to Tintagel in North Cornwall. She knew in her own experience that rushing headlong into information gathering without the necessary planning would result in failure.

She rang the place where William was being held, and arranged another visit. He was the closest and had the most information to guide her. He became much more upbeat when Wilomena told him that she had taken on Sir Charles who was heading up his defence and he wasn't at that time aware of the date of his trial.

In her conversation with William, he directed her to his recent employer Alex Deville who had arranged all of the surgery and knew that he would be the first to get the surgeons names and reports. He remembered that before he had his back surgery, the theatre nurse took several pictures of him. He suggested that Wilomena go to see Alex and his family, rather than just ring them.

As she sat on the train, impressed with William's positive attitude, Wilomena was fired up to collect as much background information as possible. She watched as Reading Station sped by on the Great Western line heading back to Truro in Cornwall, pleased that she was able to connect to dear Adelaide by mobile phone as she sat in her seat in the train. She congratulated the aged actress on her prowess to pull some strings for her son and that they had secured the best defence lawyer available for him.

The Woodman's Quest

She also briefly outlined the task in front of her to enhance Sir Charles's defence by getting the very best character references for William. She thought it better not to complicate matters by telling her about the operations he had undergone recently. Overall his mother was buoyed up by the latest news, and had told her young friend that her remission had given her a positive outlook on life again.

One other phone call to Zeta with the progress of William's case had another cheering effect and she was happy to meet the young American on the Truro platform. Zeta told her that her sister ran a small B&B in Tintagel, but as the signal on her phone had weakened somewhat she didn't have the time to explain what a B&B was to the American.

Zeta rang Alex Deville's home at the Heron's Roost to let them know that Wilomena, William's lawyer, wanted to see him. The whole family was happy to welcome the two young women to their house and invited them to lunch with them, to which they accepted.

After their meal Wilomena accompanied Alex into his study so that they could discuss her requirements for the defence brief. She told him that the main reason for seeing him was that William's barrister wanted her to construct a good character profile for him, and he was the first person that William had recommended.

Alex told Wilomena that he desperately wanted to help the man because what he had done for his daughter as well as the great job of forestry management he had performed to date. Wilomena had quite a shopping list of items for Alex to do, so she was apprehensive that he may have considered

The Woodman's Quest

not helping. On the contrary, he already had plans to contact the two hospitals that William had attended, and felt very confident that a comprehensive dossier on the operations would be forthcoming from them.

Alex also mentioned that his very good friends who lived on the Tintagel high street would be willing to testify that they had witnessed the miraculous saving of his daughter Hannah, from underneath the fallen horse. He added that they would also submit a written document to back this up.

The Woodman's Quest

Chapter 29

The trial

The trial of William Gilpin for the murder of Luigi Forzani and Enrique D'Amato was a long and arduous one, with both the prosecution and defence teams scoring equally as well. The jury had a seesaw parade of witnesses, of which the prosecution produced some which according to Sir Charles were bordering on perjury.

The most damaging witness for them was the detective sergeant, who described the carnage of the two victims. It was the most damaging to William's own case of self-defence as his description made no mention of them impaling themselves in the spiked fence as William had described. He said that the whole evidence reflected that the two dead men were victims of a violent robbery.

The police witness also focussed on the fact that the defendant had absconded from the scene and disappeared out of London and that it had taken three years to find him. It was the police's view that it was in fact an admission of guilt.

The other big setback in the defence's case was that somehow Michael Corleone, the man who employed the thugs that attacked William that night somehow got wind that he was being investigated, and then suddenly disappeared. He was suspected of leaving London to a hideaway somewhere on the north side of Majorca.

The Woodman's Quest

In the summing up, Sir Charles elected to go after his prosecutor's and he knew that it was going to be a very close thing. The defence council in their summing up, played heavily on the fact that William had absconded and in doing so had thrown doubt on his own claim of self-defence.

Sir Charles did his utmost to rubbish the prosecutor's claim that a disabled man could not in any way attack two much larger men on the pretext of robbing them. He also focussed on William's character witness who proved his compassionate nature in saving the young horse rider from being crushed to death.

He also focussed on the autopsy done on the two deceased men which apparently had been unclear on the cause of death and that the prosecution was hinged on supposition and lacked any clear witness of the accused deed.

Finally the judge in the case charged the jury to retire and reach their verdict, and reminded them that if there was any doubt in their minds they must return a verdict of not guilty.

As the jury filed out of the court, Wilomena looked behind her and saw Zeta and Phaedra sitting in the back row, and they were not looking very happy. She excused herself to Sir Charles and went to join them.

'I'm sure that he will be acquitted, that was an amazing summing up, and didn't you think so?' Wilomena asked them.

The look of doubt was obvious on the two spectator's faces and Wilomena could see that Zeta particularly had been most upset with what she had witnessed. After all of the negative

The Woodman's Quest

questions that had been posed by the prosecution, no amount of comforting could dispel the fear that she had, for the future of the man she had come to love.

Sir Charles very kindly had persuaded the clerk of the court to allow William to speak to his two visitors before he had to be taken downstairs to his cell. This in turn allowed Wilomena to speak to the QC and try to get some sort of reaction, but she was surprised that his tone seemed rather sombre.

He was still upset about the man who was the centre of his case to abscond abroad. He also said that he felt the police officer had been got at, but somehow there seemed helplessness in his tone. All that there was left to do was wait, and no matter how long, for the jury to decide.

'You must be Wilomena Ruzinski; I have a special message from a good friend of yours.' A tall good looking black man said.

Unfazed, the young woman answered that she had wondered when Adelaide would make an appearance at the Old Bailey, and then shook his hand in a warm greeting. He then introduced himself as Rufus Brown and something in Wilomena's memory clicked, she recognised that surname, was it a coincidence?

Sir Charles came over to them and Wilomena introduced him as the messenger from America where his mother resided. Sir Charles looked a little bemused with that statement, so Rufus tried to explain that he had come to see Sir Charles's performance. The QC waved his hand and walked away somewhat disinterested.

The Woodman's Quest

Wilomena then walked over to Zeta and Phaedra who looked as if they were ending their conversation with the accused. There was just enough time to catch William before he was taken away into custody so that she could introduce Rufus to him.

Rufus grabbed William and hugged him strongly. As he stepped back from the surprised William, he gave him a sealed envelope and told the clerk of the court, that it was a private letter from his mother in America.

With great relief all round, the clerk obediently stepped back from the group and let him keep it. William stood slightly apart from the group for a moment as he tried to take in the earth shattering moment. He looked at the scrawled writing on middle of the sealed envelope;

'To my dear son William'

The clerk of the court then intervened and summoned the orderly to take him downstairs, with enough time for Zeta push through the crowd and hold William briefly and whisper in his ear.

'I love you, and I'll wait for you, no matter what.' That was the most touching moment for all to see, and there wasn't a dry eye in the immediate vicinity.

A week later the court had re-convened, as the Jury had requested that they were unable to get a unanimous decision, but the judge had given them the weekend off and then to reconvene on the Monday. He then assisted them in allowing a majority decision when they considered their verdict.

The Woodman's Quest

The Tuesday after the Jury's return to decide on their verdict, the court was recalled and they delivered their verdict:

'By a majority of 10 to 2 we find the defendant is guilty as charged.' The jury spoke, but the whole court remained in an eerie silence.

Wilomena looked at Sir Charles's face as he took it in and it was ashen, he couldn't believe that he had lost the case. It was the first case that he had lost for over ten years and still there was not a single sound emanating from the gallery.

The judge dismissed the jury and said that sentencing would be given in ten days, and with that final statement he told the guards to take the man down. Zeta was in the arms of her friend Phaedra, unable to look, as William slowly disappeared from view.

Chapter 30

Don't give up

'You did everything that you could Wilomena, I thank you for that.' William said and seemed very calm as he sat in his cell and considered his awful fate.

'It is not over by a very long way William, I have got much to do on this case, please don't give up whatever you do, don't give up!' She answered determinedly.

It was very tight, but she had ten days to make a difference. Rufus Brown, the messenger from Adelaide was going to be a huge help for her. Wilomena was told by Rufus that he was the son of Senator Brown of New York, the same one who rattled the ambassador. Together they had hatched a contingency plan just in case the jury had given that verdict of guilty.

Wilomena had found quite an attraction to this young man and realised that they had a great deal in common. The first one was of course Adelaide, she had known her several months and he for several years. Rufus told her that from university he had found a calling to help the needy in the inner city of Los Angeles. Deep down she envied him as felt that she too wanted to kick the rat race, and do something for the community.

Over a meal, she explained to Rufus the situation of a possible miscarriage of justice in William's case and explained to him that the police statements seemed far from the truth

The Woodman's Quest

and conflicted greatly from William's view of what happened that night.

Rufus was particularly struck that Adelaide's son had been convicted on mainly circumstantial evidence, but it was his view that the jury must have chosen the police's view of what had happened. Rufus did not have an international call feature on his mobile, so Wilomena gladly offered hers.

Before he rang, he told her that he had not spoken to his father in six years and his Dad was not particularly happy that his son hadn't taken a profession, rather than charity work. He firstly checked the 'caller numbers' on his own phone and then chose the last one of the three numbers identified as 'dad' and then manually keyed it on Wilomena's phone.

It seemed to Wilomena that the conversation between father and son was rather frosty, but Rufus handled the awkward call with aplomb. He swiftly told his father about the verdict and what Wilomena had told him about a possible miscarriage of justice in William's case. Rufus passed the phone to Wilomena telling her that his father; Senator Brown wanted to speak to her.

She asked the Senator to tell the US Ambassador in London that the trial at the Old Bailey was a travesty, and to instruct the Ambassador to call her. The Senator said to her that was just what he intended to do, as soon as they had finished speaking. She put his son back on the line and somehow, when father and son had resumed speaking, it seemed to Wilomena, that by the tone of Rufus's voice, a few bridges were being mended with his father at long last.

The Woodman's Quest

Wilomena, how is it going? Can you get over to the 'big house' today please? Harrison would like to see you.' Harry Sinclair said in an authoritative tone.

On this visit to the American Embassy, Wilomena was ushered straight into Harrison Letts's office, accompanied by Harry Sinclair. He was not aware that Wilomena knew that the Senator had rung him, so she showed a high level of surprise when he told her that he had urgent instructions from Senator Brown, to get her views on a possible miscarriage of justice for Mr. Gilpin. He then asked Wilomena if she had any ideas on what steps could be taken to correct the situation.

Only three days after Wilomena's visit to the ambassador, Gordon Allen-Jones a Chief Inspector of police at Scotland Yard had called Christopher Speke into his office and he sat opposite the high-ranking officer. Christopher noticed that another officer was sitting in the corner of the room, but was not introduced to him.

He first assured the detective that it was good news that he had for him. He was being selected for a promotion based on his excellent performance at The Old Bailey recently in the Gilpin murder trial. Christopher asked what post was on offer, and was told it was a high ranking position in the fraud squad.

The Chief inspector carefully observed the candidate for any reaction to the job description, but there weren't any. Another half hour's discussion around the candidate's suitability had concluded amicably and Christopher got out of his chair and began to walk to the office door, and courteously nodded to the other officer in the room.

The Woodman's Quest

'Oh Christopher there's just one more thing, could you please come back and let me show you something.' Gordon asked amicably.

When he had sat opposite him again, he opened the manila folder that lay in front of him on his ornate desk, took some papers out of it and turned them around for the candidate to read. The Chief Inspector then asked him if he recognised them. A frown came onto Christopher's face as he saw several copies of bank statements, which had his name and home address on the top.

The inspector pointed to two identical credits of two thousand pounds on the first copy, and pointed out that two other credit entries had occurred within a seven day period. He then turned to the next statement which had the same amount for two further weeks. In response, the detective smiled at his interviewer and then told him that it was a loan to his brother to which he was repaying.

'Which bank does your brother's use, can I ask you that Christopher?'

'I don't know.' He replied.

The Chief inspector shook his head, and then asked how much had he loaned his brother, but the detective could not answer him, because he knew that the game of deceit was up and he could no longer fool his superior.

'How much did Corleone pay, for you to lie in court Christopher? Was it this figure here?'

The Woodman's Quest

He pointed to a credit of ten thousand pounds on his bank statement which happened to coincide with the date when he went into the witness box and perjured himself. Christopher hung his head and sighed loudly; he knew the game was up for him.

The day after that interview in the police inspector's office, the prosecution team were standing in the Judge's chambers being told that their star witness had lied in his testimony and that he was recalling the court and the members of the jury immediately.

The court was re-convened, and without any preliminaries, the judge summarily dismissed the case against William, but under the Official Secrets Act he couldn't at that time disclose the reason, except that it was a very important admission of a falsely given submission, during the court proceedings.

'William Gilpin, in my responsibility as judge in this case, I am dismissing the charge of murder on you and on behalf of this court, we are sorry that you have been dragged through all of this and please accept my humblest apology.' The Judge stood up as he said the statement and smiled directly at Wilomena on the front row.

'You are free to go Mr. Gilpin, free of all blame and this to be recorded at the end of this sorry case.'

The whole of the room was uproarious in its response from the judge. Journalists were racing out of the courtroom to get their story printed, and William was surprised by the number of people that were crowding around him, congratulating him heartily. He shook hands with people he had never met

The Woodman's Quest

before, but he was searching the whole room for a special someone.

Suddenly the melee of people parted like the Red Sea as he spied Zeta coming forward, at that moment it was his greatest wish.

'Hello Zeta, I'm so glad to see you, is Fay not with you?' William asked as he held her in his arms.

She told him that Phaedra had to go back home, there was something important she had to do although she didn't tell Zeta what it was.

'William darling let's find Wilomena, it's all down to her that this has happened. She wouldn't rest until you were free.'

They were unable do what Zeta hoped, as the young lawyer was in close conversation with a smiling Sir Charles McLeish, and they found out later that he was offering her an immediate senior partnership in his illustrious firm. They watched as Wilomena looked over her shoulder in a lovingly gaze at a dark handsome man standing behind her.

'Thank you Sir Charles, but I'm going back to the States to start a new life, aren't I Rufus?'

As the crowds dispersed, William and Zeta were standing alone in the large courtroom. Zeta asked him what he was going to do next. In response to her question, he said nothing, but handed her the letter that Rufus had brought him earlier.

They sat together as Zeta read his first ever letter from his mother.

The Woodman's Quest

'Dearest William, I have seen the photo that Wilomena sent to me. I am praying that you will come to see me here in Los Angeles. Meanwhile I have to say how sad I am that you have to be dragged though this trial right now, but you will prevail. I know that, because you are my son. I have much to tell you son and I hope to be able to tell you before.... Maybe you could call me when things are better and you get the time.
All my love to you son
Your loving mother.'

The couple looked at each other, but Zeta knew instinctively what William's next question was going to be. She felt that it wasn't her place to answer the one about when he should go halfway around the world to see a mother who had abandoned him at birth. William looked at her and he knew that there was nothing to say, it was too painful for both of them. For the moment however, he was satisfied that the truth had finally come out, and that was enough for that day, at least.

On the court steps, William watched Sir Charles McLeish professionally handle the press on his behalf, and was so relieved that he and Zeta were met by Wilomena and Rufus, who whisked them away in a taxi.

'Where are you staying tonight William?' Wilomena asked, he shrugged and he looked at Zeta for the answer.

'Driver, take us to Paddington Station if you please.' Zeta said. 'We are going home, that's right William, isn't it?'

The Woodman's Quest

Chapter 31

Time to change

Phaedra was tired from the travelling to and from London, a place that she always found to be full of bad memories. Every man in the street with a dark skin would always remind her of Ali. She loved him once, but his attitude towards all women in general had always been domineering and had made her feel a second class person. He became quite violent and in fact in the end, he had met with a violent death.

After a good night's rest at the cottage in Tintagel, something strange happened to Phaedra. It was as if a veil had been lifted from her eyes. The dark moods seemed to have disappeared, but she was unable to understand why. As she turned the kettle on, the feelings in her heart had somehow changed. Usually she would call up Bopoh the great raven, but this time she didn't want to.

Her first reaction was to wash her hair in the rainwater container with the special herbal essences she used as a shampoo and then eat her breakfast. The act of washing her hair seemed to wash away the old fears and depression that she often felt. She then stepped out of the door and breathed in the morning air deeper than before. It smelled of fresh daisies, and so decided that she would take a leisurely stroll barefoot in the grass-covered meadow that led to the cliff top.

She seemed to be walking away from her dark existence as she walked away from her little stone cottage. Even at that moment, new thoughts were rushing into her head, she couldn't help it. When she finally returned from her walk she

The Woodman's Quest

felt clean and lifted up somehow. For the first time she wanted to get some space between the cottage and her.

The feeling that she was experiencing was the same uplifting freedom as when she walked on the Palisades Park in Santa Monica. She thought of Sarah, Lewis and their twins and suddenly missed their company. She turned the ignition key of her old Land Rover and headed it to the next cliff and the Castle Hotel. Somehow she needed the company of people, noisy shouting and laughing people.

It was still too early for lunch, and yet she felt hungry, not for vegetarian food but for the old English style of lunch; roast meat and vegetables with roast potatoes, and perhaps a glass of red wine. The head waiter stood outside of the empty dining room, welcomed her and said that lunch would be served in 30 minutes. He suggested if she would like a drink at the bar in the meantime.

He offered her a table for one, near the large window to enjoy the sea view, but she asked for one in the centre of the room. He looked a little puzzled with her answer, but shrugged and said one would be made up for her. She asked the waiter for a small glass of red wine and sat quietly at her table listening intently for the sound of fellow diners that were beginning to trickle into the well-lit room.

The room was nearly half full by the time she had ordered her starter of soup, followed by the main course of roast lamb and accompanying vegetables. Phaedra had eaten there several times before and had never been disappointed with the standard of their catering.

Before the soup arrived, a slightly overweight man came to her table and asked if he could join her for lunch. At first she

The Woodman's Quest

was unsure whether to accept or reject but when he smiled, she remembered that he was the man who was staring at her from that very table, when she was with her two friends recently.

She accepted and just before sitting opposite her, he introduced himself as Bernard Boussant. In return she was just about to introduce herself; he smiled that disarming smile again at her.

'I know who you are Phaedra. I have noticed you from the first time you had visited this hotel, but I don't know your surname.' He said.

She held out her hand to shake his and told him it was 'Norman'. He said that she looked Greek or Italian, with her tanned looks and black hair. Over lunch they discussed their heritage, and he explained that he was part Cornish with a 'dash of French' added for colour. It was so easy for Phaedra to laugh at the smallest of his funny comments; even at times she had to stop herself. In fact it was the nicest and most enjoyable lunch that she had had for many a year.

'Can I look at your hands Bernard please? She asked.

He self-consciously laid one open hand on the top of the table and she leaned over to it and held it gently. He could feel a sharp electric shock go up his arm but fought valiantly not to show it.

'I can tell you that you are an artist but not a painter.... You are a sculptor, am I right Bernard? Phaedra looked directly into his smiling eyes whilst still keeping hold of his hand.

'I would like to show you something after lunch Phaedra; it's in the next room to this one.'

The Woodman's Quest

They rose in unison from the table and he led the way. The door along the hallway was closed but not locked, and they entered into what looked like a library. In the far corner there was a white marble plinth on which there stood a bronze bust of a woman with long curly hair. As they approached the statue, Phaedra took the lead and Bertrand followed close by. Her beautiful black hair bounced off her shoulders and he caught the faint aroma of wild flowers coming from it.

She was about ten feet from the bronze bust when she stopped abruptly as she recognised who it was, and then turned towards him and smiled.

'How could you get a likeness of me like that, when you hadn't even met me?' She asked, and felt sudden warmth in her heart towards him.

It was breathtakingly exact. The expression on the bust seemed rather severe though, but when she thought about it, maybe that was how she really looked to him at the time. She realised that he was right, until that day when she shook off the darkness in her life.

Totally out of character, she was so overwhelmed and flattered, that she pulled him close and kissed him on the lips. He stood there with both arms to his side, until she held one of his hands and brought his arm around her waist. It was his cue to pull her towards him and kiss her back.

When she eventually stood back he gazed at her beauty and tried to tell her that her actions were a total surprise, but he was unable to speak. Instead he offered her coffee in the lounge, in order that he could get his breath back from his utter shock.

The Woodman's Quest

'Now we have got to know each other a little better, I now want to cancel my trip and be with you Phaedra.' He seemed to be rather pensive when he said it. 'I've been invited to America as a guest of the famous Laguna Beach gallery in Santa Monica in California; I was excited about it until now.'

He told her that the gallery was staging an event where his work was being showcased, particularly five bronze busts of her.

'Do you mean that you have done four other busts like that one in the library Bernard?'

'I don't suppose you would like to accompany me to America, would you? They would go crazy if I was to tell them that the subject of my latest work was also going to be there.' He just smiled at her thinking that it was an impossible dream on his part.

'I will think about it overnight and let you know.' She answered with a coy smile on her face.

He quickly told her that there were two couples joining him for dinner the following night and if she would say yes, would be most welcome to come as his guest. His wonderful smile had become irresistible to Phaedra, so he she found herself saying yes. She did tell him that she wasn't much of a person for dressing up for dinner and he immediately put her at ease by replying that it was a 'come as you are' dinner and not to worry about it.

When she got into her car to make her way home, she knew that there was so much to think about. In just a matter of a few hours she had met someone, had lunch with him, and even kissed him. Initially the shock made her mind reel, but

The Woodman's Quest

then she remembered how she had felt when she got up that morning, and that feeling was still with her.

Since she had recovered from the terrible accident where many times the thought of coming out of it alive did not seem conceivable, she never considered herself attractive to anyone in any way. It was overwhelming to Phaedra that someone who held her in such esteem, had not only sculptured her once but five times.

She drove slowly towards her little cottage in the valley with her mind buzzing; her first reaction to seeing the roof appear was not the usual one. In fact for a moment she didn't even want to go there. It seemed dark and foreboding in as much that for the very first time, she considered what a visitor might think, especially when they entered its little dark rooms.

As Phaedra was getting closer something reminded her of the visit by the American lawyer Wilomena to her cottage and the look on her face when the raven appeared. Even when she took her back to her hotel, the woman must have been horrified. She got out of the Land Rover and looked up at the roof; Bopoh the raven sat there and looked at her with his black shiny eyes, cawing loudly.

'Go away Bopoh, and don't come back!' She shouted in Russian, and waved her arms at him.

She opened the cottage door and then turned back to look outside at her lovely surroundings. The sun was still shining on to the silver sea, and the breeze blew in her face but she was for the first time, unmoved by it all.

This sudden change in her thinking had prompted her to take a chair outside in the sunshine and think deeper that she had

The Woodman's Quest

done in years. All the past bad experiences had been wiped from her thoughts; instead all she wanted to think about was her future. She felt at that moment as if she was sitting on the edge of the cliff and wondering whether or not to jump.

Phaedra left the cottage door open and she strode over to the cliff edge and stared at the crashing rocks below. That sight of the great waves had focussed her mind, and somehow it seemed as if she had been washed clean from every negative thought. The only memory that seemed to appear as she stood on that cliff was her walk along Palisades Park in Santa Monica and the lovely meeting with Sarah and her twin girls.

He mind was made up; Bernard's offer of accompanying him to Laguna Beach was going to be accepted. She sang happily to herself as she returned to her cottage, and couldn't wait for the following evening's dinner date.

The Woodman's Quest

Chapter 32

A new outlook

They alighted from their train at Truro Station and found Zeta's little Peugeot in the car park, but William wasn't sure where they were heading, as Zeta wanted to surprise him. The only time that he had met Zeta was at her shop in Tintagel, he knew that she lived somewhere else, but never asked her where.

Each time he looked at her from the passenger seat, she would give him a cheeky smile. Whatever they were going to do, or wherever they were heading, he was happy not to know, in fact he was just happy to be free at last.

Zeta drove through Tintagel and took the right exit at the roundabout and headed out of the village. In only five minutes they were in the hamlet of Bossiney and they soon pulled into the small drive of a small modern semi-detached house on a quiet road.

'Here we are William, I hope you like it. Would you like to stay here with me until at least you know what you want to do with your new life?' Zeta asked, and kissed him on his cheek as a welcome.

'I'll tell you what I want to do with myself Zeta!' He answered loudly, and lifted her up in his arms and as she unlocked the front door, he carried her over the threshold.

The next morning Zeta asked William if he would like to visit the most romantic place she had ever been. In fact, very few of the Tintagel's residents neither knew of it, nor had ever visited it. She told him that it was called Saint Nectan's Glen,

The Woodman's Quest

and although it was difficult to get to, it was really worth the visit. How could he refuse her?

They followed the River Trevillet, through small woodland. The ancient river had carved its way through the local slate, creating wonderful eddies in its flow until they arrived at the sixty foot waterfall. It was truly magical, and as they walked, Zeta told him of the ancient legend of Nectar and his fight to protect his Celtic beliefs from the marauding Romans. William was utterly overcome with it all.

'Zeta, please be quiet for a moment will you? I've got something to ask you. In the spirit of Saint Nectan and by his most beautiful waterfall I want you to marry me.' William tried to kneel on the wet slate but he slipped and fell into the deep pool of crystal water below.

Instead of trying to pull him out, Zeta jumped in beside him, reached and snaked her arms around his neck and said; 'Yes, Yes I will!' as loudly as she could.

Practicalities soon had to take precedent over the romantic view, as they realised that getting married has so much to do with cost. William had to think about how he would support his new bride. The job he loved most was in forestry and so it was necessary to go and visit Alex Deville and hoped that his job with him would be still available after his trial in London. Zeta realised very quickly that they couldn't live together immediately as he could not drive at that time, which made it difficult to commute from Bossiney to the Heron's Roost.

These were in fact quite small problems when compared to the biggest one that they had still not discussed together. William had laid the letter from his mother onto the little kitchen table at Zeta's home. It seemed that he was putting off the decision making, because up to that time he had little

The Woodman's Quest

thought about parents, having always been brought up as an orphan.

Wilomena had told him a potted history of his birth mother before he was to go on trial, but because she was American, and her fame was of long ago, he still couldn't find a reason to feel any compassion for her. She lived halfway around the world, and in his eyes, she had waited all of his life before making contact with him.

When Zeta suggested that they go and see Phaedra and tell her what he was struggling with, perhaps consulting another person who was not directly involved, could be of some advantage for his decision. Phaedra's little cottage was only fifteen minutes away so it was a 'no brainer'.

As they drove down the track towards Phaedra's home, Zeta felt that there was something different about the cottage. Firstly, Fay was sitting outside in a wicker chair looking quite wistful, and when they came towards her she was unusually ecstatic to see them and hugged them both. Secondly she didn't want to show them inside the cottage, instead invited them for a walk on the cliff top, almost as if she didn't want to be there.

'What's happened to you Fay, you seem so different somehow?' Zeta asked.

'I've got rid of my guilt, Zeta. I felt guilty that when I was kidnapped all those years ago, eleven men, although they were bad men, were killed during my escape and I always blamed myself for the whole affair.'

'Why did you blame yourself Fay? William asked.

The Woodman's Quest

~ 213 ~

'Because I was stupid enough not to really know that the man I had fallen for was a villain. Everyone knew it but me!' She said with tears in her eyes.

She told them that one morning, she suddenly had a revelation, it happened in a flash and there seemed no reason for it. Since then she had amazingly met someone who had loved her from afar and was meeting him for dinner that very evening. Furthermore she told her visitors that he was taking her to America and proclaimed that it was doubtful she would ever return.

'Now then you two, I'm sure you haven't come to hear what is happening to me, please fill me in with your news.' Phaedra said.

Fay was delighted to hear of their betrothal, and when Zeta told her where he had proposed, Phaedra confessed she had never heard of Saint Nectan's Glen, and with only a few days left in Tintagel, doubted that she would ever get there. She also listened to the dilemma that William was in, concerning his mother. He showed Fay the letter he had received from his mother, and how he felt about it.

Fay pulled the stone attached to the magnificent snake necklace and they watched the stone glow in her hand. Zeta knew the properties of the ring and how it had affected her.

'Alex is waiting to see you both, I think you should go and see him right away' Phaedra said solemnly and that was her response.

The friends parted company, after they had wished Phaedra well in her new life, and promised to keep in touch, especially to let her know what their decision about his mother would be.

The Woodman's Quest

Zeta rang Alex Deville, at the Heron' Roost, as there seemed the appropriate time to see if William's job was still open. Alex's wife Fiona had answered the call, and promptly invited them for tea. She apologised that her husband was on his way back from a business trip in Bath at the time, but would be back shortly. Zeta asked how Hannah was, and Fiona replied that there was some improvement in her daughter and said that she had a something to show them, when they arrived.

What a lovely surprise was waiting for them as they reached the end of the long gravel drive of their house, the visitors were greeted by a young woman astride another bay horse. She seemed to have grown so much in such a very short time. Her wide grin was enough for Zeta and William to have gladdened their hearts with the sight of it. When Hannah dismounted, there were more surprises as they observed that the young girl slowly but determinedly walked over to greet them.

'I want to thank you William for saving my life that day when I fell off my other horse in the village.' Hannah said, and reached up to him and kissed him on the cheek.

Her mother was standing behind her daughter and explained that their friends, who witnessed the whole incident, had 'spilled the beans' to Hannah, not knowing that Alex had kept William's good deed a secret from her.

They had all sat down for the tea that was prepared by mother and daughter, and to everyone's delight Alex had made it back early, and it was a wonderful sight to see him hugging William like a long-lost son.

The Woodman's Quest

'Now you can hold your head up high, and stop looking over your shoulder, everything has been wiped clean my boy, how do you feel?' Alex asked.

'All I want to do is get back into that woodland and sort it out for you Mr. Deville.' William replied.

After a sumptuous tea Zeta told them that she and William were to be married soon, but as he had only proposed that day, they had no idea when 'soon' was going to be. Whilst the two men went into Alex's study, Zeta told Fiona and Hannah the full details of the way that William had 'popped the question' and the story certainly was most entertaining for them.

Whilst they were alone in the study, William broached the subject of his mother with Alex and frankly outlined his private thoughts on the matter, after he had shown Alex the letter he had received from her. Alex asked William what he knew about his mother and William recounted the short description that he had received from Wilomena, before his trial.

There was one item that Alex had picked up on; it was that she was in her eighties and at that time on some sort of remission from a tumour. In the light of that knowledge he asked William just one question;

'If you were to find out that your mother had died before you made the decision to go and visit her, how would you feel William?' Alex asked, and then without waiting for an answer, told him that it was time to join the ladies in the drawing room.

Hannah looked quite tired after her exertions of the day, so she asked to be excused. William explained to the two ladies

The Woodman's Quest

what Alex had asked about his mother dying which only seemed to make his frustration deeper. They had realised that the cost of a visit to Los Angeles at that time was prohibitive, even if he was to go alone.

Before they left Heron's Roost, William promised Alex that he would deliberate the challenge that he had posed and promised that in a few days he would let him know his decision. Alex tactfully did not press him any further as it was quite evident that William needed more time to consider his options.

They went to bed early that night and Zeta was very careful about what she said to William, as the dilemma was clearly distressing him, particularly in respect of the cost of Airline tickets, hotels etcetera. He leaned over to the bedside cabinet and reached into the top drawer and retrieved his building society passbook and his unused passport, and then passed both books to Zeta.

'As you can see, that is all I have in the world Zeta and I have decided that you and I are going to Los Angeles to see my mother. Will you come with me, because I cannot do this on my own?' He asked with tears in his eyes. She hugged him, and nodded her head vigorously, and secretly thanked her friend Phaedra's stone

The next morning Zeta found him sitting at the kitchen table looking at the letterhead on his mother's letter. She leaned over to see that it was beautifully monogrammed with her address and telephone number on it. It was enough that he had to make the arrangements to book a flight to Los Angeles, but before all that, William had to do the thing he dreaded most, which was to ring his mother and speak to the person that gave birth to him.

The Woodman's Quest

Having got the correct code, he nervously rang the string of numbers from Zeta's land line, and waited for the ringing to finally stop and a man's voice answered. The voice was a low monotone, with a definite southern drawl.

'Hi there this is the Columbine residence, Josephus speakin.'

William nearly put the phone down; he was shaking so much he couldn't get his words out. Zeta saw his problem and quickly snatched the receiver from his trembling hand. Josephus asked again, and for a moment she sensed that he also was about to put his receiver down.

'H...Hello!' Zeta shouted.

'Hi there miss can I be of service to you? The deep voice asked.

'Hello, this is William Gilpin, can I speak to...er...' He blurted out having grabbed the receiver back from Zeta.

'Mr Gilpin, can you hold the line I'll put you through.' Josephus knew who it was immediately and of course, he even knew what he looked like. After about three minutes of silence William heard the click of the line being transferred followed by a rather high pitched voice, but not an unfriendly one.

'William, is that really you? Am I talking to my son right now? How are you boy, why aren't you answering?'

'Hello mother, thank you for helping me. Wilomena has told me what you did, and I am very grateful, without you, I surely don't know where I would be right now.' William became much more confident in his speech at last.

The Woodman's Quest

Adelaide then asked him when he was planning to come over to see her as time was short. She asked where he was living at that moment and he told her that his fiancée was sitting right next to him and her name was Zeta. He then passed the receiver to her and she told his mother that they were planning to come over very soon, but they weren't rich people.

Towards the end of that momentous conversation, Adelaide asked for their full address, and promised to send them two open tickets to Los Angeles by airmail straight away, and asked William that as soon as he received them, to ring her with their time of arrival, so Josephus could pick them up at the airport in the Caddie.

'I love you son, please come to see me soon, very soon.' Adelaide pleaded.

'See you soon mum, God's blessings till then darling.'

He had spoken to his mother, and it was nothing like he had feared. He hugged and hugged Zeta, until she was gasping for breath. The joy of seeing William so happy at that moment lived with her always.

'Zeta, what's a 'caddie?' He asked, smiling.

The Woodman's Quest

Chapter 33

A new heritage

Los Angeles International Airport from a small house on the outskirts of Tintagel was somewhat of a culture shock for Zeta and William. They felt a little less exposed as they were aware that Phaedra and Bernard had arrived there the previous day and were staying not far down the coastline at Laguna Beach.

As they carried their small bags to the exit, it wasn't too difficult to spot Adelaide's car. It wouldn't be difficult to spot a pink Cadillac in a queue of dark coloured modern vehicles that all seemed to look the same, designed in a wind tunnel. They smiled at each other as the magnificent car drew alongside them.

A very large black man the age of about seventy shook both their hands genially and introduced himself as Josephus but asked if they could call him 'Joe', but not in front of Miss Adelaide. He took their miniscule luggage and placed it carefully in the Cadillac's cavernous trunk; they slid into the backseat area and felt the warm pink leather seats, feeling just like film stars who were off to a 'shoot' on set somewhere.

'How is my mother, Joe?' William asked before they set off.

'She's ok son, and she sure is excited to see you there's no doubt about that!' He shouted from the front seat, as he started the great engine up, and cruised into traffic.

They drove along Airport Boulevard for a short distance and then turned left along Route 405, where they watched as a
The Woodman's Quest

sign for 'Hollywood' on a roadside sign flashed by. At Westchester the big 'Caddie' turned right onto Santa Monica Boulevard, but Zeta was very excited as she pointed out to William the legendary sign; 'Sunset Strip'.

'Now I do feel like a film star William!' She shouted, as the wind caught her words.

Zeta hugged her co-passenger as they turned into Carmelita Avenue. She remembered that was the name on his mother's letter head and the nerves suddenly kicked in as she knew that they were close to their destination.

As the Cadillac pulled into a somewhat overgrown driveway they looked up at this tall wooden structure and Zeta whispered to William if he had seem the classic Hitchcock horror film called 'Psycho'. William shook his head, but there wasn't the time to tell him what she had meant. Zeta was imagining that the interior of the house would resemble the one that Miss Haversham lived in, in the Charles Dickens's novel 'Great Expectations', but was pleasantly surprised how light and clean it was.

They entered a small private lift and Josephus closed the ornate wrought iron doors and in a matter of seconds, they found themselves in a very large bedroom. Two thin arms were held out in welcome from a four poster bed and William strode into them with no hesitation.

'At last I have my beautiful boy in my arms.' Adelaide said theatrically.

'Hello mother, at last we meet.' William said tearfully and looked over to Zeta. 'This is my fiancée mum, she would like to say hello.'

The Woodman's Quest

Adelaide reluctantly let go of him and reached for Zeta. There was no doubt this was a momentous meeting; an old film star in Hollywood meets the long lost son and his wife to be, Zeta's mind was seeing a film director in her mind's eye, and she was smiling at the thought.

The old lady was finally overcome with tiredness and she dropped back onto her pillows utterly exhausted. Although it was only four in the afternoon, it was very late in the UK so they both felt just as tired themselves. William and Zeta stepped back from the bedside for a moment, and soon she was fast asleep.

They returned downstairs in the lift to meet Josephus waiting outside still. He told them that a room had been made up for them and they followed him up two flights of red-carpeted stairs to where they were to sleep.

Zeta took out her mobile phone and rang Phaedra, whilst William was having a well-deserved bath. Phaedra had answered whilst she was on the veranda of her hotel which looking out to the Pacific Ocean. Quietly, so as not to disturb William, Zeta told Fay the sequence of events that took place prior to their arrival to their bedroom.

Phaedra asked when they could meet, and just had time to tell her that she and Bernard were about sixty miles down the coast or about an hour in the car. That reminded Zeta to describe the amazing mode of transport that had brought them from airport to William's mother's house.

The next morning, still groggy from the travel, the voice of Josephus from behind their door summoned them to Adelaide's presence for breakfast. They hurriedly dressed, walked down one flight of stairs to observe Joe, standing outside of two ornate mahogany double doors slid silently

The Woodman's Quest

open into her bedroom. They both greeted Adelaide with a hug, and she pointed towards a fully prepared breakfast table situated at the side of her.

A full plate of ham and eggs was served piping hot, followed by hot pancakes with maple syrup. Normally they would never eat such a gargantuan breakfast, but in deference to William's mother they just about consumed it all. William picked up his mother's tray from her bed and placed it on the table, and then they both pulled up their breakfast chairs, one each side of the bed.

Adelaide asked Zeta if she liked jewellery, noticing only a small gold necklace around her neck. The old lady then asked Zeta to go to the dressing table and open the top narrow drawer. The light that reflected out of the drawer when she pulled it was dazzling. It was full of all sorts of diamond jewellery, but for just fun Zeta picked up a tiara and placed it on her own head. William laughed out loud at such a preposterous sight, and his mother copied his mirth.

'I'd like to give it to you Zeta, but it's not real, just paste. It was part of the costume that I wore in my last film in '65, with Stewart Grainger opposite me; he was my favourite you know.' Adelaide went dewy eyed when she had spoken his name.

Sadly the name of the film had eluded her, but her visitors didn't mind. William just dreamed of what it must have been like to have grown up in such an amazing house in an equally amazing place, Hollywood.

'Can you tell me mother, something about your parents, my grandparents?' William wanted to take advantage of the moment, at a time when his mother seemed quite lucid and bright.

The Woodman's Quest

She told him that her mother was a socialite in the thirties, and before the great stock market crash was quite wealthy. Her name was Alice, and she married the love of her life, a man called Herbert Columbine who was from an oil family and a pioneer aviator. He was killed in the Second World War as a fighter pilot; she vaguely recalled it was over Germany in 1943.

Then he asked about his father, to which the old lady's eyes went dull, but after a short silence told him that he was a film director called Solomon Qirk, and that he had died on set in Tunisia just before William was born. William didn't press her for more information as he could tell that the subject was too painful for her.

Once again, Adelaide seemed very tired quite suddenly, so she rang the bell at the side of her bed, and asked Josephus if he could give them both a guided tour of the house, and asked them to come back later to see her when she'd had her nap.

The butler dutifully guided them around the ground floor of the house pointing out all of the interesting paintings, but he had no idea who the painter was. Zeta noticed that there was a picture of a dusky woman in a jungle setting, and when she looked closely at the signature, was sure that it looked like 'Gauguin'.

All the rooms were full of old fashioned furniture but of the highest quality, and each room had at least one tiffany lamp in it, which made each room to be bathed in a beautiful multi-coloured glow.

Zeta asked William if his mother would like to accompany them to visit Phaedra and Bernard at the Laguna Beach hotel.

The Woodman's Quest

She had to admit to William that she had rung Fay whilst he was in the bathroom. They asked Joe if that was possible to get Adelaide out of the house at all, but he seemed unsure, as she had become very frail and hardly left her bedroom those days. However, he did think that the fresh air it would be good for her, so he suggested that William himself broach it with his mother after her dinner.

As they wandered around the garden at the back of the house, William commented that it must have looked beautiful some years before, but it had sadly declined, with few flowers and the trees and bushes needed a great amount of attention.

'I could really do a lot for this garden Zeta if only...' He looked wistfully at his fiancée, and she immediately got his drift.

'I think I know what you are thinking darling, but that is out of the question surely, isn't it?' Zeta knew that William was a single minded man, but the chances of moving to America permanently at that stage seemed fanciful at the least.

Dinner was set in Adelaide's bedroom again and William could see that the rest she had, did not do much for her stamina, and that was even before she'd had her meal with them. William considered that it was still worth asking his mother about Zeta's proposed trip.

'Mother, what do you think about taking a small trip to Laguna Beach with us tomorrow? We have some friends over from England who would love to meet you.

'I will think about it William, although sitting in the back seat with you two in the Caddie sounds exciting, I'll let you know tomorrow.' She answered reflectively.

The Woodman's Quest

Chapter 34

A sad goodbye

'What a beautiful day, my dears.' Adelaide was sitting between her two young visitors and feeling on top of the world. The hood was up and they were bathed in the morning sunshine, heading south towards Laguna Beach.

The previous evening after dinner, Zeta rang Phaedra at her hotel to tell her that there might be three guests for lunch. Fay was excited at the prospect and hoped that she would get the chance to meet William's mother as she had heard so much from Wilomena. Zeta handed the phone on to William who told her that they were having a wonderful time at his mother's and said that she had surprised him with her energy, considering her age and health.

He also asked Fay what she had been doing at Laguna and she told him that Bernard had been quite a success, but he seemed to think that it was because she was with him it had made a difference. She explained that he was exhibiting five different bronzes of her, and it was a sensation to the gallery owners that the live model of his work on show too. William told Fay that health allowing, he hoped to take his mother to see them.

Josephus had glided the pink Cadillac to the front door of the prestigious hotel which was right on the Pacific Ocean front. The sun shone on the vivid pink Cadillac which drew the attention from all the guests that were nearby, it was an incredible sight. Many people came over to the car to say hello, and for Adelaide, so used to the attention, lapped it up. Just before they disembarked an aged couple approached the car and recognised William's mother.

The Woodman's Quest

'Hi there, you must be Adelaide Columbine the great actress, I'm right aren't I?' The gentleman that leaned over to Adelaide was dressed in a smart black sports jacket and white trousers.

Adelaide reached over to the man and let him kiss her hand, and then the couple went on their way. William and Zeta were completely bowled over by his mother's nonchalant way she had responded, obviously in the past it would have been quite normal to get that sort of greeting from total strangers.

Phaedra and Bernard were standing on the steps of the hotel in genuine awe and waited for the old couple to leave before they came towards their car and introduced themselves. Adelaide was utterly pleased with the 'fan' and visibly moved by the fact she had been recognised.

As soon as Josephus opened the trunk to take out the old lady's wheelchair two hotel staff appeared from nowhere to help her into the chair and carried her into the vestibule, and then disappeared just a quickly. Bernard then accompanied Josephus to the car park at the rear; he intended to show him up to their suite personally.

Adelaide remarked that their rooms were similar to the suite that had been reserved for her in Dallas Texas but the view front her veranda, was not as inspiring as the one she was currently looking at. Their suite was on the sixth floor and the view of the beach and Pacific Ocean was utterly breath-taking.

They ate their lunches on the wide veranda, but after the lunch, Adelaide asked if she could lie down as it was usual for her to rest after a meal. Josephus elected to stay with her and said that they would be very happy to relax in such a

The Woodman's Quest

beautiful environment. William promised not to be long at the gallery and Bernard whispered that they would be back very soon to Adelaide, who was already falling asleep in the spare bedroom and managed a feint nod.

When they had arrived at the gallery, Bernard excused himself for a while as the owner wished to speak with him. Fay led them into a room that was dedicated to Bernard's work. It was clear that his forte was in sculpturing busts, but in particular they saw that one side of the room was dedicated to an amazing display of Phaedra's likenesses and there were no mistaking them.

Five bronze sculptures were placed on plinths in a rough circle 9 feet in diameter. Phaedra then walked between two of them and stood in the middle. The whole part of the floor that housed the plinths was a like a carpeted plate, so that when a switch was pulled the whole thing slowly rotated.

William and Zeta then approached her as she cheekily made faces at them. On closer examination of the work as they passed by them, it was clear that he had sculptured her in very different yet expressive moods.

'Bernard did these before he had even met me, scary or what?' She asked them, smiling.

After another twenty minutes or so, Bernard returned to the room apologising for his absence but he was not smiling. William swallowed hard, he knew in his heart that somehow, all this pleasure was about to end. Nothing was actually said, but Bernard gestured for the three of them to follow him outside.

'It's Adelaide, she has taken a turn for the worse, and Josephus has taken her to the recovery centre of The Mission

The Woodman's Quest

Hospital just along the coast' we must go there now!' He
urged.

They were soon at the side of Adelaide's bed and William held
her tiny hand. She looked so small and seemed lost in the bed
somehow. The doctor quietly came alongside William and put
his hand on the young man's shoulder.

'So sorry son, but the tumour has returned with a
vengeance, the remission has come to an end.' He said in his
ear.

William got onto the bed and lifted his mother to a sitting
position and slid her back onto his broad chest. He knew that
the time was close, as her breathing came in short bursts and
then there was a period when it stopped, and then a deep
breath again. The nurse stood on the other side of the bed
looking at mother and son.

'Is that you my son? Adelaide said in a barely audible
whisper.

'Yes mum I'm here.' William said.

The nurse had a tear in her eye as she watched Adelaide
finally draw her last breath in her son's arms. William didn't
want to let her go, but finally realised that she was gone from
him forever.

As William left the bedside and walked into Zeta's arms,
Phaedra and Bernard clasped their arms around the couple in
their bereavement. When they all turned back to his mother's
bed, the nurse had neatly repositioned her in the bed, so that
she looked as if she was sleeping again. Josephus then came
into the room and kissed her on the forehead and William

The Woodman's Quest

hugged him and thanked him for what he had done that day for her.

They said their goodbyes to Fay and Bernard at their hotel and drove back to the house from Laguna. As they sat on the back seat, they looked at each other, and then at the vacant space between them. William thought about how happy his mother was, when that old man recognised her and even kissed her hand, as they arrived at the hotel. Even that had seemed like a goodbye somehow.

Josephus or Joe, as he then wanted them to call him, asked William if he would like him to make all the arrangements for the funeral of his mother. He also inquired when they were thinking of returning home, but William said that he wanted to stay until things were settled. Forgetting himself for not asking Zeta, he looked at her for a response to his answer, but she just nodded, realising that he was still getting used to the idea that his long lost mother who he had just found, was now dead.

Zeta had got out of bed early the following morning, but not soon enough it seemed, as the other side of the bed was empty. There was no need to search of any of the rooms in the big mansion for William; she knew instinctively where he was. His yellow striped dressing gown gave him away; she spied it through the trees as he wandered aimlessly in the garden trying to get his head around all of the events that had happened since he had arrived in Los Angeles, the 'City of the Angels'.

'I had a dream last night Zeta, I dreamt that the little fawn had come into our room and it spoke to me.' William looked at his fiancée, and she could see the hurt in his eyes.

The Woodman's Quest

She remembered that roe deer kid and three women who had quietly entered the woodman's cottage, and after a little coaxing it came up to them and allowed each one to stroke its mottled coat. She knew that 'butch' as he called the young deer, was calling him home. Simple happiness like that could not be bought with any sum of money, no matter how large.

William felt the wisdom of her as she held him, but she refrained from speaking because he already knew what needed to be done. When all of the decisions concerning his mother's will had been settled, they would be on the next plane to home.

The first hurdle for William would be the funeral service that dear old Joe had organised. Joe knew Adelaide better that anyone and she would not want any fuss to be made at her funeral. He asked William to compile list of friends or relatives who might attend and told him that it would be conducted in the Chapel of Rest at the crematorium on Woodman Avenue Sherwood Oaks near to Ventura Boulevard.

Joe also said to William that deep down in his mother's psyche, although she had been a film star, Adelaide loved to do things quietly and in secret. He told her son that it was Rufus Brown whom she particularly supported for many years in his charity work.

That statement from Joe about his mother's character initially hit William very hard, but of course he had no idea at all about his mother's kindness over the preceding years. So he soon pulled himself together, and realised that there had been no time to find this out about her.

Around six in the evening they received surprise visitors to the house which lifted both of them. Four people stood on the

The Woodman's Quest

doorstep and William couldn't believe his eyes, it was Phaedra, Bernard and Wilomena with Rufus.

Phaedra had insisted that they were there to support William in his grief, and asked if they could attend the service. Fay also added that on William's behalf, she had invited Teddy, Lewis and his family who wanted to also be there. William said that although he had never met them, he was overjoyed with the prospect of meeting some of her friends. Fay had planned another surprise for the service, which she hoped would be acceptable, but for the time being, had kept it a secret.

The date for the cremation had been set for two weeks' time, on a Sunday morning. Adelaide's private lawyer had arranged to conduct the reading of her will at the house, roughly a week after the funeral service. William had finally lost all of his foreboding, now that the important dates for winding up his mother's affairs had been set.

There were only twelve seats in the chapel and apart from her small staff including Joe, every other seat was filled. Phaedra introduced Teddy and his new partner Yolanda to William and Zeta and then Lewis Owen and his family were introduced next.

After the short service by the minister, there was a short silence in the room and after a signal from him, three members of the mourners stepped up onto the small dais. A small piano was set in the corner and Teddy squeezed his tall frame onto the stool. His blonde partner Yolanda took up her stance at the side of him, carrying her violin. Phaedra then positioned herself in front of the two musicians and said to the audience that she felt that Adelaide would approve of her rendition of 'You'll never walk alone' from the musical 'Carousel'.

The Woodman's Quest

Later in the afternoon, Joe had organised a small 'wake' as he called it, at the house after the service, and all were invited. This was William and Zeta's best opportunity to get to know all of the guests and to thank them for supporting them so well.

At one point Bernard was having a conversation with Lewis about his career as a conductor, but soon they were to find that they had a great deal in common. Lewis's father was born in the same town as Bernard's, it was an amazing coincidence.

Bernard told Lewis that his step-father, John Harrison, after a spell in the British Army had qualified in astronomy and was very proud to tell everyone that for his work in that field, he had just been recognised in the Queen's Honours for that year.

Lewis and Bernard's fathers' ages were so similar; they could have possibly gone to the same school in that small Derbyshire town called Ilkeston. Phaedra was listening intently to the conversation between the two men, and as soon as she heard the name of the town, she called Teddy over, who revealed that his grandfather was also from the same place.

Teddy introduced his partner Yolanda to William and told him that she was the third violin the same orchestra that he worked, and from that time they had fell in love and were planning to get engaged very soon. Although an American citizen, her ancestors were Chinese in origin.

Eight days later, the gathering at the house was a small one for the reading of Adelaide's will, William, Zeta, Rufus and Wilomena and of course her loyal staff. The lawyer had

The Woodman's Quest

informed every one that Adelaide's will had been altered quite considerably, only two weeks before she had died, and pointed out that it had been duly witnessed and filed in the courts according to the law.

Wilomena, with her prior agreement, had been appointed as the executer for the will and had the responsibility to ensure that all of Adelaide's wishes were to be carried out to the letter. Adelaide had made a special commendation to Wilomena for all the work that she had done to find her son William Gilpin.

The first bequest was made for her staff, a generous endowment for life for each of them, with a particular mention of her 'dear Josephus'.

The next bequest was concerning the charity run by Rufus Brown. In that case, she charged Wilomena to oversee the liquidation of all her investments and to set up a charity fund with the proceeds, in the name of The Adelaide Columbine Foundation. That fund was to be set up for the sole use of Rufus's Children's Charity work in Los Angeles.

The final bequest was that the house and its contents were to be sold, and the proceeds to be passed to her only son Mr. William Gilpin.

'And that is the end of the reading ladies and gentlemen. I hand the affairs over to Miss Ruzinski attorney at law.' The lawyer dutifully passed the document to his fellow legal practitioner and left the room.

Wilomena told the staff of the house that they would receive a cheque that day which covered their severance pay, and their monthly payment as outlined in their individual letters would continue 'in perpetuum'.

The Woodman's Quest

Rufus inquired what the value of the foundation would be, and Wilomena answered that at the last valuation of the stock, it stood at just below one and a half million dollars.

Before she left with Rufus, Wilomena told William that the Sotheby's valuers would be arriving at the house tomorrow, but if they had a specific item that they would like to choose to remember Adelaide by, then as long as they informed her there would be no problem.

Joe came up to William and Zeta and told them that he was quite aware of what had been planned for him and he was very happy to have served such a wonderful employer. William hugged Joe and thanked him for the great help that he had given them and told him that he would never forget his kindness.

William had absolutely no idea of what he wanted, that would remind him of his mother, however Zeta mentioned about the paste tiara that was in the dressing table. The item was a film prop that reminded Adelaide about the film she made with Stewart Grainger.

William smiled for the first time, and agreed wholeheartedly. Wilomena was just about to leave when he called her back for a moment; meanwhile Zeta had rushed up to the old actress's bedroom and retrieved the tiara. William told her the reason for their choice and Wilomena kissed them both in approval and promised to keep in touch.

The Woodman's Quest

Chapter 35

Quest achieved

Three weeks after returning from America, William was determined to get back to his life as a forester on Alex's woodland. The only difference to the job was that he didn't stay in the woodman's cottage anymore. He would drive the tractor to Heron's Nest and his fiancée would pick him up there.

One evening they drew up at the little semi, but she was unable to get the car in the drive, a large black limousine had blocked their path. William was the first to the driver's side of the car as the window slid down revealing a smiling giant of a man. He got out of the car and offered his hand to William.

'Hi William, my name is Harry Sinclair and I would like to tell you about the man who sent those 'goons' to frighten you that night, Mr. Michael Corleone. I have some news about him; do you think we could go inside for a moment?' He asked.

Zeta went into the small kitchen to put the kettle on as Harry introduced himself as the chief security officer at the American Embassy in London. This information meant nothing to William.

He told William that Corleone, had gone into hiding in Spain and sadly, British police were powerless to bring him back. In secret, the ambassador had issued instructions for a covert mission to bring him back through their own resources. Off the record, two secret American agents were despatched to 'persuade' Mr Corleone to give himself up to the police in the UK, and to admit to them that he had sent his men to hurt

The Woodman's Quest

William severely. This he did, and because of his admission, William's record had been cleared off of the police files.

William then asked what had become of Corleone, and at that question Harry smiled. He told them that as he was about to board a plane back to Spain, he was re-arrested on a charge of double murder. Two children had been burned in a shop fire. They were in the flat above it, and reliable witnesses had seen the same two henchmen leave the shop just before it had been torched. Mr Corleone had been found guilty and sentenced to thirty years minimum term at Wormwood Scrubs. Justice had at last been done.

A year had passed since their fateful journey to Los Angeles, and although William hadn't heard much from Wilomena; he had been too busy to worry about it. Mr. & Mrs. Gilpin had changed their lives without any need to resort to inheritances.

They had got married in St. Nectan's Chapel near Lostwithiel, with Alex Deville acting as William's best man and his wife Fiona proud to be Zeta's maid of honour. Their daughter had carried Zeta's wedding gown's train perfectly, for William that was the icing on the cake.

When they had returned from their wedding reception which was held at the Heron's Roost, there was a letter from America and they both knew who it was from. The post mark was Los Angeles and William asked his new wife to open it. She read it out loud to him.

`Dear William and Zeta Gilpin,

Congrats on your marriage and my apologies that Rufus and I couldn't be with you both for the ceremony. We wish you great happiness in your new lives.

The Woodman's Quest

*I've finally got the funds that covered the sale of the property
and its contents. I hope that you are sitting down when you
read this as the sum is;*

$2,850,000

*This sum represents the net funds, after State taxes, the
whole amount is sitting in Wells Fargo Bank here in L.A.
awaiting your instructions.*

*Best regards from your good friend, Wilomena Ruzinski
Attorney at Law and Trustee of Adelaide Columbine's last will
and testament.'*

William shook his head in disbelief and humbly said to his wife
that whatever she decided to do with it would be fine with
him. They opted in the first place to leave it in the American
bank.

More importantly, with Alex's help, William had passed his
driving test, and it happened to be very good timing, as Zeta
had told him only six months before, that she was expecting
their first child.

A surprise package arrived at the little house in Tintagel
received by special delivery postmarked Los Angeles USA
addressed to Mrs. Z. Gilpin – Addressee only. The sturdy box
contained a well-read book, a separately wrapped smaller box
and envelope addressed to Zeta. She opened the letter first
and was not surprised to see that it was from Phaedra.

*'My darling Zeta, now that your life has found meaning at
last. I want to tell you how happy I am for you. So sorry that
I was unable to get to your wedding, but I do hope that this
will make up for it'*

The Woodman's Quest

Zeta undid the silk ribbon and she then unwrapped the box. Inside this box, was another one shaped like a pink jewellery case. Before opening it, she looked underneath and it was stamped with the makers name; **Tiffany's on Vine – Hollywood.** Her anticipation grew as she slid the cover off the box.

Lying curled up on a purple velvet cushion was a perfectly formed snake bracelet at the end of which was a magnificent dragon's head clasp fashioned in bright yellow gold. Two sparkling rubies had been set for the eyes. On the other end of the chain was of course the snake's tail made out of tiny rings of gold separated by minute diamonds

Zeta offered the tail to the dragon's head and felt a soft 'click' as it held firmly shut. She was then apprehensive about releasing the tail but as her finger touched the back of the head, and out popped the tail. It was a marvel of micro-engineering and could only have been constructed by the finest of jewellery craftsmen.

Zeta pulled out the chain to see what was attached to the centre of it, and smiled knowingly. It was the strange stone that Phaedra always wore, and was so surprised that she would give it to her. Looking back at the note from Phaedra she noticed a 'p.t.o.' at the bottom and turned it over.

'As you know I have worn this chain since Teddy gave it to me, so that is why it comes in a box from Tiffany's; Bernard insisted that only the best jewellers in town would be allowed to clean it and they did a great job eh?

Zeta, now place the stone in the palm of your left hand and if it glows, I know that I have passed it onto the right person. That done, then read the book that I sent you, written by

The Woodman's Quest

Teddy's grandfather called 'The Mystic Stone' it will give you all you need to know on its history and relevance.

Love you
Phaedra'

Zeta closed her left hand around the stone, it quickly felt warm and an orange light was shining out between her fingers.

Chapter 36

A call from afar

A year had past since the twins Rowena and Sara had received Brucie into their home in Los Angeles and as their father had promised them, it was big and black. In fact it was a Labradoodle; a cross between a Black Labrador and a woolly black Standard Poodle. Lewis knew that if he didn't insist that the dog undergo a long intensive training programme, then its strong character would take over and the girls would have been overwhelmed.

Al, the dog trainer told Lewis that the twins also needed intensive dog-handling training at the same time as it was extremely important for the dog to know who is the 'boss' in their relationship with him. As an exuberant and large dog, when it gets over excited, will forget all of its training unless the owner is very strict.

For instance, pulling on the lead is the first thing that had to be broken in him. Al told the girls to remember the 'carrot and stick' method; carrot for reward and stick to reprimand. The gun-dog gene in Brucie was strong and within only a few weeks he was eager to please them. He was extremely good on the word 'Heel' and calmed down immediately after the first week he had been successfully trained to overcome the temptation to jump up to approaching strangers.

Initially his biggest weakness, was when the girls took him to the beach. As soon as he was off the lead, he would run and run and no amount of calling would get him back. Al, the trainer soon introduced the solid rubber ball to the dog, and that had changed that habit for Brucie forever.

The Woodman's Quest

Of course, Brucie was extremely lovable with his shaggy head, bright eyes and wonderful black curly coat. Because he was part poodle there were no traces of dog-hair on the furniture. Also being that he was part Labrador, he was a great calming influence on the whole household.

Apart from when they attended college, he just about shadowed the girls wherever they went. If Lewis could have taken him to his work, where he was the conductor of the L.A. Philharmonic, and he was sure they would not appreciate a big black dog on the rostrum, he probably would howl anyway.

Lewis used to be a workaholic, which reflected on his orchestra, he was a very hard taskmaster when it came to rehearsals. Since Brucie came on the scene Lewis became more tolerant and even smiled when they succeeded in getting the right notes etc. When things were going well his mind often drifted to the beach where he imagined throwing that ball and the eager dog's face as he would promptly return it to him.

'Look Dad, someone has remembered Brucie's birthday' one of the twins shouted.

Lewis was munching on his toast in the kitchen and as he looked down a shaggy head that had rested on his knee with a brown paper parcel in his teeth, and his huge tail wagging like a black flag.

'Give' Lewis ordered, and the big dog slowly opened its massive jaws enough for Lewis to extricate the parcel. This was pure instinct in him, having that game-dog gene. Lewis looked at the box and was amazed that there were no teeth marks at all, the dog had held it so gently.

The Woodman's Quest

The postmark was Southampton England and he immediately recognised that this was from Mark Bussell, his late father's solicitor. Inside the box was a hand-written note and a paperback novel. He settled down at the kitchen table and read the letter.

'Dear Lewis,
I do hope that you find the time to read this letter as I'm not sure how you will react to it.
I recently had a telephone call from Phaedra Norman who says that she had met you and your family when she was over there in L.A.
There is so much that I would like to say about your father, but instead I include this book called 'Lewi's Legacy' Most of the book is concerned with your late father's colourful life and as far as I know, most of it is true.
As you well know I knew your father very well, both as his lawyer and on a personal basis. I can honestly say that I've never met such a kind man.
I do hope that this book may tempt you to come and see me in Southampton. I do have so much to tell you.
Accommodation for your visit could easily be arranged for you and your family for as long as you wish.
Please consider and come
Best wishes
Mark'

Lewis glanced at the book, considered reading it, but then remembered that he had an important meeting with the music director at the Walt Disney conference centre. His wife stood near, as he was looking at the cover of the book and frowning.

'Do you think you could do me a favour Sarah, I'm very busy this morning what with meetings and rehearsals? Could you please read this letter from Mark, and if possible, read the

The Woodman's Quest

book that he sent with it. I'd be very interested in your opinion of it.' As usual there was only time for a quick goodbye kiss to his wife and the twins and tousle of the shaggy head of Brucie, then he was gone.

After dropping the girls off at their college she headed to the usual spot on the sunny beach with Brucie and prepared to concentrate on some serious reading. The title of the book, 'Lewi's Legacy' was already making her curious as in her view that made three spellings of the same name – Lewis her husband, Louis his father and now Lewi. According to the letter from Mark, it was mainly about his father. She found a nice shady spot and made sure Brucie was ok and soon got into to the first chapter.

That same evening after dinner Sarah asked Lewis what he knew about his father and held her breath. She had already endured many years of being unable to talk about his past, but he did ask her to read the book, so she sat and waited for the explosion that did not come.

'You remember the last time we saw my dad in Buxton over ten years ago. He mentioned that I had Jewish ancestry in me and for forty odd years since my birth, I had no idea. Secondly, a year or so before that, he had introduced himself as my father, in the strangest circumstances as my mother had always said he was dead. For these past ten years that we've been in the USA I have been confused to say the least, but as you also know, since we met Phaedra I do feel that it's time to learn more, hence the letter and book from Mark, I suppose.' Lewis gave her a smile as he answered her. With a little relief, Sarah then recalled some of the facts in the opening chapters in the book 'Lewi's Legacy'.

'Did you know that your father's early childhood was a very difficult one? He was brought up by his father, your

The Woodman's Quest

grandfather, as a single parent, as his French mother died at childbirth. Additional to that, he was born a cripple and struggled until he was ten years old until miraculously cured by an old gypsy woman.' Sarah told him, carefully watching her husband for his reaction.

His reaction was very clear, Lewis picked up the book, sat in an easy chair and started reading it. In fact he was so engrossed in it that he had let two cups of coffee get cold and Sarah had to remind him that it was time to go to bed. He dropped off in bed with the book open on his chest, the last chapter unfinished.

The next morning Lewis asked Sarah to find out the old waistcoat that he always wore after he had been appointed conductor. The red waistcoat was duly found with Sarah commenting that it was time to clear out some of the clothes that he hadn't worn for such a long time.

She watched him search the front pockets and exclaimed with delight having found what he was looking for.

'Can you remember reading about this in dad's book Sarah?' Lewis said as he showed her a little brown envelope.

Sarah quickly retrieved the book and re-read the passage to her husband;

'Magda held out her hand to him and he looked down to see it. A small brown envelope was nestled in her bony palm, he saw that it was no more than an inch square, made of brown parchment, with what looked like two words written in a strange language. He took the envelope, turned it over and saw that it was sealed. Magda explained to him that the writing was

The Woodman's Quest

in the language of the ancient Greeks - ῾γνῶθι σεαυτόν᾽.

She also told him that inside the little envelope were some tiny seeds. 'Keep them inside and do not take them out. I tell you this because in the bag they are powerful, but to let them out they will just become seeds, and will forever lose their power.'

Finally, she told him that he would always know the whereabouts of the little package, as the power will remind him wherever he went. She also told him that it would be alright to give it to another person, if he wished to. Good fortune would follow this person if the seeds remained in the envelope.'

'Well darling, this is that very same envelope that dad gave me when we moved over here to America. He also explained the meaning of the Greek script – it was an ancient saying from the philosopher Socrates, and it means; know thyself"

After the weekend, his head was full of the history of his father, and had been enlightened with some of the reasons why he hadn't contacted his son before. By the Monday Lewis had already formulated a plan, and immediately went to see the Director of Music at the L.A.P.

'Jonathan, I know this is short notice, but I need to take some leave. It is an urgent personal matter which requires me to visit Europe in two weeks time.'

The director's face showed concern, as there were new performances scheduled and of course it was paramount that his conductor be there. Lewis had already thought of that and gave Jonathan a list of three excellent conductors who were willing to substitute for him.

The Woodman's Quest

The next part of the plan was much simpler. He asked Teddy if he and his new wife Yolanda would come to dinner on the following Wednesday. Teddy knew a great deal of the area he was planning to visit and although not related, knew his late father enough to be a beneficiary in his will..

That Monday night there was a family meeting over dinner and Lewis revealed his plan to everyone, including the dog. Sarah told her husband that the problem of taking the girls out of school and finding someone to look after Brucine for four weeks would be very difficult, so she suggested that he visit the UK on his own this time. That would give him the flexibility that he would surely have needed.

After the dinner with Teddy and his wife on the Wednesday he was then confident enough to ring Mark in Southampton to tell him of his plans. Mark rang him back to say that he had cleared his day for the first Monday of his visit, and that Phaedra's mother and father had offered free accommodation at their house in nearby Lyndhurst. Mark also told Lewis that the house that they lived in was previously owned by his father Louis.

The excitement was at fever pitch. It had been nearly eleven years since he had been living in the UK and it was the first time that he had visited the South Coast of England and 'wow' only a week to go, he mused to himself.

The Woodman's Quest

Chapter 37

A shock all round

Marcy and Mikhail, the new Mr and Mrs Norman arrived back in Philadelphia from Bermuda after a four-week long honeymoon, and still had stars in their eyes. As they headed back to her parents' mansion, she was remembering the huge reception at that house after their wedding, and particularly how her new sister-in-law Phaedra and Teddy performed such a beautiful musical tribute to her and her husband.

They stepped out of the yellow cab and approached the impressive white marble steps that glinted in the afternoon sunshine and as they climbed in unison up the steps, Mickey suddenly felt the grip in his new wife's hand.

'What is it Marcy, are you nervous or something?' He asked.

'I can't explain it, but I suddenly felt like something is wrong.' Marcia answered, and struggled to take another step.

Mickey managed to coax her to the top of the steps, tried the front door without success so he then pushed the large button embedded in the wall beside the great double doors. It seemed like an age before Barbara the housemaid pulled open one of the great double doors. The look on her face said it all to them, there was definitely something wrong. As they stepped into the white marble hall it seemed cold and so quiet. No greeting from Helen or Hugo as they expected. Without speaking they walked into the lounge and sat down in one of the massive sofas.

'What's going on Barbara? Where is everybody?' Marcy pleaded for an answer.

The Woodman's Quest

'I'll bring you some tea, have you eaten?' Barbara seemed to ignore the question.

'Just tea please Barbara and we would like an explanation when you return.' Mickey answered.

As they waited for their refreshment, Marcy sighed deeply and just held hands with her husband, fearing the worst. Within a few minutes, Barbara appeared with a tray and Marcia indicated that the maid sit on the sofa opposite. Fighting back the tears Barbara told them what had happened since they had gone on their honeymoon. It transpired that just one week after they had left, Mr Hugo had stormed out of the front door laden with two big suitcases, and quickly drove away.

'What about my mother then Barbara, where is she then?' Marcy asked, as her head craned forward toward the maid.

'The lady of the house left just a week ago also with suitcases and got in a taxi. I've heard nothing from either of them since.' Barbara answered and held her head down so as not to look them in the face. 'Oh, and she gave me this note for you'.

Marcy could not see, her eyes were full of tears, so Mickey read the small note out loud for her.

'If you want to contact me, I'll be on this number. Say sorry to Marcy and Mickey and tell them I love them – Helen'

'Is there anything else you can tell me Barbara, anything at all? Marcie pleaded.

'Well, not long after Mr Spiros had left, your mother had a visitor, a young woman called Ruzinski, ah yes her first name

The Woodman's Quest

was er..Wilomena I think. Sorry but that is all I can tell you.' Barbara ran out of the room visibly upset and closed the lounge door after her.

'Give me that note Mickey, I'll get mom on the phone right now!' Marcy shouted angrily.

'You can't ring her now darling, because it's already 4pm here but it'll be midnight in Lyndhurst with the time difference'.

'What? Mom's in England, why? What's going on?' It was all too much for Marcia, the floodgates had opened and she buried her face in his chest shaking with emotion.

Helen Spiros sat in a window seat on the American Airlines flight to Heathrow and even after the most tumultuous four weeks of her life, she still could believe what she was currently doing. Three weeks before, after the usual row in which her husband Hugo shouted her down once again, little did he expect that for once in his wife's life she would not lie down and let him 'walk over her'. To his great surprise she got out of her chair and pushed him to the wall and pinned him there by the neck. Where she found the strength from she would never know, but if she had been holding a weapon at the time, she would have killed him of that there was no doubt.

Of course that action was the tipping point for their marriage. He blurted out that he was having an affair and was going to leave that day. She had tried to ask him how long it had been going on, but didn't get a chance, he was upstairs packing, and within an hour was storming out of the door and drove off to goodness knows where. At least she had the time to make one statement to him as he was opening the front door;

The Woodman's Quest

'Good riddance I don't want to see you again except in court, you overbearing old goat. She's darn welcome to you!' She shouted at the top of her voice.

She knew that being the senior partner in a large law firm, he was probably on strong legal footings, but she knew that whoever represented him, would soon find that she was on the moral high ground and come hell or high water she would take him for everything that she could get. She knew that would get him where it hurt the most, in his pocket.

Her new found strength did not leave her either. She knew immediately who would represent her, a young lawyer, who had recently changed an impossible dream to reality for an aged actress called Adelaide Columbine. Against all the odds, Wilomena had found her son, who had been lost for thirty four years and was living on the other side of the world. Added to that, because of the health of his mother, Wilomena had very little time to complete such a complicated task. That certainly was a good enough reference as far as Helen was concerned.

Wilomena Ruzinski had recently attended the wedding of Helen's daughter as the guest of her son John. So Helen did the logical thing and rang him to get the lawyer's phone number and at the same time had to break the news of his parents' split.

His response was a great relief for her and showed no great surprise. His was aware that his father had always been a difficult man having defied his father's wishes and refused to follow him into law, instead went into publishing. He worked at the LA Times as a sports correspondent which just about finished any relationship with his Hugo.

The Woodman's Quest

'What I know mom, is the Wilomena has left the law firm in LA and is now working in some charity organisation. I'll try to get hold of her and call you back'.

In fifteen minutes John was back on the phone again to his mother, with bad news. All the contact numbers for Wilomena were non-starters and sadly he had no idea of the charity's name or where it was.

Helen's heart sank, having failed at the first hurdle. Normally Hugo would quickly sort out such a problem for her, but she laughed at that idea, knowing that Hugo himself was now the problem. As she sat with a coffee in the easy chair, she racked her brains to identify anyone who might know where Wilomena was. She had to admit, it was a bigger task than she had imagined.

As she made her way to the bedroom, no ideas had come to mind. For Helen, usually sleep often shook away the dross in her mind and sometimes the solution to the problem would present itself in the morning. It was much before that however that the solution came. In the night's darkest time around two am, she had woken up with a start.

'What was that young woman's name who seemed quite close to Wilomena at the wedding? She asked herself. 'Her name was Phaedra and she was the one who sang so beautifully with Teddy at the piano' She smiled, as she also remembered that after the reception, Phaedra had left to get back to LA with Teddy. The thing that triggered her memory, was that they were trying to get the same flight as John and Wilomena.

She knew that Phaedra was the sister of her new son-in-law Mikhail and the daughter of Victor and Lydiya who went back to the UK, and they had had left their contact details

The Woodman's Quest

somewhere. All she had to do was then to find those details, the first place she looked was her purse. She emptied the whole contents out and what a relief, there was a card – one of Hugo's, with the phone number written on the back. It was still in the dead of night in Philadelphia, but looked at the wall clock and calculated that it would have been about nine in the morning over there.

'Hello Victor' Helen said tentatively.

'Is that Helen? Let me pass you over to Lydiya, hang on.' He had felt the urgency in Helen's voice and he had to admit that his wife was far more able to deal with pressure than he was those days.

The American gave a brief outline of the seismic events that had recently occurred and even had left Lydiya gasping for breath Helen then realised how difficult for Lydiya to grasp what she was saying so she slowed down somewhat and asked that she needed to speak to her daughter Phaedra, hoping that she had a phone number for Wilomena.

After the call had ended, Lydiya had contacted Phaedra by text with instructions for Wilomena to ring Helen Spiros in Philadelphia, ending with – 'VERY IMPORTANT'. Thousands of miles and four long hours of agonising and waiting, Helen had finally obtained Wilomena's contact number.

The news of John Spiros's parents' split came as a great shock to the young lawyer in Los Angeles. The shock soon changed to deep compassion, as she soon realised how desperately Helen had needed her help. So to Helen's relief, Wilomena accepted her request to take the brief and promised to be with her in 24 hours.

The Woodman's Quest

'Don't worry Helen we'll get this sorted for you, see you soon.' Wilomena said reassuringly.

Later on that same day, the phone rang again and to Helen's relief it was Lydiya ringing from her home in the New Forest, asking whether or not she had gotten hold of her lawyer. Helen took the opportunity to tell her in greater detail about the way that Hugo had treated her.

Lydiya replied that she was not at all surprised, and recalled that she could see the writing on the wall at the wedding. She also mentioned that she had noticed how little her husband had spent with his wife. Lydiya told her that at one stage she was so curious that she once followed Hugo out of the main reception room and was sure that when he had gone into another room, she clearly heard him lock it. Lydiya said that she could hear voices inside that room, but then with everything happening that day, thought no more about it.

'Helen, should you want to come and stay with us, as I had mentioned to you before, we have lots of room and you can stay as long as you like, please come.'

Helen promised to keep in contact and promised that she would ring her back once Wilomena had made her visit to the house.

The Woodman's Quest

Chapter 38

A friend in need

As soon as Lewis had landed at Heathrow, the euphoria that he had felt at LA International with all of his family waving him off and wishing him well, had soon worn off with the jet-lag. There was no-one at the airport to meet him, although he knew exactly where he was headed and how he was supposed to get there. Mark Bussell had emailed full instructions of how to get to Waterloo and onward transfer to a small station in the New Forest.

Having collected his large suitcase he trudged along the wide concourse and headed for an empty bench. It was Sunday morning so he was unable to speak to Mark, and goodness knows what time it was in Los Angeles, he thought to himself. With one hand on the suitcase handle, he could feel himself dropping off to sleep.

'Are you Lewis Owen by any chance?' A softly spoken American voice woke him out of his slumber.

A well- dressed woman in her early sixties sat next to him on the bench, smiling disarmingly. He tried to smile back but tiredness laced with a dash of disappointment weighed heavily on his shoulders.

'My name is Helen Spiros, and I believe we have both been invited to stay with the same people, Victor and Lydiya Norman in a town called Lyndhurst in the county of Hampshire, am I right?' She asked.

'Er.. Yes that's right but how on earth did you find me amongst this crowd?' Lewis asked, he was finally waking up.

The Woodman's Quest

'Mark Bussell sent me a picture of you to my phone. Here it is, very smart may I say, were you attending some dinner of some kind? The dinner jacket and bow tie really suits you'

'Actually no Helen, they're my working clothes, I'm in the LA Philharmonic.'

Helen knew where he had arrived from as Mark had given her the LA flight number and its arrival time at Heathrow. It just happened that her flight came in two hours earlier. She asked him what instrument he played and was astounded to hear that he was the leader of the orchestra.

'How long are you in the UK Helen? He asked.

'I guess just as long as it takes.' She answered solemnly, and Lewis didn't pursue that line of questioning as he could immediately see that it was the wrong question to ask.

After the rather harrowing connection between Heathrow and Waterloo rail station, they were both finally boarding the Bournemouth train and chose a table at the dining car sitting opposite each other coffee with cup in hand. At last they could relax for a while.

As she talked, he studied his travelling companion. She was quite attractive for her age and to him, displayed a sort of nervousness which is not evident of a woman of the world. He sensed that she was escaping from somewhere, as if she needed a sort of sanctuary. When she stopped talking for a moment, he smiled at her and she smiled back.

'I wasn't sure what sort of person I would meet at Heathrow Lewis, but I'm glad it was you.'

The Woodman's Quest

He reached over the table and gently held her hand, and she squeezed his hand if not a little self-consciously. For about fifteen minutes they said nothing to each other, sometimes looking at the others facial expression, sometimes looking at the countryside flying by, but during that time their hands remained clasped.

For a brief moment Lewis wanted to get out of his seat and kiss her, but he fought off the temptation, and fearing the consequences. Instead she must have sensed something and began to talk about the recent marriage of her daughter in Philly. She quickly mentioned two names that shook Lewis for a moment.

'You know these two people well Helen? He asked.

When she explained that Phaedra was the sister of her new son-in-law, he laughed heartily as he realised what a master stroke Mark Bussell had made in bringing them both together. The journey time from London to Brockenhurst had passed so quickly. Most of the time they were locked in conversation and without any effort at all, they seemed to find each others company so comfortable. In fact, it wasn't too long before they had willingly spoken about their most private feelings. As they approached the station, a voice from the tannoy was warning them that their destination was near, when they looked out of the window they could see that the area showed a much more rural part of the country that the one they had left an hour or so ago.

The train was applying its brakes and they rose out of their seats at the same time, and as they stood in the aisle, Lewis took the opportunity to give his fellow passenger a hug, she readily hugged him back. Their faces were very close together and he could smell her perfume, almost tempted to kiss her, but he knew that it was the wrong time and place. When he

The Woodman's Quest

looked at her smiling face though, he felt that she wouldn't have resisted him.

'Thank you Lewis for a most stimulating journey, and considering what I've been though, I needed that hug.' Helen said and smiled as she looked for her suitcase.

As they alighted from the train, two railway porters grabbed their heavy suitcases and silently led them over that small iron footbridge towards the station exit. As they were crossing the line they noticed just one large black car in the car park and thankfully a slightly built man standing and waving to them.

Helen recognised him as Victor, the father of Phaedra and Mikhail who had attended her daughter's wedding a month or so before. Lewis lifted their suitcases into the back of the SUV whilst Helen hugged Victor and then introduced him to her travelling companion.

'You've never met me Lewis, but I feel that I know you very well. I count myself fortunate to have known your father such a long time. I am going to take you both to our home, which I do hope that you will treat it as your own. Please come and go as you please whilst you are here, and I promise you that you will lack for nothing.' Victor said as he pulled out of the station car park and headed for Lyndhurst, a mere three miles away.

The visitors sat in the back seat, totally relaxed and watched the thickly wooded countryside glide by. Helen looked into Lewis's eyes for a second and reached for a comforting hand. A small tingle rushed up his arm, and once again had to control a strong urge to kiss her again. Her smile told him that she had read his face very clearly as she squeezed his hand very slightly.

The Woodman's Quest

A raven haired woman was standing on the gravel drive in front of an impressive Edwardian mansion with superb mock-Tudor gables and oak entrance.

'**Добро пожаловать в наш дом**.' She exclaimed to her guests and gave each one a powerful hug.

'Lydiya likes to traditionally greet anyone in her native Russian tongue, it means 'Welcome to our house" Victor laughed at their visitors' quizzical looks at each other.

Lewis instantly liked this woman, she seemed off-beat and brave and yet most endearing, quite different to anyone he had ever met before, except of course her daughter Phaedra.

Victor led Lewis upstairs to where he was to be staying at the house. He was given a small suite of rooms; bedroom, cloakroom dressing room and a small sitting room. As they looked out of the mullioned window of the sitting room, Lewis could see that it overlooked a small clearing of heathland surrounded by a stand of white trunks of silver birch trees.

Victor explained that although the area is called New Forest, most of it is heathland, cleared by the eleventh and twelfth century English kings for their sport of deer hunting. At this point he put his arm around Lewis's shoulders and told him that his father, who once owned that house, would be so very proud that he was standing looking out of the window at that very moment.

This immediately brought a lump to Lewis's throat as he quietly stood looking out of the window. The evening sun still shone on the lush grass of the clearing and Lewis was taken aback by its simple beauty.

The Woodman's Quest

'Now Helen, can you first bring me up to date with the situation at home in Philadelphia?' Lydiya asked as she led Helen into the library and asked the maid to bring tea for them.

Helen told her that in the short time that Wilomena, her newly appointed lawyer had been at her house, she had already made some exciting headway. She had firstly mentioned to the young lawyer how strange and secretive Hugo had behaved at the wedding reception.

This gave Wilomena an idea to ask Helen to retrieve all of the hundreds of photographs that had been taken during the reception that day, and armed with a magnifying glass meticulously asked Helen to identify every face that was captured in them.

Her client was mystified why they had to go through that laborious task, until when they looked at some of the group pictures; there certainly was one young woman's face that Helen had not recognised. This face appeared on two other pictures and in all of them Hugo was standing right beside her. In one particular picture it could be defined that he was holding her hand, and looking at her more affectionately that anyone would to a stranger.

'You mean that your husband took his 'floozy' to the wedding of his daughter without your knowledge?' Lydiya was shocked.

Helen outlined what Wilomena had planned to do following their discovery; the first one was to investigate the full details of both his current and historical extra marital relationships, going back at least five years. The second, to take the form of a thorough investigation into his financial affairs including a valuation of his pension holdings which she would expect to

The Woodman's Quest

have a lien on. Just before she left, Wilomena promised that no stone would be left unturned, and promised to construct such a case that he would not be able to defend it.

'Helen, you have him like a piece if raw meat seasoned and ready for the searing barbeque. I can't wait for the next instalment.' Lydiya giggled with delight.

Chapter 39

History revealed

The day after his arrival at Lyndhurst was the day Lewis chose to go to Southampton and meet Mark Bussell, his late father's solicitor. Victor offered to drive Lewis there and if he wished, attend the meeting with him, to give him some support.

On the journey, Victor recalled the time that he had spent with his father when Louis lived in Alsace on the Franco German border. It was there that Louis was to discover his Hebrew ancestor Lewi Levi. Lewis stopped him there, as he had told him that only a week before he had read the book 'Lewi's Legacy' kindly sent to him by Mark.

What Lewis didn't know was that his father had provided the means for Victor's daughter Phaedra to be rescued from certain death whilst being held by ruthless captors in London. Just as they arrived at the solicitor's car park Victor said that even Mark the solicitor they were about to meet was enlisted to help.

Lewis suddenly felt nervous as they entered the building, realising how he had badly misjudged his late father and now two years after his death, this seemed like a day of reckoning.

'I'm so glad that you have brought Victor with you today Lewis, because there will be quite a bit to take in and I know Victor will be a great help to you'. Mark said reassuringly.

Mark led his two visitors into a private conference room, indicating to his secretary to bring refreshments in an hour and before that time, they were not to be disturbed. As soon as they had sat around the table, Mark got straight to the

The Woodman's Quest

reasons for their visit. With Lewis's permission, he went through all the provisions of his late fathers will, just as he had done two years before.

The list of beneficiaries and the values of their bequests astounded Lewis, and on more than one occasion he had stared at Victor for confirmation; to which he received a knowing smile. After a period of fifteen minutes, the room went silent and Mark looked solemnly at Lewis, who then realised what was coming next.

'It is my bequest that a sum of money from my estate be set aside for the benefit of my only son Lewis. I have instructed my lawyer Mark Bussell to keep secure this sum for a reasonable period. If however he is reasonably satisfied that my son does not respond to his persistent efforts, then this sum will be left for dispersal to the charities that I hereby list below.'

'What is the reasonable period Mark? Lewis asked.

'The two years since the reading of your father's will, had expired one month ago, and for your information the sum involved was....' Mark looked at Lewis in a serious manner; Lewis held his breath and looked at Victor.

During the ensuing silence Mark got out of his chair and approached Lewis, who had by then put his head in his hands, fearing the worst.

'The sum is two million pounds Lewis and here it is.' Mark slid the banker's draft on to the table in front of him. 'Yes I used my discretion and held this back for you, all because of Phaedra. She told me that she had faith in you and that you would come through.'

The Woodman's Quest

Not usually one to show a great deal of emotion in his life, he was more likely to hide his feelings, but this was different. In the presence of Victor and Mark, he was suddenly crying like a baby. Without speaking, his two companions knew exactly the source of these emotions. There was the loss of so many years before he had even known his father, but even more than that, the following bitter years when Lewis had rejected him. It was at that point that he realised that his dear father had never given up on him, just as any loving father would do.

The wait was a long one but eventually Lewis stood up, first to hug the waiting Mark and then turned to do the same to Victor. In all it was a very emotional moment, one that all three of them would never forget. He realised that both of these two men, had known, loved and were held in the greatest trust by Louis, his father.

Mark's secretary, with impeccable timing, came in the room laden with a large coffee pot and tea pot for them to take a well deserved break. Mark nodded appreciatively to her and then nodded again is if to signal to her. Ten minutes later she returned with a large bunch of flowers and laid it on a space in the table. Lewis looked up at Mark, somewhat bleary-eyed.

'I thought that you might want to visit the grave where some of your family are buried, including of course your father. I'm not sure if you know Lewis that my family is also of the Hebrew faith on my mother's side and I regularly attend the synagogue in Southampton.' Mark smiled at the man as he spoke.

He told Lewis that he had made arrangements to clear the day's business and would be honoured to take him to the Hill Lane Cemetery in Southampton, to which Lewis agreed and Victor was happy to go too.

The Woodman's Quest

In the documents that Mark had given Lewis, there was also a simple hereditary line showing the details of all his past relatives from his original ancestor, Lewi Levi. As Lewis looked at the official looking document, he marvelled at the painstaking work that Mark had gone into, knowing that his family history was a highly complicated one. However he was then of no doubt of his Hebrew heritage, and for the first time felt so proud of it.

'I hope you like the document Lewis, it has been on my mind to construct it for you for a long time. I do hope that it will help you to understand the very important heritage that you possess.' Mark said with pride.

The Woodman's Quest

Lineage of the House of Levi

Lewi Levi/Hanna ------ **Moshe Levi**/Ruth (no issue.)

I
Louis Levi/Bridgette

I
Rochelle Levi/Henry Owen

I
Louis Owen/Esther

```
_____ I _____
I                 I
```
Leah-May Owen (D)   **Lewis Owen**/Sarah

Please note;

Lewi Levi had another issue in his advances years, of a female child called Leah, born to an un-named mother in 1945. Leah, I believe, still resides in the Alsace region of France, but no detail has been obtained at this stage.
M. Bussell.

The Woodman's Quest

Victor drove Lewis and Mark to the cemetery and he guided them to two plots lying next to each other. They had walked passed many headstones, some that were written in Hebrew and English. The area was kindly donated to the Jewish community by the council and Mark pointed out that many of the deceased were related.

They finally approached the first memorial stone which Mark interpreted the Hebrew script as for Moshe Levi and Ruth Levi, Lewis's great, great Uncle and Aunt. Lewis stopped to look as he had remembered the passage in the novel where his father was very close to Ruth, and she was instrument in helping his father accept Judaism.

The second memorial contained three names; Esther Owen, Leah-May Owen and finally Louis Owen. Mark took his leave for a while as both his parents were buried nearby, and Victor stood back allowing Lewis to have some time with his closest relatives.

A great deal went through his mind as he knelt there, as he looked at the flower tribute he placed on the memorial, he looked at the family tree that Mark had provided, and noticed that there some names on the document, that were not on the gravestones, and wondered where they were buried, so he proposed to ask Mark if he had done any further research. His eyes looked again at the footnote that mentioned Leah. She would be about the same age as his late father, mid-seventies and realised that she was probably the sole surviving Levi apart from himself.

The Woodman's Quest

Chapter 40

Lost and Found

Helen's first day in the New Forest was quite different to
Lewis's. She had spent most of the Monday leisurely strolling
around the small town admiring the quaint shops and
enjoying the mundane things that Lydiya had to do. She was
also impressed how friendly the local folk were, and in some
cases Lydiya made the effort to introduce her guest to a few
people who knew her. There was one young man, tall with a
full beard sheepishly asked Lydiya about her daughter
Phaedra. This somehow made Helen even more relaxed,
having met Phaedra.

'Yes young man, Phaedra's brother Mikhail is married to my
daughter and they live in Philly.' She proudly boasted to the
man. His face screwed up, showing his lack of knowledge.

'Oh, sorry I mean Philadelphia in the USA'. Helen explained.

'I was just going in Sally's Café; would you care to join me?
He asked nervously.

Without hesitation the two older ladies linked arms each side
of the young man and he led them across the road. Lydiya
looked and smiled at Helen as she jokingly whispered that he
was quite a good catch.

Helen had been in Lyndhurst for nearly a week and had
become a changed person. This was encouraged by Lydiya
and often they would be found exploring the small villages in
the area, taking in the rural atmosphere. In all this time Helen
had hardly mentioned any of the problems at her own home.
They could be often heard laughing out loud as Lydiya

The Woodman's Quest

indulged her guest, and in such a very short time, they had become a very close friends.

When she had arrived at the house a week before, Lydiya noticed how tired and introverted she looked, but by the end of the week, she was vibrant and her face was full of colour.

Lydiya even persuaded her to visit the hairdressers and have any traces of grey removed, to brighten up her flagging blonde hair. By the Saturday, Helen had to admit it herself she had shed at least ten years from her demeanour. On the Saturday, in the same Sally's Café, she was turning heads as they both giggled like little schoolgirls.

On that bright Saturday afternoon, the two women were strolling arm in arm in the garden at the back of the large house when a loud call from the French windows made them halt their conversation.

'Helen, there's a call for you from Wilomena, I think!' Victor shouted.

Wilomena had been very busy, and by the sound of it, so had Hugo. The investigation into her husband's private life, had uncovered some startling facts. He had been unfaithful to Helen for at least four years. Maria Ortiz was the mother of a three year old son and was currently pregnant with a second child.

Hugo was at that time, living with his new family in a flat in Boston, quite openly, and they were often seen at the local Walmart shopping for groceries. Wilomena also mentioned that her other investigation was still underway concerning his financial situation and was hopeful to conclude this by the middle of the following week. She did warn Helen not to have

The Woodman's Quest

too high an expectation on settlement as initial findings were not that good.

This last piece of news, the financial one, was somewhat of a bombshell, but Lydiya told her not to be too downhearted as her lawyer seemed highly competent, and Hugo was a very highly paid if not just a little stupid. Helen decided, subject to Victor and Lydiya's agreement, she would like to stay on at their Lyndhurst home for some time yet and their response was most comforting to her.

In that same first week Lewis had been rather busy too. After a long telephone conversation with his wife in Los Angeles, he had said that he needed at least two weeks to sort out his mind, he was pleased with her response. She had even suggested that he must take his time, considering that the girls were still wrapped up in their studies, and were not pining for his swift return.

With Victor's offer to use the Lexus, Lewis decided to make a trip to the Midlands and try to find the grave of his grandmother Rochelle who had died giving birth to his father, in a small maternity unit in a small town in South Derbyshire. That information had been unearthed by Mark after he had telephoned him requesting more information.

Victor had found a small hotel in the centre of the town and after a journey of four hours or so he found himself in the small market town called Ilkeston. The centre of the town was situated at the top of a hill, dominated by a large parish church. From the book 'Lewi's Legacy' which he had with him, it described how his father lived his life in the area, but didn't mention about where his mother was buried.

Over an evening meal at the small hotel, the owner directed him to the local Cemetery but firstly advised him to call into

The Woodman's Quest

the council offices, where they would direct him to the person who held the burial records.

Half the day was spent going from one office to another until finally he found himself at a large cemetery on a hill, with acres and acres of land covered in graves. The council officer had provided him with a map of the area and kindly marked the plot of Rochelle Owen's grave was situated. Lewis spent over an hour searching and was just about to give up, when he saw a large clump of tall weed-like grass near some iron railings.

Right in the middle of the wild grass and bramble, he reached down and was able to feel a small headstone, about two foot tall with a rounded top. With his feet and hands, he pushed the undergrowth away from the stone face and rubbed it hard with his hand.

His heart was lifted when the faint writing on the small monument was revealed:

Here lies the body of
Rochelle Owen (nee Levi)
1925 -1944

Lewis sank to the ground, his knees were being pierced by the nearby brambles, but he never felt anything. His hand held the top of the small headstone and bitter tears coursed down his face.

'Grandmother I never knew you, but you know me. You were left here and forgotten, but I have now found you and I vow to bring this little spot where you are buried to a state worthy of the Levi blood that is in me.' He said though his tears.

For the next two days, Lewis had restored the whole forgotten corner of that burial ground, fit for the woman who

The Woodman's Quest

sacrificed her life in birth of his father. He didn't seek permission; instead he purchased a strimmer, spade and a range of cleaning items from the local hardware shop.

Also, he obtained all the items he needed to construct a fitting memorial around the plot, obtained from a local garden centre. At the end of his efforts, the place where his grandmother was buried shone out like a beacon against the grim surrounding area. Lewis had also trimmed a few of the adjacent overgrown plots for easier access.

On his last visit to Rochelle's grave, having placed some flowers in the new holder that he had secured firmly at the front of the shiny headstone, Lewis stood back and took several photographs both close-up and from the main pathway so he could show his family and friends back home.

Just as he was leaving, he looked back at the great improvement to that little plot, when he was startled by a voice coming from the side.

'That's a real good job you've done there son, effort well rewarded I'd say.' Lewis looked around to see an older man with a wheelbarrow looking up at him. An idea then came into his head.

'Are you here regularly sir?' Lewis asked.

'Oh yes, every day.' The man replied.

Lewis took the opportunity to ask the gardener if he would tend his grandmother's grave on a regular basis for a fee. He explained that he lived on the west coast of America and may not be able to return that regularly. The man agreed to do the task, but not for pay, as he was so impressed with the work already done by Lewis.

The Woodman's Quest

Asking the man to wait, he quickly ran to get all the tools that he had purchased that still in the Lexus, and he gave all of it to the gardener in grateful thanks. Lewis took a couple of pictures of the new carer of his grandmother's plot and for once in his life, felt that he had really achieved something on his own.

As he sat in his car, which was parked on the roadside next to the cemetery, Lewis sat for a moment. In the top pocket of his jacket he found that tiny envelope of seeds, given to him by his father.

'Now, I really do 'know myself' – thank you dad.' He whispered.

Buxton was only twenty odd miles further north, so he quickly went back to his small hotel to clean up and rang Sarah's parents to ask if he could come to visit them. Although they were somewhat disappointed that he had not brought his family with him, they soon understood the reasons why, when he explained his quest to them..

Lewis also had shewn the pictures that he had taken at the Cemetery pointing out the Levi connection. At last he could tell them that there was the evidence that he always longed for. Although he hadn't told Sarah at that time, he omitted to tell her that he was thinking of a further European visit, to trace his great, great grandfather's grave.

Lewis had started his small pilgrimage on the Tuesday of his first week in the UK and by the Friday he was back in Lyndhurst in the beautiful New Forest sharing the wonderful experience and photographs to his three new friends. Using the latest technology on his phone he was able to send all the photographs that he had taken to his wife in chronological

The Woodman's Quest

order, starting with the wild bramble-filled corner, to the finished work. He even sent pictures of the local gardener who had promised to keep the grave in good condition for him.

Sarah rang him back to confirm that she had received all the pictures and was greatly moved to see the reference to the Hebrew family of Levi on the memorial stone. They agreed it was very emotional that he could at last see the irrefutable evidence of the connection to his Hebrew heritage.

They discussed at length what Lewis was planning to do next while over in Britain, but his wife was not at all pleased when Lewis told her of the plans for his next visit. She considered that he might be exposed to danger whilst over there, and warned that it may not be as easy as he imagined. As an afterthought she had suggested that perhaps her father would like to accompany him.

Victor proposed that the four of them visit his favourite pub in Burley called the Queen's Head for Sunday lunch. Lewis said he would pick up the tab in grateful thanks to their hosts kindness to him and Helen, and he took advantage of the gathering to explain what his plans were for the following week. Over coffee at the pub, Lewis outlined his proposed pilgrimage to Hagenau in Alsace to search out the memorial to his great, great grandfather Lewi Levi.

'Do you think that I might come with you Lewis?' Helen asked. 'What would you think about that?'

The diners fell silent as all eyes were on Lewis pondering his answer, but instead he just smiled and said he would let her know later on. After a short walk around the picturesque village of Burley, they passed a small cottage where Victor and Lydiya used to live, situated along a leafy road.

The Woodman's Quest

Victor said that his father and mother were the previous residents and also told them that his father was an accomplished painter. Not far away from Burley, Teddy's mother lived in a remote cottage and above her fireplace she owned the best painting that his father had done. It depicted the view from the cottage window, over Burley Moor.

The painting had depicted two figures in the mist, one of which was Victor as a boy, with his faithful collie Sally. Suddenly Victor seemed very tired and wistful; Lewis gently held his arm and suggested that he would drive them back to Lyndhurst for a well-earned rest.

It was still quite early in the afternoon and the sun was shining brightly over the forest, so he suggested to Helen that they go on a little mystery trip. Previously Victor had told him of a fairly new nature reserve called Cranford Lakes, not very far from Lyndhurst, that was worth a visit that few people knew about it at that time. With simple directions Lewis easily found the lakes and was pleasantly surprised to see only two cars in the car park.

They followed a gravel path flanked by numerous trees and the undergrowth between the trees had been purposely left to grow wild, good cover for the badgers and foxes in their night-time hunting.

They passed signs for various hides and seeing one close to the path, they ventured quietly into a wooden hut. The windows covered the whole of the wall area with bench seats beneath them. Bird feeders abounded so as soon as they had settled, a myriad of small wild birds attacked the seed fillers. Just below the windows, on a shelf were plastic covered notes identifying each species and together they had great fun identifying each one.

The Woodman's Quest

Helen was about to leave when Lewis touched her arm. She looked back to see a great spotted woodpecker in all its glory fly up to one of the feeders, not more that three foot away from where they were sitting. The two companions were utterly spellbound.

On the path again they noticed a large lake surrounded by reeds and occasionally part-sunken tree branches. Helen spotted something move on such a branch, and as they peered at it she knew that it was a grey heron looking from its perch into the still deep water. They stood transfixed as suddenly the heron dived into the water directly below it and just as quickly back onto the dead branch.

The fish that it had caught was quite a large one, but with one gulp it was gone head first, past the sharp beak and in seconds the heron had enjoyed a nice fish tea; a reward for its patience.

They continued on their walk on the gravel pathway which came to an end abruptly at another hide, but this time they went past it. They followed a right turn onto a boardwalk over a swampy area which had a quite different atmosphere. Helen held onto Lewis's arm as they passed over onto the other side of the lake, she was not so enamoured about that route but after crossing a small bridge, they were back into the sunshine again.

They reached a sign which indicated to go back to where they had begun but this time on the opposite side of the 'heron' lake, but Lewis indicated that he wanted to go left, as Victor had told him about a secret bench. Through a metal gate and about four hundred yards further, Helen spied a beautiful bench just off the pathway in a little opening. The sun was streaming though and in the rays of light that filtered through the trees it looked so peaceful.

The Woodman's Quest

Lewis cleared away some fallen leaves and seeds from the seat and they thankfully sat to rest for a while. They were on a bank where a small stream passed by beneath where they sat. To the left was as old fallen tree which had made a natural bridge over the little brook.

They looked to the right, to see that the stream had taken a natural bend at that point and which had caused a small island to form. The sun shone directly on the island from a gap in the trees where some foxgloves and other woodland flowers were which had attracted a large number of flying insects.

Helen identified butterflies, dragonflies, damsel flies, worker bees and large bumble bees with white tails. Suddenly something bright caught the corner of her eye, sitting on the fallen trunk over the stream was a kingfisher all in bright green and gold, its head transfixed, looking into the water. They both held their breath as they watched him catch a stickleback and fly off. At that moment Helen felt really close to her companion and she shuffled a little nearer to him.

'What a good idea of yours Lewis to come here, it is so beautiful and yet not crowded with people, it seems like we are part of nature somehow. Whilst we are here, are you going to answer my question about your journey to France?' Helen looked deep into his eyes.

He was going to speak, but instead she pulled him close and kissed him on his lips. His eyes looked surprised, but soon closed them as her hungrily kissed her back, and then pulled back blinking.

The Woodman's Quest

'Helen what are you doing?' He whispered, and Helen responded by kissing him harder and at the same time putting her arm around his neck.

'Yes Helen I do want you to come with me, but you do realise that it would mean at least two nights away and...' He tried to say more but she kissed him again.

'Helen please, just let me say that I'm a married man, and you're a married woman, well at least for now anyway. In different circumstances I would take up that obvious offer you are making but I know it would be not the right thing to do. It's obvious that if we stayed in a hotel one thing would lead to another. You know what I mean don't you?' He blurted it all out in a rush so that she wouldn't try that tactic again, nice as it was.

'I do understand that Lewis, I don't want any long term involvement.' They both stood up from the bench as she spoke. 'I don't see anything wrong in a short-term one though.' Helen gently looked into his eyes, and at the same time pulled his willing body close to her own. She could feel him respond to her closeness and even felt the thumping of his heart as she snuggled up with her head on his chest.

When they arrived back to where they were staying, Lydiya noticed that there was something different about them. They weren't holding hands or anything as obvious as that, but sometimes she was able to sense that aura between two people that had never been there before. Perhaps it was where they had just been, had awoken something. She shrugged it off just as quickly and went to organise some tea for her returning guests.

Around ten that evening the phone rang, but as was still Sunday, Helen was surprised to hear Wilomena's voice at the

The Woodman's Quest

other end. Her lawyer has some spectacular news. Apparently Hugo had telephoned her from Boston to say that he capitulated and would agree to the terms that Wilomena had emailed him with. He wanted a quick settlement and for it not to be drawn out.

He had offered to Wilomena, over the phone, that Helen could take the mansion and a sizable monthly allowance. The call from her young lawyer that day was to ascertain whether her client would be amenable to the offer. Wilomena had said that it was worth considering and then after a quick divorce, each party could get on with their separate lives. She then proposed that Helen return back to America on the next convenient flight to Philadelphia and she would fly from L.A. to see her in then next couple of days with the full details of the settlement.

Her advice went further, that Helen book herself in a hotel for the time being as the house had been temporary closed up, as Hugo had paid off their staff at their home. There was a seat available on the flight back to Philadelphia on the Monday, and as Helen had initially purchased an open return, it was much easier to organise.

The next day Lewis stood at the boarding gate for her flight, passed Helen her hand luggage, after he had hugged her and put his hands each side of her face and tenderly gave her a kiss.

'I still have mixed feelings about you accompanying me to Hagenau, Helen. I even feared that you might have crept into my bed last night'. He said smilingly.

'What would you have done if I did?' She asked.

The Woodman's Quest

'I suppose I would have screamed, or then again, perhaps not!' Lewis kissed her once more and as she passed through the terminal gate, the American turned just once more, with a grin on her face, and then disappeared.

The Woodman's Quest

Chapter 41

An independent woman

After an uneventful flight back to Philadelphia International and taxi back to the place where she had brought up her family, she climbed the marble steps to the imposing double front doors under the shelter of a Greek style portico supported by black marble columns.

She knew that the mansion was all locked up and secure, but had no problem in entry with her own set of keys and ability to disarm the alarm. She stood in the huge hallway and looked up at the disappearing staircase and for once felt nothing. To her now it was just a pile of stone, there was no intrinsic beauty of the architecture, nor the warmth of the welcome that it always had for her.

The silence was deafening as she stood for a moment and sighed deeply. Only the day or so before, she was enjoying the nature reserve in the New Forest with someone who had awakened some feelings in her that she thought had been lost forever.

'Mother, so glad that you are home, I want to see you, can you come over?' Marcy her daughter seemed rather frantic in her question over the phone.

Helen resignedly accepted the request to visit Marcia and her new husband Mikhail at their flat in the town centre, and decided to wait outside the house for her daughter to pick up outside. She wouldn't say out loud to Marcy, but it wasn't her immediate plan to go visiting and endure the tiresome small talk that would ensue. It was great to see the young couple and Helen was pleased that what had happened to her and Hugo, had not changed them.

The Woodman's Quest

'Look you two, I'm not made of glass, and I want to say that your father had not only betrayed me, but at the same time he had betrayed you and your brother too.' Helen's strength was beginning to recover from the jet lag.

'We would like you to stay with us Helen, there is a spare room and...' Mikhail began to say.

'Thank you but no, I need time to be on my own and think all this through. I'm grateful that you both are making a life for yourselves, but I learned something when I visited your parents Mickey; that I'm not too old to start again.

May I also say that they were great hosts to me at their home and I learnt a lot about how two people can be happy through all their own life's trials?' Helen just blurted out the truth and felt stronger and that there was not any need for any pretence to them.

She told them that Wilomena was handling the divorce and would be flying over from LA in a couple of days, meanwhile she will be checking into a hotel in Philly and as soon as she is settled there she intended to ring them with contact details.

Mikhail told his mother in law that when his parents came over for their wedding he put them in the Holiday Inn on Columbus Boulevard, they liked it because it was close to the Delaware River. He passed his mother in law his phone which displayed the hotel number and when she had booked a room, she then rang Wilomena to tell her to call her at the hotel as soon as she arrived from the West Coast.

As soon as she had settled in her hotel room she asked the concierge to arrange a personal laundry service for all of her clothes she had packed into her large suitcase and at the

The Woodman's Quest

same time ordered dinner in her room. For once in her life she felt that all the decisions she would make would be for the benefit of her own future, and that she had got so much wasted time to catch up on.

At breakfast the next morning, she had had the best night's sleep for a considerable time. Smiling to herself, she visualised waking up at the side of Lewis in some romantic hotel in Alsace France asking him to make love to her one more time.

A wonderful fantasy, and as she looked around the dining room, there was not even one hotel guest, half as good looking, or even interesting enough to distract her attention. Helen wistfully sipped on her second cup of coffer when a waiter came towards her carrying a telephone.

'Helen, it's Wilomena here, I'm just getting in a yellow cab and hope to be with you very soon, are you busy?'

The two women sat in their easy chairs in a quiet part of the hotel lounge after Helen had waited excitedly for her lawyer to arrive.

'My, Helen you look great, who's your personal trainer. What have you been up to since I last saw you?' Wilomena asked with a wry smile. 'Please call me Mena, all my friends do.'

'For one thing Mena, I very nearly fell in love. Firstly with a place called the New Forest in England, and then with someone who lives in your city, but I'm not going to tell you his name 'cos you might know him.' Helen's new found confidence was unmistakeable.

The Woodman's Quest

Wilomena booked a room on the same floor as her client and went to refresh before meeting her client, two hours later in her room.

It transpired that Helen's husband surprisingly had folded like a pack of cards when that tigress Wilomena presented him with all of her findings. It was a 'fait accompli' Hugo really didn't have a leg to stand on. He had agreed to all of Wilomena's conditions for the divorce and was then awaiting Helen's approval of them.

As both plaintiffs were to agree on the marital settlement Helen's fear of having to go to court and see Hugo was greatly improved by the offer of her lawyer offering to represent her and all she needed to do was scrutinise the details of the settlement and sign the form that Wilomena had provided and the rest would follow in due course. The mansion would take a while to sell, but Wilomena had several valuations already and Helen wisely chose the lowest one of them.

The two women happily talked together for what seemed a short time, but when Wilomena looked at her watch she was shocked to see that it was nearly six pm and they hadn't eaten all day.

They planned to meet up again in the hotel foyer at seven thirty and Helen promised to treat her friend and lawyer to a meal she would not forget in a hurry. In that time she had booked the best table in the rooftop restaurant at Liberties bar. This definitely had the best views in town.

As the two women looked over the Philadelphia skyline, the last vestiges of light from the setting sun painted the high buildings of the business district into a bright shade of scarlet.

The Woodman's Quest

The smiling eyes of the young successful lawyer also had an unusual brightness to them.

'You've done it again Mena, you found that long-lost son of that aging actress after thirty odd years and now this. I can't believe that you stitched up my overbearing husband even though he's quite a big noise in the legal world. I imagined he would be bloody-minded enough to make the whole thing drag on just to hurt me.' Helen reached over and they held hands.

'To think that he now can get back to changing the kid's diapers and all the other stuff that he probably thought had gone out of his life. I don't suppose in today's world his new partner will let him get away with just doing his job, he'll certainly have to pitch in now even though he is sixty two!' Wilomena said with a mischievous grin.

Helen didn't reply to that comment, but more than anyone she felt totally justified at that moment. Not to ever see that ogre of a man again, would be her biggest reward, especially for all those years of subjugation.

Wilomena had to revert back to business mode with Helen as she mentioned about what her client wanted to do once the decree had been finalised. There was a great deal of money involved in the settlement and she suspected that Helen's financial dealings had always been left to Hugo. Helen however if not the greatest mathematician was very quick in reading the signs that Wilomena was showing.

'Mena, I want to retain you do all the work in relation to my income and the eventual proceeds from the house sale. I know that you have done a lot of work already and I do have some money of my own, so I propose that when the decree is finalised, you send to my your bill so far, and I will transfer

The Woodman's Quest

the funds to you, and then bill me each quarter until the details are all wrapped up for me. Is that a deal?' Helen asked as she stretched out her hand.

'You don't know how much my first bill will be.' Wilomena looked a little serious.

'Will it be more that twenty grand Mena? Helen asked.

Wilomena shook her head and laughed out loud. They held hands as they waited for the next course, the lights on the tall buildings were all on and the darkness fell around the rooftop restaurant. Helen had found the best friend and lawyer anyone could have ever wished for.

No one can live in a hotel forever, even if it is a nice one, especially when the staff goes out of their way to look after you. Hotel life is a temporary one, the novelty soon wears off and most people look forward to getting back to normal in their own home.

For Helen however she had no home to go to. The fact was, that the home she had lived in for thirty odd years was up for sale with prospective buyers coming and going, asking all sorts of intrusive questions. She had tried to live there for a few days but her privacy was short lived, as the real estate man was for ever bringing new people to the house, and one couple even asked if she was the maid.

Her son John had rung his mother, inviting her to Los Angeles where he was the sports editor for the LA Times. Helen had seriously considered it, but she knew what John would have been like; she would have been asked to get the dinner ready, get his laundry sorted, and keep out of the way should he bring someone back to his flat. No thank you was her reply.

The Woodman's Quest

Things appertaining to the divorce seemed to be on a go slow, and not any call to Wilomena was going to speed it up, she was resigned to the fact that it was 'just one of those things' the young lawyer would apologetically tell her client.

Six weeks seemed like a lifetime but finally all the t's were crossed and the i's were dotted. All at once she was 'an independent woman with independent means', so the Sinatra song went. Life and love was waiting for her, but she had to get out there and find it.

The Woodman's Quest

Chapter 42

Nature often speaks louder

Victor, Lydiya and Lewis decided to have their evening meal on the patio of the house in Lyndhurst. The evening was quite balmy and a blackbird was singing his heart out, just out of view. On the opposite edge of the large green clearing there was something the size of a large dog, but it was grazing on the lush grass. Victor passed Lewis a small set of field binoculars and pointed in the animal's direction.

'That's a muntjac deer Lewis, once brought into the country from China to Woburn Park in the early twentieth century. Since then they somehow escaped and now they're a common sight around here.' Victor told him.

Victor took advantage of the quiet evening alone with his hosts to ask their advice on something that was weighing heavy on his mind. Having had a successful visit to Derbyshire and the encouraging find of his mother's grave, it had kindled something inside him. He wanted to continue to explore the possibility of discovering more about his ancestry which as far as he could see, would mean going to Hagenau in France.

He added that he was quite wary of travelling so far on his own. He had considered asking his father-in-law to accompany him, but he was then of advancing years, although competent in both French and Hebrew languages. Having told them all that, he said that he would very much like to know what they thought of his idea.

Lydiya at once said that his father-in-law was already two hundred miles away in Buxton, even before they would be attempting such a long journey as the one Lewis was

The Woodman's Quest

envisaging. Her advice was that although he was flushed with success that his best option was to get back home to his family. The grave of his ancestor will still be there for another time. Maybe they might go there for a holiday, as she reminded Lewis that Sarah was Jewish too.

Victor mentioned that Lewis could stay as long as he wished at their home, but he had to agree with his wife, that perhaps he might want to take another walk at the lakes, where he had been with Helen and sit upon that bench to think about it. Whatever he decided was ok with them.

Lewis locked the loaned Lexus in the Cranford Lakes car park. It was quite early in the morning and there were no other cars. He noticed a different pathway disappearing into a thick clump of trees and decided to take it. He had only walked twenty yards when he came upon a small bridge over a stream and as he crossed it there were a few steps which led to another path alongside the rippling stream.

The stones in the stream were covered in a deep red colour which he assumed was the hue of the sediment that the stream had uncovered on its journey. The dappled sunlight that had filtered through the trees shone onto the water and made the water a pale blood colour. Lewis couldn't take his eyes off the inspiring sight.

The narrow twisting footpath ran close to the stream as it meandered its way through the hazel trees and overhanging ferns. He had only taken a few steps and an overwhelming sense of calmness took control of his mind, increasing his senses. The steam was only about four yards at its widest. There were shallow parts where the clean water tumbled over the sunken pebbles, making the flow seem rather quick, yet almost silent. A little further on, one of the larger trees seemed to jut out of the bank where it created a small eddy.

The Woodman's Quest

The water there was darker in the shadow of the tree making a deeper pool effect. A fallen leaf from an overhanging branch had fell into the water at this point and the eddy somehow made it go round and round in a continuous whirlpool. Lewis stood and watched, as another leaf joined it and soon they were both thrown into the main current, bobbing their way downstream.

He followed the gurgling water carefully picking his way along the narrow path where an even larger tree was forcing the stream to turn abruptly. The water near bank had formed into a dark pool, almost making it silent and still. As the wind gently moved the leaves above, a shaft of light penetrated the dark water for a moment and he saw the reflected fin of a brown trout, but only for a brief moment.

The little gurgling stream continued on its course for another fifty yards until it disappeared under a large fallen tree. At this point the track moved away from the stream and uphill in to a thick copse of hazel where he notices hundreds of hazelnut shells on the forest floor. He picked one of up and observed that the shell had been neatly opened; the work of squirrels, no doubt.

The dark little copse soon opened and standing before him was the biggest tree in the wood, an ancient English oak, its gnarled bark inviting him to touch. The mighty tree stood in his way, unmoving and silently powerful.

Lewis had experienced something in that short time in that secret part of the forest. Next to the huge oak there was a smaller tree trunk that was covered in moss and he smiled to himself as it seemed to beckon him to sit a while. His feet sunk into the forest floor made by centuries of fallen leaves and giving out a sweet and yet powerful aroma.

The Woodman's Quest

It was still quite early in the morning and his mind travelled six thousand miles to his home on the East Coast of America. Sarah and the twins would still be asleep, blissfully unaware that he was allowing the very basic elements of nature give him the utter peace that he had craved for such a long time, allowing him the clear mind so that he could make the right decisions that would shape the rest of his and his family's life.

The memory of the two leaves bobbing their way in the sparkling current of the stream made him realise that constantly trying to recreate his own past was fruitless, he had to go back home and create a new future. Lydiya was absolutely correct; it was the right time to move on, not back. Lewis could have walked further in the pristine woods, but he knew that he had already found the answer; it was right in front of him.

'Thank you dear old friend, I have listened to your still voice and I now can see my way forward.' The solitary man laid both hands on the great tree trunk, looked up at its great oak boughs as they disappeared into the sky, then turned back and picked his way through the lush fern-covered track. He thoughts were again flying to his home, on the other side of the world.

Only two days later, he was walking through the exit doors of Los Angeles International airport greeting his family once again Sarah and the girls, how much he had missed them it was his wish that they stop off at the beach before they returned home. He wanted to feel the soft Pacific sand through his toes and he knew that the waiting Brucie would certainly thank him for that.

Sarah had anticipated her husband, as she had brought towels to sit on and of course the big black labradoodle was

The Woodman's Quest

waiting in the back of the car with the hard blue ball firmly in his jaws.

Rowena and Sarah also were prepared, they had their swimming costumes underneath their summer dresses, so as they rushed into the foaming surf, Lewis hurled the ball as hard as he could for the dog so that he might have a few minutes to lie in the sunshine with his wife. Some hopes however, Brucie was soon back and shook the sand all over them.

'Glad to be back darling?' Sarah asked sweetly.

'I've had a wonderful time in the UK and met some great folks in the New Forest, but yes it's so nice to see you.' He gave her a long kiss, just as Brucie dropped his wet ball on the back of his head. In a short while, peace was shattered as the twins rushed out of the sea and clamoured for their beach towels.

'Dad, how much did grandpa Louis leave us in his will?' Sara asked as she dried herself.

'I'll tell you all when we get home.' Lewis answered and threw the ball one more time for the big black dog, and whilst chased after it, the family gathered up their belongings and prepared to stash them into the car boot. He considered that that information wasn't for any bystanders to hear.

Lewis still had the banker's draft in his wallet that Mark, his father's lawyer gave to him. He passed it to Sarah who showed it to their children, then only at that time was he aware that they were now millionaires. Sarah calculated that when they had changed the sterling draft into dollars they had just under three million. Lewis had always left the family

The Woodman's Quest

finances to Sarah, as quite simply, she was much more adept at handling money.

'I don't want either of you to mention this to your friends, this is to be kept firmly within the family and no other, do you swear?' Their mother pointed to one twin and then to the other waiting for their solemn promise.

The excited twins went to bed chatting together about what they were going to spend their money on, but as they left the dining room, Sarah shouted a reminder to them about their promise, as if to hammer the subject home.

Their parents spent much of the evening discussing what to do with such a huge sum, and Lewis as usual asked if she could make some suggestions. Sarah immediately thought of the girls and said she would like to put a lump sum for each of them in a trust until they were twenty one. That agreed, they began to talk about what to do with the remainder.

'What would you say if I said that I wasn't happy at the LA Phil?' Lewis asked in a sort of throw away question.

She didn't directly answer, but she did suggest that they should invite Teddy and Yolanda over for the weekend saying that Teddy was the only other Englishman that she knew in California, and it would be great to get Teddy's input. Lewis had to agree with that and also mentioned, that two years before, Teddy had also been a beneficiary in his father's will. Enough was enough for one day, so they retired to bed having had one heck of a day already.

The Woodman's Quest

Chapter 43

Mystical messages

William sat outside the little woodman's hut on the outskirts of the large stand of trees that was his job to manage. He recalled the time when he had no future, in fact he was a fugitive from the law. Two years before, had it not been for a split second decision on his part to help a young girl that had fallen from her horse, he knew that his future was going to be even worse than bleak.

The girl's father was the owner of the estate where this wood was situated and he had celebrated his first year as the improver of the wood and he could already see then fruits of his labour. Of course all woodsmen would agree, that the work that they do to improve the health of their trees is a long term one, and in some cases they never see the completion of their heavy toil. Some say that good woodsmen are visionaries for the forthcoming generations.

Even so, when William compared the state of the area when he started, only twelve months before, it was evident that great inroads had been made. Much of the dead and dying trees had been carefully removed and some of the out of control foreign species like rhododendrons had been attacked with vigour. New saplings had soon taken hold in the spaces that he had left within the wood, so William took pains to surround each one with a chicken wire fence. This would deter the local deer from feasting on the new shoots and give the young trees a chance to survive.

His love of working with wood was re-energised when his wife Zeta suggested that he start going to a local woodworking class at the local college. That prompted him into thinking

The Woodman's Quest

about the possibility of making craft furniture, especially that he had a great deal of raw materials so close to hand.

William also had a gift that no man should be without; a woman who loved him dearly and a six month old son who they had named Uther Edmund Gilpin. Zeta had suggested the boy's name because she wanted his names to retain his mother's Celtic and Cornish heritage. Zeta had fallen in love with the legend of Uther Pendragon and had always promised herself to call any son that she might have after this king. The legend also said that Uther was the father of King Arthur who had such an attachment to Tintagel, where they lived. When she had asked William to agree to name their son Uther, he was all for it.

Zeta continued to run her gift shop in Tintagel where they had originally met, and apart from a trip to California, where William had finally met his aged mother, they had not even considered moving from the mystical and beautiful area of North Cornwall.

There was one another person in this jigsaw that also had some influence in both William and Zeta's lives; Phaedra Norman. Just before they had married, Phaedra, who lived nearby, went to California with a sculptor and she had told them that she was not intending to return. Only a week before, Zeta had sent a letter to Phaedra and had enclosed an up to date picture of their baby Uther so that she could share in their joy.

Whilst writing, Zeta held her stone and sent a subliminal message to Phaedra to do what both she and William wanted for their friend most of all; to get Phaedra's amazing voice recognised, and that it was to come soon. She whispered this wish to the picture of her smiling son and then sealed the envelope.

The Woodman's Quest

At the same time that William was sitting outside of his hut, the postman had delivered a letter to Zeta at her shop, postmarked 'Laguna Beach CA' and Zeta immediately recognised Phaedra's writing. Inside was an invitation to her wedding, but Zeta's heart sank as she knew that William would decline the invitation, and yet she loved Phaedra dearly and missed seeing her. Zeta sat in her empty shop, pulled Uther out of his buggy and cuddled him.

'What shall we do Uther, I know your daddy won't want to go and it is so very far away, but I do miss her.' The little boy looked up into his mothers eyes as if he had understood and started to cry. She unconsciously held the beautiful necklace around her neck and squeezed the mystical stone.

It just happened that day, that the tourists didn't seem so interested in buying, so Zeta closed the shop, picked up some shopping and drove home to prepare a meal for the three of them. It was still quite light when William arrived back home much earlier than usual.

'How did you know I was at home William?' Zeta was surprised to see him.

'I was sitting outside the hut thinking and suddenly a thought came over to me that I needed to be at home.' He answered and at the same time picked up his son who was holding both arms out wide.

Before Phaedra had left for America, she had given Zeta a special present of a mystical stone on a fabulously beautiful gold and platinum snake chain. Zeta it seemed was destined to wear that particular gift as in the past had been involved in the spiritual world of séance meetings. He smiled as she held

The Woodman's Quest

the stone from around her neck and witnessed it glowing through her fingers.

'I know, you sent me a message through that stone didn't you. You wanted to see me, am I right?' Still holding the boy, he drew his wife to him and kissed her. She passed him the letter from Phaedra and he sat on the couch and read it, still cuddling his son.

'I know what you are going to say William, and I quite agree, what with Uther being so small, and the cost as well.'

'Are you trying to read my mind or something? Well that thing around your neck doesn't control every thing, does it my boy?' Uther screamed and giggled at his father. 'As it happens Zeta, I should love to go, why don't you contact Mena and tell her to send us some money for the tickets, by the look of it there isn't much time before the wedding date is there?' William asked and then laughed.

Zeta looked at him astonished with his answer; her eyes wide open in surprise. Then she ran into the kitchen to see to their meal, tears of joy steaming down her face. After their evening meal that night, Zeta found the last letter from Wilomena, and found her contact number should they need it.

During their transatlantic call, Zeta purposely kept the mood of their initial conversation to less controversial items before handing the receiver to William. He spent the first part of the conversation telling her about his work and ambitions, but not for long.

'Did you know that Phaedra is getting married soon?' William asked.

The Woodman's Quest

The young lawyer had known and was excited to tell him that she and her partner Rufus Brown had been invited to the celebrations at nearby Laguna Beach on the Pacific coast. Wilomena was stopped in her tracks when William told her that they had also been invited and were intending to accept.

'But how are you going to get here with the baby and all, William?' Mena asked, so William handed the phone back to Zeta, as he could hear the screams on the other line.

Zeta had told Mena that they had made their minds up that day and rang her because they wanted her to wire sufficient funds so that they could arrange the air fare for the three of them. This was the best news that Wilomena had heard in ages. She asked Zeta to give her bank details, as she was still the official executor of William's affairs in respect of his mothers will. Amazingly she could access the account in Wells Fargo Bank in L.A. and do a swift transfer to her account so that the funds would be available to use the very next day.

'How much do you think that you need Zeta?' Wilomena asked.

She looked at her husband and he mouthed 'twenty'. The bank was still open in Los Angeles and Wilomena took immediate action. Zeta promised to let the young lawyer know when she knew the arrival date and time at LA International, and just before the phone was disconnected, she distinctly heard Wilomena shout Rufus's name to tell him the news.

Now that they had made the arrangements to attend their friend Phaedra's wedding, William considered that it was time to do something about the rest of his inheritance, from his deceased mother in Los Angeles.

The Woodman's Quest

William was greatly touched by the foundation that had been set up for deprived children that Wilomena and Rufus were involved in. Often, when he had taken a rest from his work, he had realised how wonderful his life become, and having such a huge sum of money in the bank in America was of no use to him at all. In fact, it was of no benefit to anyone.

With Zeta's help, they had formed an idea that would suit all concerned. Firstly, William would try to purchase the plot of land containing the woods and the little cottage, about twenty acres in all, from Alex Demille. The bulk of the remainder would be spent setting up a disabled centre in Tintagel, to serve the surrounding area in North Cornwall.

For over thirty years, having suffered so much with his disabilities, it was certainly the most logical and beneficial thing that William and Zeta could do for their own community.

Chapter 44

An opening at last

Phaedra had soon settled in California, even though Bernard was often out and about in the area, organising his work to be shown in local galleries who were clamouring for him to show his work. He stood firm however, with his promise to Phaedra that at he would only work in California. This had still left her with a great deal of time to explore the Laguna area, and could often be found on some secluded beach in the area of Laguna, of which there were quite a few of them.

Having such intense spiritual power, which had been passed on to her from her mother Lydiya, there was a great peace as she wandered alone, along some of the deserted coves on the Pacific Coast. Her favourite cove at the time was called 'Table Rock Cove'. She had taken a letter with her that she had just received from her friend Zeta, and was so grateful to receive such a photo of their beautiful boy inside it.

As she read that the boy's first name was Uther. 'Uther' she knew was of Celtic origin and only after research did she discover that it was the name of the legendary King Arthur's father. She shouted the boy's name against the roar of the Pacific surf, and then suddenly began to sing loud and clear. Something had opened her mind, as she continued to sing for some time.

After such an exhausting time, she climbed upon the escarpment to rest, when her mobile phone rang annoyingly. She looked at the name displayed and was very surprised to see the name 'Teddy' displayed. Phaedra walked away from the roaring surf so that she could hear him, as he seemed quite agitated.

The Woodman's Quest

He had just received a call from John Spiros telling him that there was an opening for a classical trained soprano at Herbst Theatre in San Francisco. An urgent replacement was required. Renee Fleming had recently cancelled her concert with them due to contacting a throat virus. Apparently the director of music was a surfing buddy of John's and of course was in a panic as the concert had been planned for the very next day.

'Renee Fleming? You're kidding aren't you Teddy!' She shouted. Do you know that she's one of the top five soprano's in the world? Well, the answer is NO!' She shouted again at her mobile.

'Well John doesn't think so Fay, he was bowled over by your performance at Marcy and Mikhail's wedding in Philadelphia. Why don't you give it a try Fay? The guy wants to see you today, can you get there?' Teddy asked, hoping that might swing it.

She rushed back to the house on Bluebird Park and was lucky to see Bernard reversing out of their drive. After a couple of calls, he was able to clear his day, and within an hour they were driving to San Francisco and the concert hall. After a single aria from Madam Butterfly by Puccini the man seemed happy enough, and by the power of the internet, the exclusive London school of music where she had studied, were happy to email copies of her pass certificates and a glowing reference from the principal. These were sent direct to the Musical Director's laptop.

Bernard and Phaedra were back at their home just after lunchtime with Renee's new replacement clutching a copy of the playlist of arias the celebrated soprano had planned to perform. She knew three of the six and Bernard quickly downloaded the other three recordings by the great soprano

The Woodman's Quest

and Phaedra practised them into the small hours of the following morning.

Bernard was extremely proud of her when after just a few hours sleep; she was refreshed and ready to go. Most people would have panicked and crumbled at the though of what she was about to do, but not Phaedra. There were no sign of nerves at all, she didn't even ask for his opinion when she had completed all six arias in the car on route to the venue in San Francisco.

Unbeknown to Phaedra, John, who worked as sports editor for the LA Times had severely twisted the arm of the head of music reporting, to attend the concert. Teddy in turn, asked if Lewis Owen, his conductor would go incognito to get his views also.

The next morning at the breakfast table, Bernard searched the arts reviews page of the LA Times and he could see that Phaedra's career had from that moment taken off with a big bang.

'Phaedra, will you marry me?' He asked, getting down on one knee at the breakfast table. 'If I don't ask you now, you will be swept away with all this.' He then passed her the reviews that he had just read.

'I guess it will have to be soon Bernie, by the look of this, I guess the phone might be ringing off the hook soon.' She nodded and he got up off his knee and kissed her tenderly.

The Woodman's Quest

Chapter 45

Coming together

That night after she had eaten quite a large dinner at the hotel with Wilomena, Helen went to bed early. She lay on top of the bed for a while assessing her situation. He new life beckoned, but what was it going to be? She imagined she was a child again going to the local sweet shop and looking at the counter – so much choice and yet being unable to point at which delicacy that she wanted, they all looked so good.

Inevitably she drifted off to sleep, but it was not a peaceful one. The most vivid dream came to her where she was called by her grandfather to join him and her grandmother in their motor home. They were going to the Grand Canyon, yet another trip around the USA.

Helen was a third generation Greek, who came as immigrants to New York not long after the end of the Second World War. Her grandparents owned a restaurant in Athens, sold up and were soon settled in Astoria a small area in New York situated between the Bronx and Manhattan. Three generations of her family ran a very successful restaurant in the Greek Quarter, so much that in the mid sixties her grandfather sold the business to his daughter, Helen's mother, and went travelling in their new motor home.

Occasionally they would return to New York, during the school holidays and take Helen on a min-adventure. For a young girl growing up in the sixties, to go travelling with free-wheeling grandparents would forever generate the most wonderful memories for her.

Before the divorce, Helen often recalled some of the adventures as a young girl, she had had in that motorhome to

The Woodman's Quest

Hugo. She had tried to explain to him that work was not the 'be all and end all' of life, but sadly it was like talking to a brick wall. Little did she realise at the time, that he was getting all the adventure he needed with someone else.

Her subsequent visit to Victor and Lydiya in the UK had rekindle that spirit of adventure in her, so that following morning after that dream, she made her mind up that whatever she did with her life thereafter, it would reflect that spirit that her grandparents so enjoyed.

Some of the time she had spent in the New Forest village of Lyndhurst with Lydiya, Helen had been told about Lydiya's daughter Phaedra. There were harrowing times in her headstrong daughter's life when she had diced with death, all because she had fell for the leader of an Iranian gang in London. Many people including Mikhail, Helen's son-in-law had risked their own lives to save Phaedra.

After that incident, her daughter had gone into a sort of hermit like existence in Cornwall, much against Victor and Lydiya's wishes. Finally Lydiya had told Helen that there was a happier ending for her daughter as she had found someone that suited her, a sculptor whom she had moved to California with recently.

Over breakfast at the hotel in Philadelphia, Helen felt drawn to the idea of meeting Phaedra, and decided that she would like to know some more about her. It was fortunate that she was the sister of her own daughter's husband Mikhail, so that would be a good enough excuse to look her up.

She rushed up to her hotel room to rummage into the side pocket of her suitcase and there was the telephone number that Lydiya had given her before she had returned home. All this had been triggered from the dream about her

The Woodman's Quest

grandparents and now she was really excited that there was a new spring in her step, she was going west!

Los Angeles was even more attractive an idea because her son John, would be overjoyed to know his mother was planning to visit. She thought again about Lewis and how close they had become in such a short time, was this fate? She thought to herself.

'Hello, is that Phaedra?' Helen asked introducing herself. There was a distinct silence for a few seconds that seemed like an age to her.

'Helen? You mean you're Marcy's mum, is that right?' Phaedra answered in a shocked tone.

Helen explained briefly what her new life situation was, but was relieved to hear that Phaedra's brother Mikhail had called and told his sister all the developments with his mother-in-law a week or so before.

Helen then said that she was planning on visiting her son John in LA and wondered if she could visit.

'Come to visit? We'd be honoured if you could come and stay with us here at Bluebird Park. It's just a short walk from Laguna Beach. We've just rented a large ranch-styled bungalow, you'd have your own room and bathroom, please come.' Phaedra seemed so excited about the prospect.

During the phone conversation, Helen was overjoyed to hear that Phaedra had finally taken on the career as a classical soprano in San Francisco. She recalled the traumatic time that Phaedra's mother Lydiya had told her about, during her recent visit to the New Forest in England.

The Woodman's Quest

Phaedra also told Helen that she and Bernard were planning to get married in two weeks time and that Helen's daughter Marcy was going to be her maid of honour. In passing she also mentioned that, as Bernard had no living relatives, someone called Lewis Owen was going to act as the best man for him.

'Who is going to be the best man Fay, sorry I didn't quite get the name?' Helen asked meekly.

'Lewis Owen, you probably might not know him Helen, but he's a good friend of ours. He works with Teddy as the conductor of the L.A. Phil.' Phaedra answered.

'Oh I see' Helen gulped. 'I'll see you soon then, bye.'

18762349R00173

Printed in Poland
by Amazon Fulfillment
Poland Sp. z o.o., Wrocław